Folder

A Novel

by
Raymond Bolton

Folder
Published by arrangement with the author.
All rights reserved.

ISBN-13: 978-0991347193

Young Adult
Urban Science Fiction

For information about Raymond's other books, go to:
https://www.amazon.com/Raymond-
Bolton/e/B00HMY0B6U/
Or e-mail him at **author@raymondbolton.com**.

Bolton, Raymond (2020-01-01). Folder. Regilius Publishing

ACKNOWLEDGEMENTS

The book you're holding is the result of the efforts of several individuals. *Folder*'s remarkable cover is the work of graphic artist Amalia Chiricea, née Chitulescu, of Bucharest, Romania. If you're reading this on your Kindle, Nook, or other electronic device, you can thank Clare Ayala, who resides in Southern California, for her excellent formatting skills. If you find that the story keeps you engaged, it's due in part to the developmental edits of Sabine Berlin, Senior Editor at Eschler Editing, located in the Salt Lake City, Utah area. Aside from the advanced vocabulary of the story's protagonist, Eric Folder, who is both a physics major and poet to boot, the fact that the dialogue between characters in his age group remains true is due to the critical eye of beta reader, Kaidyn Paakkonen. Because she's a private person, I'll just tell you she lives somewhere in Colorado. I would also like to thank Toby "October" Santerelli, whom I met in 2018 at the Superstars Writing Seminar in Colorado Springs. After hearing me read the first page of the manuscript, he contacted his sister, the aforementioned Kaidyn, and enthused about what he had heard, thereby gaining me her assistance. Friend and former client, Janet Basu, allowed me to name Eric's course advisor after her late husband because

(1) his name is exceedingly rare, even in his native land, India, and (2) because readers who knew Basab would immediately associate the professor's high ethical standards with her husband's integrity and virtuous makeup. When we were kids, my recently departed childhood friend, George "Pooge" Pryor, would sometimes joke about a fictitious character he liked to call Joe Dexter, whom he knew would never exist in any author's book. Pooge would be pleased to know Joe now resides in Chapter Three.

PROLOGUE

I'm lost.

I don't know if I should laugh or cry when I say this, because I sound as if I'm repeating words from a hymn or I'm in need of a compass, or else I've given up completely. The thing is, I'm terrified because all these things are true and I don't know how to fix them. I would say a prayer if I thought someone could hear, but even if they did, I don't think this is a place where prayers get answered. If I had a compass, knowing whether I'm facing North or South wouldn't take me away from this place, let alone back to where I started. In fact, no one can get me out of the mess I'm in, except maybe me, and I'm as scared to try to change what has brought me here as I am afraid do nothing.

I remember when my friends and I were kids and we hid in the bushes and pretended there were monsters coming after us. Well, now the monsters are real. I've been listening for what seems an eternity to their angry snorts and the clatter and scratches of their claws on the large stone surface where those creatures are gathered. Every now and then, one of them hisses and another does the same in response. The rate of their footsteps escalates and I imagine two of them colliding and squaring off in an expression of indignation. It's too dark to see whether this has actually happened, or if it's just my imagination, but the pounding of my heart in face of the impending danger keeps me riveted on what's happening.

As I hide in a clump of bushes and the minutes pass, I'm more than a little relieved that they're taking so long to find me. Unexpectedly, the full moon peeks through a break in the cloud cover and the scales on the bodies of several great beasts glisten. Each is twice the size of a bullmastiff and I count six of them several yards from here. Their eyes glow whitish gold and appear to have vertical slits, although it's hard to be sure at this distance. As they circle a spot where I was standing a short while ago, sniffing the ground in several directions around it, one of them raises its head and opens its mouth, baring rows of long, needlelike teeth. I expect the creature will howl. Instead, a rasping reptilian sound emerges and I shudder, wondering what kind of beings they are.

Although I've recently arrived, from my earlier experiences and the landscape's layout, I recognize this place as being near where the street car used to stop in a time that's lost to me forever. The place where I'm hiding used to be the parkway where Park crosses Mill—or what used to be Park and Mill before everything transformed into this new reality. There aren't any streets anymore and I'm surprised there are even deer trails to mark where Park and Mill once intersected. This used to be Portland State University, but now everything's grown over and forested. The clock tower has vanished, as have the student union and the rest of the buildings that were part of the campus.

Without warning, a thought bubbles up from a world I'll never see again and I almost cry out loud. Cursing this lack of control, I force my idiot self to keep quiet. Still, there is some truth to the thought that this situation is what Dad would have called a mixed blessing. It's because it rained so hard that those things haven't discovered me already. Here I am, kneeling on a thick bed of leaves. If they weren't so soggy, they would crackle each time I move and announce my location. Instead, their wetness muffles whatever noise I might otherwise make. On the other hand, because the night is so cold and water is starting to soak through my pants, I'm beginning to shiver and I'm afraid I might sneeze any minute. If I do, those creatures will certainly hear and I know I will die because I'm sure they can out-run me.

The breeze that's been chilling me starts to increase and I wonder if another storm is building. The last of autumn's leaves whip though the air and there is a sharp crack above me. The creatures turn in my direction and two cock their heads. A third one starts walking toward me and I hold my breath, wondering whether it will continue to advance, when a second crack drops a large bough into the bushes a few yards to my right. The creatures stop and stare at the spot where it landed. Then, apparently satisfied they understand what caused the disturbance, they resume their search in the original location. Realizing I've been holding my breath and that I need to breathe, I inhale deeply, then exhale. My breathing is starting to grow normal when something grabs my shoulder.

Chapter
One

My name is Eric Folder and my family and I recently moved to Portland, Oregon from Santa Fe, New Mexico, two places that couldn't be more different from one another. The day I became able to fold, as I like to call it—partly because of my name and partly because of what doing it seems like— the sky was the uninterrupted blue dome that so often accompanies warm summer days in the Pacific Northwest. Nothing about it gave even a hint of how life-changing that day, and the event that became part of it, would turn out to be. But before I tell you about the occurrence that altered my life forever, I'd like give you some idea of how I lived, so you can understand how profound were the changes that followed.

Before we relocated, I was a student at Santa Fe Prep and we lived just outside the city in a residential development called Eldorado. We were by no means wealthy, as are the majority of families who send their kids to Prep and live in some of the richest parts of town—places like Wilderness Gate and Las Campanas—but we were doing all right.

Back then, my dad, Walter Folder, worked as a professor of creative writing at UNM in Albuquerque. Even though maintaining our house in Santa Fe meant he had to endure more than an hour's commute in each direction, he did so because of the education my sister, Trish, and I received at Prep and because Beatrice, our mom, or Bea, as Dad and her friends like to call her, had a really good job at a financial firm on the north side of town.

The firm where she worked was one of the country's finest, until its mortgage division went bust when the national economy collapsed back in 2008… about the time I was eight and Trish was six. Fortunately for us, the company's investment division survived and she managed to hang onto her job. After that, however, she seemed a lot more stressed whenever she came home and Dad, even though he had tenure, didn't smile as much either.

Before that happened, we used to vacation in either Bermuda or Hawaii a few weeks each year and Mom and Dad were a lot more fun to be with. Yeah, Trish and I would still hang with our friends after school and on weekends, pretty much as always, but the trips disappeared. Instead, we'd drive out to places like Bandelier or Madrid and sightsee with the tourists. Most weekends, however, they would just take us out for brunch on the Old Las Vegas Highway or at some café near the Plaza. Things stayed pretty much like that until last winter when, suddenly and without warning, everything starts getting better.

Mom receives an offer to serve as an assistant controller with Portland's largest sportswear manufacturer. I mean, how cool is that? Especially since their employees receive special deals on footwear and gear. Next, Dad does an online search and finds there is a professorship open in Portland State University's MFA program. He applies for it, then is quickly told that it's his. I've always done well enough in school and on tests that I wind up with a National Merit Scholarship. That pretty well cinches my application to the same university when I apply online. Once we learn I've been accepted, Dad becomes especially excited because I have more than enough time to enroll. Suddenly our house is up for sale and we're packing our furniture, along with the rest of our stuff, for a move to the Pacific Northwest. Naturally, Trish is bummed because she will be leaving her friends just as they're getting psyched about becoming juniors, but I suspect she'll get over it.

The cross country trip takes four days to complete. Although Dad insists we can make the drive in two, Mom is determined not to let the trip exhaust us. On top of that, since we have to wait for the movers to show once we get to our new home, we agree not to hurry.

The scenery through Utah and Nevada is not all that much different from the New Mexican landscape, but it starts changing as we drive through southwestern Idaho and move into eastern Oregon. As we cross the Cascades heading westward, it feels as though we're passing out of one world into an entirely different one. The landscape grows increasingly green and, as we follow the Columbia River, my jaw drops. I have never seen so much water except in an ocean. The river must be half a mile wide.

It is late afternoon by the time we leave the Columbia Gorge. We hit the freeway into Portland and the number of cars on the road is amazing. I had heard about the freeways and traffic on Oahu, but since we had spent all of our time on Kaua'i, I had never seen such congestion: lanes filled like parking lots with all of the cars creeping along in unison.

I glance beside me and see Trish has her feet on the seat and her arms wrapped around her shins. The sunlight that is turning her auburn hair copper makes her frown hard enough that her eyes are reduced to slits.

All at once she asks in her angriest tone, "Is this Portland?"

"Yes, Dear," Mom replies.

"Is it *always* like this?"

For a minute, Mom doesn't answer. She's turning around to face her, looking totally confused, when Dad jumps in.

"You mean the traffic?" he asks, almost laughing.

"Yeah."

"No, dear," he replies. "This is just rush hour," he assures her and Trish seems to relax. "There are a lot more cars and people here than you are used to, but most of the time things move along better than this."

Dad should know. He and Mom spent a couple of weeks checking out houses before they settled on ours. Trish nods, but continues frowning.

Twenty minutes later, we turn off the freeway. After five minutes more, we are driving along a street lined with small shops and old-fashioned houses. The conversation dies as we begin taking in this strange but interesting neighborhood with its smiling pedestrians and shops selling things like pizza, bicycles and chai. At one point, we round a corner where a nationwide coffee shop stands and Trish laughs.

"Look," she says and points at a man and woman who have set up easels on two concrete islands in the middle of the street. They appear to be painting the scenery.

A couple of intersections later, people are sitting at tables outside a bakery and a man on the corner is singing and playing a guitar. We turn left onto a tree shaded street, much narrower than the others. With cars parked along either side, there is only room for one car to drive down the middle. It's a pleasant surprise when drivers coming toward us pull into the spaces between the parked cars, allowing us to pass, or else we make way for them—not at all like the aggressive situations we've run into elsewhere.

At one point, Dad pulls over and shuts down the engine. When he turns in his seat and asks, "Well, what do you think?" Trish and I exchange glances, unsure what he's talking about. It takes a few seconds before we notice the house where he's parked. Although it's designed to look like the others on the block, its wood slat exterior and peaked shingled roof appear to be new.

"Is this it?" I eventually manage.

Dad nods and asks, "Would you like to take a look?"

Since we're talking about complete opposites, I should tell you that our Portland and Santa Fe homes couldn't be any more dissimilar. Our New Mexico house was huge. It was all one story, flat-roofed and made to look like it was constructed out of adobe, the mandatory style there. It sat on an acre-and-a-half lot and backed onto a green belt—although you should know the word "green" is somewhat of an exaggeration. In fact, the land where we lived is entirely scrub-covered earth dotted with juniper trees, each of them no more than seven or eight feet high. Eldorado houses are rarely less than one hundred feet apart and more often hundreds of yards from each other, so you can imagine my shock when I see our new Oregon home.

First of all, the word "new" in this context is as inaccurate as the word "green" was in the last one. Most of the houses in Portland's Sellwood district, where Mom and Dad bought, were built between the late eighteen hundreds and the mid-twentieth century. The lots are tiny and the homes are spaced maybe fifteen to twenty feet apart. On the other hand, the trees that surround them are fifty to a hundred feet tall and almost every house has a lawn—something forbidden in Eldorado because of the almost non-existent rainfall and the limited water supply.

It takes us only seconds to pile out, arrive on the porch and gather around the front door. Mom fumbles with her purse, sorting through tissues, a change purse and the typical stuff women carry, but finally comes up with a key. When the door swings open, we remain staring as if we're about to enter a terrifying new world. My eyes haven't adjusted, so I'm unable to make out much detail, but I notice the smell of fresh paint.

"Is it new?" I ask.

Dad shakes his head. "It's a remodel. There are a few similar ones in the area."

Trish leans through the doorway and comments, "It's

kinda small."

"All of the houses in this neighborhood are," says Mom. "I know it will take some getting used to, but it's really quite nice." When Trish doesn't move, Mom takes her by the elbow. "Let me show you your room."

I guess I'm a little reluctant myself, because I remain standing in place. When the girls head upstairs, Dad puts a hand on my shoulder and asks, "Are you planning to spend the rest of the day out here?" Before I can answer, he says, "C'mon. Let's take a look."

I'm pleasantly surprised to find how much I like it. Although it's considerably smaller than where we'd been living, everything is nicely laid out. The living room, dining room, kitchen and laundry room all seem to flow together, and there is a small office in the front where Dad will be able to work. The three bedrooms upstairs each have their own baths. And while I don't spend too much time checking out Trish's room or my parents', mine has enough space for not only my bed, my bookcase and bureau, but also for my computer desk where, as a physics major, I expect I will spend an inordinate amount of time.

As you might expect, the movers don't come when they promise, so we spend the night on the air mattresses Mom and Dad brought along for just this situation. Once the moving truck arrives the next morning and our things are unloaded, it seems like forever that we are digging ourselves out of boxes, trying to find places for everything.

By the morning of the fourth day, however, despite how hard we try to keep everything organized, there is cardboard and bubble wrap everywhere and I find myself aching to leave this mess and explore my new city. I pull out my cell and, after a few minutes' search, land on the TriMet website where I find I can get on a bus a few blocks from our house and land in the middle of Portland State with only one transfer. I grin. It's a bit of a hike, but definitely doable.

I go downstairs, where I find Dad sitting in a splash

of sunlight on his office floor, tangled in computer cables, dust motes sparkling in the air around him.

"Hi, Dad! What'chuptu?"

He places the wires on the floor beside him, runs his hands through his thinning head of hair, then lets out a sigh.

"I'm trying to figure out which of these connects to the external hard drive."

"Don't you back up to the Cloud?"

"For files, yes. But if the computer's hard drive crashes, it would take too long to restore everything wirelessly and there's always the possibility of data corruption. I guess I'm old fashioned, but I still prefer a hardwire connected backup."

I get down on my knees beside him and, while I show him how to identify the USB3 connector, I tell him about my plan.

"Why so soon?" he asks. "There are still several weeks before school begins."

"I'd like to get the feel of things. Besides, I have a meeting with my class advisor scheduled for next week." When Dad's eyebrows go up, I explain, "I have to decide between the standard option, or the environmental and biomedical options for physics majors and whether I'm going to pursue a BA or BS degree."

"Really?"

I nod.

"Freshman year is pretty much the same for all of them," I explain. "But the course loads start to change in the second year and I'd like to get myself on track early."

"Your schedule sounds almost as complicated as my own," he chuckles. Then he cocks his head and asks, "How's your room?"

"It's all pretty good. I still can't find some of my books, but otherwise everything's where it should be."

"Have you checked with Mom to see if she needs any help?"

11

I nod. "I keep asking, but she says she and Trish have everything under control."

"Would you like to take the car?"

I shake my head. "Until I have one of my own, I need to familiarize myself with the transit system."

He nods, then looks at his watch and says, "It's still early enough. Do you know how to get there?" When I assure him I do, he adds, "Be back in time for dinner. Shall we say five?"

I'm so excited that I'm barely aware of the walk to the bus stop. It's only after I board that the sights begin registering. On the way to where I will transfer to the train, we pass a Taiwanese restaurant, an old-fashioned movie theater, and I get my first glimpse of the Willamette River through a break in the trees over the houses' rooftops. It's not for another fifteen minutes, however, when the train into Portland rolls onto the recently completed Tilikum Crossing, that I get my first look at the city. I lean against the window and stare.

I have never seen buildings as tall as these, colored in hues of red, pink, dark blue, moss green, gray and white. Yeah, I'm sure New York and many other cities have skyscrapers that can put these structures to shame, but until now, I haven't been a city boy and I find myself falling in love with what lies before me.

Then there is the river and its bridges. I have already said that the Columbia River is huge, but as we cross the Willamette, I'm struck by not only its width, but how deep it must be. To my right—I do a quick calculation and realize I'm looking more or less westward—what looks like a container vessel is passing underneath one of the Willamette's steel girder bridges. It makes me laugh at the Rio Grande, which you would be lucky to navigate in a row boat certain times of the year. By late summer, its water level drops so low that that it's often reduced to mud flats as it passes through Albuquerque.

I leave my seat when the train's automated system announces that we are approaching the stop at College and Sixth. Hanging onto one of the bright yellow support posts near the cabin's sliding doors, I peer through the windows and spot a green and white sign on the side of one building, marking it as the Ondine Residence Hall, Portland State University.

I'm finally here!

The train rolls away and leaves me gaping at my first glimpse of my long-awaited destination. I should be paying closer attention to my surroundings, because as I'm gazing upward to glimpse one building's upper stories, I inadvertently step off the curb and into the street. The last thing I remember is someone shouting, "Look out!"

Chapter
Two

All around, I see darkness. Out of the corner of my eye I see a shadow, a darker shape against the lightlessness around me. Someone is approaching, not just walking in the same direction, but coming after me and quickly catching up. No matter how hard I try, I can't see my pursuer's face, only her distinctly feminine shape and emerald green eyes. She opens her mouth and starts speaking, but I'm suddenly afraid and move away from her. It's then I hear the voices of a man and woman talking. I feel I should know them, but I can't say who they are for the life of me.

All at once, my perceptions shift and I realize I'm dreaming and need to wake up. Until now, I've been caught up in a bizarre series of dreams, stranger than anything I've experienced for longer than I can remember. I want to leave my pursuer behind, but I'm having a tough time climbing back into reality. Dragging myself out of that dislocated place and waking up is requiring more effort than usual. It's almost as if something is holding me there, dragging me back into unconsciousness. Even so, I fight the temptation to succumb and work even harder to remove myself. As I do, the couple's voices turn into the sounds of people alternately whispering or speaking softly. As I strain to understand them, a few words stand out.

"Walt, did you see his eyelids twitch? I think he's starting to wake up."

That sounds like Mom. I'm almost certain it is, but I'm finding it tough to think clearly. Try as hard as I can, I can't open my eyes.

"I'll get someone to help," Dad replies, sounding concerned.

The next thing I know, I hear footsteps. Someone squeezes my hand and says, "Eric, don't worry. Your father and I are here. He's gone to get help."

Frustrated, I try to sit up.

"Ow!" I cry as a sharp pain in the crook of my right elbow forces me to stop bending it.

I finally force my eyes open to see what is happening and see that I'm in a light colored, almost white room with overhead light fixtures arranged in neat, parallel rows. I'm wearing a loose-fitting patterned garment I've never seen before. There is a blanket across my chest with a sheet folded over it. I turn my head to the right to determine what's poking me and notice a ridge of skin in the crook of my elbow with… Is that a needle? It is indeed, and it's taped securely in place like the tube it's attached to. A black plastic device with a lead running from it is clamped over the tip of my right forefinger. As I continue to discover what's happening, I notice several other wires, either taped to my arms or running from under this strange piece of clothing.

"I'm so glad you're awake. Are you all right?"

I turn toward the voice and, yes, I see that it's Mom. I try to reply, but my mouth is so dry it's hard for me to speak.

"Wait. I'll be right back," she says.

In a couple of seconds she returns to the bedside, unscrewing the lid from a plastic water bottle. She puts it to my mouth and I take a sip and gasp.

"Thanks," I say as some of it trickles down my chin.

Something moving behind her catches my eye and I

look past to see a woman, dressed in what appears to be dark blue pajamas, enter the room and come up beside her. When Mom notices, she steps aside.

"I see you're finally awake, Eric. How do you feel?" the woman asks.

"Kinda woozy," I answer.

She nods and explains, "I suspect it's due to the medicine we're giving you." Then, because I probably look confused, she introduces herself. "I'm Debra. I'll be your nurse. I'll be looking after you for the next several hours. Do you hurt anywhere? Are you experiencing any pain?" she asks as she studies my eyes, shining a light into one, then the other.

I stop to consider. "My back hurts a little." I pause. "And my left hand."

When I raise it to illustrate, I see a piece of blue plastic encasing it.

"Can you wiggle your fingers?"

I comply and she nods.

"Now, the right hand."

I move them as well.

"How does your head feel?"

I scrunch up my eyebrows, unsure why she's asking.

"Any headaches?" she persists.

"Now that you mention it," I reply after taking a moment to consider, "yes."

I turn my head as I'm preparing to touch it and feel something on the back of it scrape the pillow. I begin reaching with my right hand, but again the needle jabs me. When I use my left one instead, I'm surprised to find the back of my head is bandaged.

She moves along the tubular metal railing that's encircling me and arrives at the foot of the bed. Lifting the blanket, she asks, "Can you wiggle your toes?"

When I do, she smiles and makes a note on a clipboard, then runs the tip of her pen up the sole of each foot. In response, my toes curl downward and the corners of her mouth turn up, almost smiling. She nods. Just as she is about to say something more, the curtains that form one wall of the room separate and another woman, dressed in a lighter shade of blue, steps inside. Dad follows a short distance behind her. Nurse Debra moves toward the woman and the two begin talking. Dad steps beside Mom and they do the same. I use this opportunity to resume examining my surroundings.

The first thing I notice is a piece of electronic equipment a few feet to my left, with the wires from my body running into it. It stands about four feet in height, is less than two feet in width, and is emitting intermittent beeps while a monitor on its face displays digital readouts. On the wall behind it are diagrams of the human anatomy, one of which has captions about what to do when certain situations occur. When I attempt to read the instructions, I'm surprised to find that I cannot. The diagram is shimmering, as if I'm seeing it through a moving sheet of wrinkled, clear plastic cling wrap.

On my right, a foot or so from my shoulder, is a vertical metal stand. Hooked to its top is a clear plastic bag filled with liquid and a tube running down to the needle in my arm. I'm still trying to figure out what I'm doing here when the newcomer separates herself from Nurse Debra and moves to a spot a few feet to my right.

"Hello, Eric. I'm Doctor Silberstein." In the same instant my eyes go to the plastic name badge on her chest that reads C Silberstein, MD. She glances toward my parents, then turns back to me and asks, "Do you want them to be here?"

"Why wouldn't I?"

"This is a confidential discussion and… " She glances at the clipboard. " …you're over eighteen years old and have the right to keep our talk private if you prefer."

"No," I say. "I mean yes. It's all right. They can stay."

She flashes a brief smile, then continues.

"That was quite an accident you had. What do you remember about it?"

Her comment startles me. When I try to recall what she might be talking about, my mind draws a blank and I shake my head and frown. She frowns as well, then studies me closely and asks, "You remember nothing?"

I start to shake my head again, but decide a verbal response will be better.

"No. No I don't. Is that why I'm here?"

"According to witnesses, an automobile ran a red light and struck you when you stepped into the street. It's a small miracle you've sustained only minor injuries." Her expression softens and she continues. "According to what we've been told, the car was stolen and the driver—who's been apprehended, by the way—was trying to escape the police. You bounced off the hood and the back of your head struck the windshield. Even though the CAT scan reveals nothing serious, your nurse tells me you're experiencing headaches. Can you describe them?"

I pause to consider, then tell her, "I just noticed them when she asked about them. My forehead feels tight and the sensation runs around to… "

Reluctant to use my right hand, I use the other and point to a spot a couple of inches above my left ear.

"On one side or both?"

"Both."

She asks me to rate the sensation on a scale of one through ten. When I give a relatively high rating, she asks, "Are you experiencing any other symptoms?"

I'm about to shake my head, when I pause and tell her about the shimmer that, now that I stop and see it more clearly, seems to be overlaid across everything. She steps forward and shines a light into each of my eyes, peering into them with obvious concern. After a moment, however, she comments that nothing appears unusual, but asks me a few more questions about the phenomenon. When she asks if it seems to be tied to the headache, I think about it, then reply, "I'm not sure. I've just started noticing it."

"Is he all right?" Mom interrupts.

"It's too early to tell." Turning back to me, Doctor Silberstein explains, "You've fractured a wrist. But aside from a few contusions and a probable concussion, there's nothing obviously wrong with you. Your vital signs are strong and your tests came back normal. Under other circumstances, there'd be little reason to keep you, but this shimmering, as you refer to it, as well as the headache concern me. Until I'm certain they don't indicate something more serious, I'd like to conduct a few more tests." She makes a few notes, then turns to my parents. "I've decided to admit Eric. I'll need you to help with the admission process."

"Is anything wrong?" asks Dad.

"It's too early to say," repeats the doctor. "I need keep him here for at least one or two more days to give us time to observe him."

"Can we bring him his laptop?" Dad asks. To the doctor's questioning look, he explains, "Eric's getting ready for school and should probably stay in touch with his advisor."

"Sure," she replies. "That shouldn't pose a problem."

Two days later, I'm back home. The tests revealed nothing and the headaches and the accompanying shimmer are starting to become less noticeable since I started taking the medication Doctor Silberstein prescribed. I'll have to admit, though, I'm not very good at taking stuff like this on a regular basis, so we'll have to see how things go from here. I still can't remember the accident. And though the gap in my memory bothers me, I have no choice but to accept it and be thankful things didn't turn out worse. As far as I can tell, I still have all my mental faculties, which I verify by playing a few rounds of computer chess. At my usual settings, I still win about half of the time, which is normal. Unable to come up with anything better, I go about preparing myself for the coming quarter.

… … … … …

A week later, I climb aboard the bus to keep the appointment with my advisor. When I transfer to the Orange Line and sit in one of the train's shiny blue seats, I can't help but notice the cute brunette sitting across from me.

She's wearing a short skirt and has her legs crossed. The left side of her hair has been buzzed to half an inch or closer. The rest of it, however, perhaps eight to ten inches of curls, has been cut into a ragged, almost spherical corona with one longer stray lock falling over her forehead and past her right eye to a point almost touching her cheek. There's a small silver ring piercing her left nostril and a tiny ruby stud on her right upper lip. It's her eyes, however, that catch my attention. An unusual shade of brown, like pieces of amber I once saw in a museum, shaded by the longest lashes ever, they stare at me without the slightest flicker of uncertainty while her lips curl into a smile.

My initial impulse is to avert my eyes downward, and I almost give in. It's only because I'm afraid she will interpret the reaction as fear—which it's not, just the habitual attempt to try to remain PC—that I catch myself and continue to maintain eye contact. I manage a smile before I pull out my cell phone and try to become a little more private. It's a useless attempt. In the seconds that follow, she crosses the aisle and drops into the seat beside me.

"Hi," she says. "My name is Erin. What's yours?"

"Eric," I reply.

"Really? That's almost the same as mine."

Although her aggressiveness startles me, I glance up only enough to notice her impish grin, then return my eyes to my phone.

"You a student?" she asks.

I feel my backpack move and it feels as though she's handling it. Although I find her physically attractive, people who have no respect for boundaries have always turned me off. As a result, I'm torn between my body's telling me to get close to her and my growing irritation over her aggressiveness and lack of respect.

"Um hmm," I reply.

"PSU?"

I nod.

"What's your major?" she asks.

I hear myself mutter, "Physics."

"Whoa!" she says, then giggles. "You're a geek?" When I don't respond, she says, "You're too cute to be a geek."

I'd really like to cut the conversation short, so I turn toward the window. Unfortunately, when I do so, the maneuver puts my pack squarely in front of her. There is the rip of Velcro releasing before I feel her remove something. I turn back toward her and see she is holding my notebook.

"Give that back!" I say and try to snatch it away from her as she begins turning pages.

She turns away from me and asks, "What are these? Are they poems?" All of a sudden, she giggles and says, "Yes, they are. This is poetry." Glancing over her shoulder with a suspicious look on her face, she asks, "Who wrote them?"

I start to turn my head away.

"Don't tell me these are yours."

I nod.

"No way. You, a physics major, writing poems?"

She turns her back again and I hear her thumbing through them. I find myself flattered by her interest. I've never shared them with anyone else before, not even with Dad, who I'm sure would enjoy them, so I allow her to read, curious as to what she will think about them. She pauses and studies one page in particular, twirling a lock of hair around her finger and looking thoughtful.

"Here's one I think I like," she says and starts reading

out loud.

> Reminder
>
> A bolide, heavenly fireball,
> Streaks earthward
> Through an electric dusk.
> "Oh, look!" I cry.
> But the inarticulate replies
> Of Michelins on asphalt
> And wind in my ear
> Are as empty as
> The seat beside me.

"You wrote this?" she asks, cocking her head when she finishes. When I nod again, she shakes her head and counters by saying, "No way a physics major did this." When I nod a third time, scrunching my shoulders up near my ears, she frowns. "Physics and poetry don't go together. How could you have produced this?"

"I guess some of my father rubbed off on me," I reply and explain what he does for a living.

"I'll say he did! And you have a vocabulary, too. Can I ask what inspired it?"

I've never been good at keeping secrets, so I tell her about the girl named Melissa who broke my heart back in Santa Fe.

"Sounds like she meant a lot to you."

I grimace and acknowledge she did. "It hurt a lot. I've never felt anything like it before."

"Have you gotten over it?"

"More or less."

She smiles broadly and says, "That's good, because I think you're really cute."

At this point, I want to tell her I think she's really crazy, but I restrain myself. Instead, because she is talking over the train's automated announcement, I look up to determine which stop we're approaching. A sign on the building's exterior says Portland Opera and I can see that we haven't crossed the Willamette River yet, so we have a few more minutes before we reach Portland State.

Erin is apparently giving either me or my poetry a little more thought, because she's lapsed into silence. As for me, aside from the fact that she's a little bit psycho, she's seriously beautiful and I'm having more than a little trouble getting back into my smart phone. She's also well-endowed—probably a D cup or larger—and is wearing one of those synthetic tops that clings to her breasts to the point I don't even have to guess what they look like. To make matters worse, her nipples poke through and the neckline plunges so low I can almost see her navel as I glance down her cleavage. It couldn't have been more than a second or two, but at one point she notices and tugs her lightweight sweater across them in an attempt to cover up. She scowls as if I've committed some hideous offense.

This is one element of certain women's behavior I don't understand: dressing provocatively, then acting offended when some man responds to his natural instincts. I mean, it's not like I came onto her. And besides, given half a chance, in another second or two I would have turned my eyes elsewhere.

Erin glares at me, stands up and throws down my notebook as she moves back to her original seat and we spend the rest of the ride pretending the other one doesn't exist. I'm both angry and confused—angry over what her actions imply about the kind of person I am, confused as to how I can undo the damage this unintentional glance has caused.

Despite the fact that I'm now miserable, I'm aware enough that this time, when I step out at SW Sixth Avenue and College Street, I make a point of watching where I'm going and avoid doing something that might get me killed. I turn toward the campus proper and find I'm a few yards from

Sixth, looking toward Park. I start off walking when I think I hear someone calling. Glancing around and seeing no one else responding to the hail, I see a girl with wavy, shoulder length, honey-colored hair running toward me and holding my notebook overhead.

Breathing hard as she catches up to me, she gasps, "You forgot this."

Surprised, both by my carelessness as well as her consideration, I reply, "Thank you."

She grins as she hands it over and says, "I see you met Erin. Did she shake you up?"

I nod, unsure how else to respond.

"She has that effect on people." She smiles, then starts to turn away.

"Wait," I say, wanting to know more. "How did you know… ?"

"Erin's kind of a… " She stops speaking, apparently to consider how to phrase what comes next. "Let's just say she's kind of unconventional, and you wouldn't be the first one she's pounced on."

I smile and reply, "Really," as a statement, but with a hint of a question in my voice.

"Really," she replies, then nods and starts to turn away again.

"Do you go to school here?" I ask before she can leave. She admits that she does, so I follow up with, "Do you think you could show me around?"

When she cocks her head and asks, "Are you new here?" I explain my situation.

Alex, as she calls herself, comes from the San Francisco Bay area and is starting her second year at PSU as a graphic design major. When I ask about our "friend" Erin, she replies, "Last year, she majored in Black Studies. This year, however, I hear she's changing over to Sexuality, Gender, and Queer Studies." I give Alex a questioning stare, to which she replies, "It's not that there's anything wrong with either program, but sometimes I think her intention is just to do whatever will provoke a response."

We spend the rest of the day getting acquainted while Alex shows me around the campus. We share quite a bit about each of our families, as well as what interests us. Both of Alex's parents are attorneys and we laugh about how someone with creative inclinations came out of that kind of household. It's almost as peculiar as how my interest in things subatomic developed from mine.

While the train ride left me shaken and wondering what kind of place my parents had chosen to move to, by the end of the day, I believe I have a good understanding of how everything at PSU is laid out, and I also feel I've made a new friend.

Chapter
Three

After the meeting with my course advisor, I descend the stairs from the Science Research & Teaching Center and step onto SW 10th Avenue. Glancing back at the large lime green sign in its window, I wonder whose brilliant idea it was to paint the building's inside walls the identical color. Shuddering at how much time I'll be spending in the physics department amid the Center's vivid interior, I'm at least grateful how well my initial interview went with Professor Basab Basu. I like the man. In fact, I like him a lot. Even though he has already told me he will hold me to high standards and that he expects good work and thinking outside the box without cutting corners, since I intend to give this effort all that I have, I find that we are very much in agreement. He has also given me a lot to consider about my degree path. It's confusing enough that I'm unable to make an immediate decision except that I'm aiming for a Bachelor of Sciences Degree rather than pursuing a Bachelor of Arts. Even so, I find myself intrigued by that side of the equation, because it's an unexpected approach to earning a degree in one of the sciences.

Since I have several weeks in which to occupy myself before plunging into the hard stuff, I remember there is a book I've been wanting to read. I've heard about Walter

Isaacson's biography of Albert Einstein and believe it might be just what I need to keep myself occupied. And while it's available for download as an eBook, I would prefer to read it in physical form. Unfortunately, it's way too spendy—as Oregonians like to put it—for my limited budget. Google Maps tells me that, if I follow SW 10th to Taylor, I will arrive at the main branch of Portland's Public Library. It's a beautiful day, so, taking the chance they will have a copy on hand, I decide to hike the roughly ten blocks to get there.

The library is an impressive red brick and white concrete building with a low ornamental concrete fence that separates the structure from the sidewalk. On its Taylor Street side, thirty to forty feet from the intersection, the fence briefly transforms into a bench. The reason this particular feature catches my eye is that a man—someone homeless, if I'm not mistaken—is sitting there. He's bearded, dressed in a stained brown suit jacket with matching trousers, and there appears to be some sort of animal perched on his shoulder. Hoping he won't notice me watching, I approach cautiously, not wanting to disturb. When I've halved the distance between us, I can see the creature is a squirrel. Every few seconds, the man reaches into his jacket's hip pocket and withdraws a light colored morsel which he then presents to his visitor. The creature doesn't hesitate to accept it, nor does it appear to be the least bit nervous, so it strikes me that this is an established relationship. I smile and wish I could walk up and ask how their friendship came to be, but I'm afraid if I do so, I will startle the squirrel and cause it to run away. I set the impulse aside and stand where I can continue observing the pair unnoticed.

I've been viewing this display of affection for three or four minutes, when I spot a group of teenage boys approaching from the opposite direction. They are laughing, joking, and bumping into one another, and I'm certain they're about to accomplish exactly what I'm trying to avoid. They've come to within half a dozen yards when the middle one notices the pair seated between us. Extending his arms to either side, he brings his companions to a halt. Initially annoyed, the two walking with him try to disengage themselves, until he points at what he's seeing, commenting to the one on his left and then to the other.

At first, they appear uncertain, unable to determine what he's referring to. Then, as the one nearest the concrete wall spots the man on the bench, a mischievous smile unfolds and he grabs the shirt of the third, pointing with his free hand to the man and the squirrel. In only a second, that one nods and the three begin conversing and gesturing with obvious excitement. Composing themselves, they proceed in the pair's direction with an air of casual indifference.

As they draw near, the squirrel pulls itself upright, ears erect, tail twitching vigorously. When they've come to within a couple of yards, the squirrel hunches down on all fours, leans forward and appraises them. One of the teens lunges and the squirrel leaps to the ground, dashes across the sidewalk and runs up the trunk of a nearby tree. The man stares after it for a moment, then turns around and spots the teens.

"What's happening, old man?" asks the middle one.

He's lean, angular in build and a full head taller than either of his companions. He glances at both of them and grins when he finds they are snickering. When the homeless man turns away in an attempt to ignore them, the trio's leader approaches, strikes the man's back with the palm of his hand and shouts, "I'm talking to you!"

The old man hunches up his shoulders and leans away. This angers the bully even more. He grabs the man by an arm and attempts to turn him. When the old man shakes free, the two shorter teens circle to where they can face him. The second one squats. His back is toward me, but I can see him tilt his head in an attempt to look the old man in the eyes.

"It's not polite to ignore people when they're talking

to you," he shouts.

While all this is happening, a man and woman are coming up the sidewalk from the same direction the teens did. When the man notices the confrontation, he takes the woman by the elbow and escorts her off of the sidewalk and into the street. They circle a parked car, eyeing the incident warily, and step onto the curb behind me. My first thought is to criticize them for avoiding the situation, when I realize that I'm providing the man no more assistance than they did.

I glance back and see that the teens have the man surrounded, each of them taking turns at shoving and shouting. I'm afraid that, in another minute or two, matters could escalate and they might even start beating the poor soul. A part of me wants to confront them, while another part is afraid I'll be beaten too, since there are three of them and only one of me. On top of it all, I've never done anything even remotely similar. Still, I can't turn away, nor can I simply stand by and watch. Telling myself that the old man and I together make two, I take a deep breath and begin walking toward them.

"Leave him alone," I shout, but the trio are too caught up with their game to notice. "Leave him alone," I repeat, a little louder as I come to within a dozen feet.

One of them hears me and glances back, then turns around to face me.

"Dudes, check it out," he calls to his friends. "We've got a hero coming to the rescue."

The other two look up and the tall one grins broadly. As they halt their attacks and step away to confront me, the old man clutches his lapels and raises his face and I can see he has started crying. At the same time, I'm beginning to develop a headache.

"This is none of your business," says the tall one as he approaches and faces me squarely. "Why don't you just get out of here and we'll pretend we never saw you?"

He brushes several strands of hair from his eyes,

broadens his stance and curls his hands into fists. As the other two move to flank him, I gather my courage and hope my voice doesn't crack.

"I'm not going to let you keep bullying him."

"Hah!" he explodes. "*You're* not going to let *us*? You and what army?"

His two friends grin, and I'm not sure what my next move should be. Deciding that walking straight at them would be begging for a fight—one I will certainly lose, and lose badly—I move toward the old man instead. Offering my right hand, I say, "Here. Please come with me."

Number three runs at me and shoves me aside. As I collide with the concrete fence, he shouts, "Get the hell out of here!"

Grabbing the wall, I use my casted hand to catch myself, barely avoiding tumbling onto the sidewalk. I gasp out loud, briefly wondering if I've worsened my injury. Even though I manage to keep my feet underneath me while stumbling backward, my rib cage strikes the concrete's edge and I cry out again. It takes everything I have to draw myself upright. As I haul myself back up to vertical, my head starts throbbing harder, the world begins shimmering, and I blink several times as I try to see clearly.

"We gave you a chance, dude, and you blew it," the second one announces. "Now, we're going to teach you to listen."

"Teach him, Tommy," says the leader and his friend glances back at him and nods.

Tommy starts coming toward me. When he's almost in front of me, he brings his right fist around in a wide sweeping arc. I raise my left arm to block it and—despite how hard it's becoming to see through the plastic cling wrap effect—I punch straight ahead with my right. Tommy's nose flattens and I feel warm wetness against my fist. Staggering back, blood streaming profusely, Tommy reaches up to cover himself. When he takes down his hands and sees what I've

31

done, he turns to his friends and shouts, "Get him!"

I glance past Tommy and see the shapes of the leader and number three coming toward me. I'd like to run, but with my head throbbing and the shimmer intensifying, I can't see clearly enough to do so. I have no idea what's happened to the old man, but since he hasn't stepped forward, I'm sure I'm alone in this.

The leader and number three arrive almost simultaneously. Unable to see well enough to defend myself, I raise both my arms in an effort to stave off their blows. Although I'm warding off most of them, one fist grazes my cheek and another one lands square in my gut, almost doubling me over. With no other choice, I begin stepping backward, afraid to retreat very far for fear of moving into traffic.

The visual interference is maddening. If I could just see more clearly, I might have some chance to defend myself. It couldn't return at a worse time and I wish I could put an end to it as the shimmering intensifies and appears to be taking on substance. Instead of overlaying everything around me, the world now appears to be part of it, crinkling and developing creases where the light display does. Maddened by the illusion, I reach up with both hands, as if to pull it away and I'm met with a curious sensation. It feels as if I'm holding something tangible. When I pull with my hands, the scene around me seems to move with them, bending and contorting according to which way I tear. Deciding this might be the way to be done with it once and for all, I pull downward. As if the world around me is a sheet of plastic or a page in a book, it folds downward as well. When I pull far enough, I find I'm able to look behind it and see the city of Portland clearly. Unsure what's happening, but needing my vision to clear, I continue to fold the previous situation aside until it's completely out of the way. Gone! Vanished completely!

Breathing heavily, I find I'm standing on the sidewalk

by the library fence with no sign of the trio. A few feet away, the old man sits on the bench in the concrete wall feeding peanuts to a squirrel. I look behind me and see the couple who passed by earlier. They are crossing the street, smiling and laughing, without a glance backward to indicate they are aware of what had happened only seconds before. When I look down the block, I see the same three teenage boys crossing SW Taylor on 11th, giving no indication they intend to turn in this direction.

What just happened? I don't know what to make of it, so I stand in place, drawing in chestfulls of air. Everything else looks the same as it did earlier, but there's no sign of anything dangerous. My side and left hand no longer hurt and the cast appears to be undamaged. After all that just happened, I'm not yet steady enough to visit the library. Instead, I remain on the sidewalk watching the man take care of his animal friend.

It doesn't take long for the old man to notice me. He smiles and motions, with a quick tilt of his head, for me to join him. I'm not sure if I'm ready to interact with anyone else yet, but when I remain where I am, the man motions to me again. I study him a moment longer. When I see that he shows no sign that he's aware of what had just happened with the three teenage boys—he seems calm and relaxed—I decide to do as he's suggesting. In the hope I still might learn something useful about the event, I walk toward him. When I arrive where he's sitting, I'm pleased to find that, although the little squirrel stops and studies me, it doesn't scamper away.

"Hi," I say.

"Hi, yourself," the old man replies. "I'm Joe Dexter and this here's Wally."

"I'm Eric Folder."

"Pleased to meet ya, Eric. I notice you've been watching us."

"I'm sorry. I didn't mean to stare." Unsure how to

33

bring up the incident with the teens, I add, "I, uh… I was just curious about the squirrel… I mean Wally."

"He does attract a fair amount of attention." Turning to the animal, he says, "Wally, say hello to Eric."

Instead, Wally goes from being perched on his hind legs, to dropping onto all fours on Joe's shoulder, looking expectantly at Joe's coat pocket.

"Would you like to feed him?" Joe asks.

When I nod, he reaches inside and withdraws a peanut, shell and all, then hands it to me.

"Don't be afraid," he says. "Wally don't bite. He's a friendly little critter. Just give it to him."

I accept the tidbit and present it to the squirrel. It extends both forepaws and snatches it away, then proceeds to chew through the shell, spitting fragments onto the sidewalk and Joe Dexter's coat. When it liberates a nut, it starts munching.

"Wally and me have been friends for a couple of years now," Joe replies when I ask how the two got together. "I used to sit here pretty regular, offering him peanuts until he eventually decided he could trust me. At first, I used to set them a few feet away. Little by little, I'd move them closer until, one day, I held one between my fingertips, waiting for him to take it. By then, he'd developed quite a taste for 'em, so it didn't take long before he decided he would risk it." Joe smiles and says, "We've been buds ever since."

Joe and I spend quite a while getting acquainted. When he confides that he used to be a Navy Seal, he seems surprised when I don't question his claim. Instead, I tell him, "Back in Santa Fe, there was a man who kept all of his possessions in a shopping cart and hung out in the Coronado Shopping Center. Word had it he also had served as a Seal." I look at Joe and add, "I guess it takes a lot out of you."

He nods, but elects not to elaborate and I decide not to press him further, not only about his time in the Navy, but also about the thugs. I mean, how could I bring up something that obviously didn't happen? I'm still feeling confused and think maybe the book that I came for will help me unwind. We say our good-byes, and I make my way into the library where I encounter a woman with a badge that identifies her as one of the library's staff. She directs me to a room on the building's ground floor and teaches me how to find what I'm looking for. I'm pleased when the computer indicates they not only carry Isaacson's *Einstein*, but also that they have a copy on hand. After obtaining a library card, I check out the book and take it with me.

My TriMet app tells me the nearest bus that will get me to Sellwood is only a quarter mile from here. During the ride home, I try to begin reading, but I can't take my mind off of what happened earlier. How did I go from being in the middle of a fight to an entirely different set of events? It was like rewinding a movie several frames, then watching it evolve toward an entirely different outcome. I once heard of experimental movies that were filmed back in the sixties, each with several possible endings. The audience was allowed to decide which one they preferred. The problem is, this isn't a movie. My one consolation is the fact that my headache is gone and, except for a residual shimmer, the world seems normal again.

Unfortunately, that doesn't last long. I'm helping Mom and Dad clear the dining room table after dinner. I've taken a stack of plates into the kitchen when it feels like my head is going to explode. I drop the dishes and grab my head as the headache escalates.

"Eric!" Mom calls in response to the resulting clatter. "Are you all right?"

In only seconds, both parents rush in and find me clawing at the air around me. I know I must look crazy, but once again the world is staring to crumple amid intersecting shards of light, making it impossible to see anything clearly. Just as before, when my fingers latch onto something tangible, I take a cue from that earlier experience and pull down once again. When I do, everything seems to fold in the same direction. I begin to experience painless clarity as I tear one reality away, only to find myself standing upstairs in the corridor just outside my room.

What just happened and how did I get here? Am I going crazy? I stare at my hands wondering what they grabbed onto to that landed me in an entirely different location from the one I'd occupied only seconds earlier. What should I do? Do I call Mom and Dad? I'm breathing hard and my heart is pounding. I need to calm down before I hyperventilate.

"Are you all right?" Mom calls from downstairs, the same question she had called from the dining room a few seconds earlier.

Why would she repeat this? Did I call out? Did I make some other kind of noise? This is very strange and I'm unable to answer. When I hear Dad say, "I'm going to see what the matter is," followed by footsteps pounding up the stairwell, I regain my senses.

"I'm okay," I call out to him.

The footsteps stop. "Are you sure?"

"Yeah. I'm just a little shaken up. I'm going to bed now. I'm sure I'll feel better in the morning."

He pauses before answering, then says, "Call me if you need me."

"I will." I seem to remember that only a moment ago, in *this* reality, we had been discussing something that had happened earlier, so I tell him, "I promise." And while I don't remember exactly what it was, I somehow know that what I'd answered was appropriate.

I'm becoming worried that the accident may have caused more damage than I, the doctor, or either of my parents realized, so I'm more than a little scared. Unsure what else I should do, I decide a good night's sleep might help. If anything else strange happens, maybe I'll need to talk it over with them tomorrow.

Chapter
Four

I love morning showers and the way they help me get my head straight.

It's the morning after the library incident and, now that I think about it, that strange thing that happened to me last night when I suddenly found myself relocated to the hallway upstairs. Vague memories are rising to the surface, as if they are trying to get my attention, but the shower feels so good that I refuse to allow my thoughts to drift to anything outside my present situation. Instead, I close my eyes, intending to let the water's flow and a good scrubbing to wake me up and help start my day. Once I'm thoroughly warmed, I reach for the shampoo and begin lathering. I'm trying to hold my left hand clear of the water to keep the plastic brace dry, when I notice it's missing. *How could it have possibly come off?* I worry that the Velcro somehow broke open while I was sleeping. But since I'm already wet, I will make a point of checking my bed as soon as I'm dry.

The hand is tender and reminds me to be careful. Taking care not to reinjure it, I start scrubbing with my right hand, going easy with my left. I manage to give myself a good massage as I work my way down to my temples and the sides of my head. Then, because the sutures still have a few weeks to go before my body will absorb them, I work gently over the part of my skull that struck the windshield.

I stop.

Something feels different.

There should be stubble growing over a bald spot where they shaved me in order to suture the wound. There should also be stitches. But as I feel around with my fingertips, separating the strands of hair, carefully probing every inch of my scalp, I can't detect anything except hair, all of which is as fully grown as the other strands. There is a bump and it's tender, but there's no sign of what the doctors did.

This isn't right.

I lift the shower nozzle from its holder and begin rinsing so I can feel my scalp better. Shampoo is getting into my eyes, so I decide to rinse off completely. Then, replacing the shower head, I start examining myself with both hands.

Still nothing.

Dripping, I step out of the tub and quickly towel dry my hair. Shoving the terry cloth into the rack, I reexamine my scalp, but it feels no different. I need a second mirror in order to verify what my fingers are telling me and the first one I think of is in Trish's bathroom. I finish drying, then wrap the towel around me and head toward her bedroom.

Empty houses feel different than they do when someone else is there with you. It doesn't just have to do with sound or the lack of it. They can be in a different part of the house. You don't even have to know they are there, but the difference is noticeable. I can't explain it any better than that and, right now, I'm pretty sure I'm alone. Even so, I call through the door.

"Trish!"

When she doesn't answer, I knock several times and call to her louder this time. "Trish, can I borrow a mirror?"

Silence.

Putting my ear against the door, I give several more knocks, just to be certain, and call once again. When she fails to answer, I turn the knob and peek inside. Just as I thought, the room is empty.

My sister has started wearing perfume and the scent of it lingers. The bedroom's decor reflects her taste. Even though Trish is one of the most feminine girls I've ever encountered, there's very little pink in either the room's furnishings or Trish's wardrobe. She has developed a preference for pale green and lavender, and almost everything that isn't ivory, like her dresser and bureau, is a shade of one or the other. No pictures of NCT Dream, or Jaden Smith, or CNCO either, even though she listens to their music almost constantly. My sister is all about neatness.

Her bathroom door is closed, so there's a chance she might be inside. If she is, that could explain why she didn't hear me. Making sure that my towel is secure, I decide to find out.

"Trish," I call.

When she fails to acknowledge, I open the door and find the bathroom is empty. Fortunately for me, Trish is not only super-organized, but she also has a passion for mirrors. When I spot one that is handheld, I grab it and position myself in front of the three-way mirror above the sink. Turning my back and looking over my shoulder, I begin parting my hair with my free hand, only to see uninterrupted growth. No matter how I arrange it, I can't find the bald spot or feel the stubble I know should be there.

I'm replacing the hand mirror, when I catch a glimpse of my back in the door's full length one and what I see shocks me. Needing to confirm my impression, I hurry to close the door, turn the latch, and let my towel fall to the floor. Retrieving the mirror, I look again and see the impossible. While my lower back and hips do, in fact, show bruises, they're not where they were a week ago. Not only that, they're bright purple, not the least bit faded, which tells me they're fresh.

This can't be.

I keep examining myself for several minutes, studying my reflection and thinking. Finally, I decide I should show Dad and Mom and see their reaction. After one long and deliberate check to insure I've left no trace of my intrusion—knowing full well that Trish would freak if she found anything broken, messed up or out of place—I return to my room to put on a pair of briefs and cargo shorts. It's then I remember the missing cast. I examine my left hand with my right, testing gently at first, then with increasing amounts of pressure. The wrist not only hurts, but it's obviously swollen. Puzzled, I start examining where I'd been sleeping. After tearing away the blankets and finding nothing beneath them, I drop to my knees and search underneath the bed.

No cast.

It was bright blue plastic, so there is no way I could miss it, but now I'm certain it's definitely gone. I sit upright, cross my legs and place my hands on my thighs, too shocked to do anything more. I know I was still wearing it after what happened outside the library, so what has changed since then? I decide to go over yesterday's events. My mind drifts back to the way I seemed to fold away the ugly street scene and, along with it, Joe Dexter's attackers, and how everything seems different after my abrupt relocation from the dining room to the upstairs hallway. Could other things, such as my cast, have changed and I failed to notice? The question makes me more than a little nervous, but rather than just sit and wait for the next thing to happen, I rise and make my way downstairs with the thought of having breakfast. Maybe a little food in my belly will help me think more clearly.

On the kitchen counter, I find a note.

Your dad and I are shopping for groceries.
We expect to be back by noon.
Call if you need anything.

Using mostly my right hand, I open the cupboard and take down a bowl and a box of cold cereal. Once I've grabbed a carton of milk and a spoon, I add sugar, then pull out a barstool from under the counter and sit down to eat. As I go through the motion of reading the back of the cereal box, my mind drifts back to yesterday evening and what seemed to be memories trying to intrude.

When I step into a new universe, I tell myself, the Eric I've stepped into must certainly have a past. He doesn't exist without a history. Therefore, I've stepped into his series of events. And since his memories are stored inside his brain, a brain which has now become my own, if I try hard enough, I should be able to access them and learn about the world I have just become part of. Even though I can't do it yet, I will need to do so if I hope to fit in without seeming deranged to the people I interact with… beginning with Mom, Dad, and Trish.

Eventually, I find myself staring at the milk and what little is left of the cereal when a voice interrupts my daydreams.

"Eric!"

It's Dad.

"Why is this mess still here?" he asks, glaring as his eyes go from my empty cereal bowel to the half empty glass of milk standing beside it. He picks up the carton and says, "It's warm. This should have been put away a long time ago." Looking at Mom, he adds, "I think we ought to toss it."

I apologize, but when I tell them I need their help, each of them pulls up a barstool and sits down to listen. I'm afraid to tell them about Joe Dexter, since I have a hard time believing it myself. Instead, I decide to ease into what happened last night by explaining about this morning and some of the events that happened yesterday, including my bus ride to the college and the interview with my advisor, they stare at each other.

"What are you talking about?" asks Mom. "Except for the quick trip you took to the library in our car, you were home all day."

I stare at them, and then start to recount my version of events. But when I lean against the counter, putting my weight on my injured left hand, I cry out, grimace and hold onto it.

"Let me take a look at that," says Dad. Taking my hand into his, he examines it. "I think it's broken. That fall off the ladder must have been more serious than you let on."

My mind flashes back to the conversation from the top of the stairs and I'm beginning to have a vague recollection of what they are talking about.

"Why didn't you tell us how bad it was?" asks Mom. "Does anything else hurt?"

"My head hurts," I say, indicating the location.

I'm about to ask them about the ladder when Dad reaches out and examines my scalp. When I wince, he turns to Mom. "Let's take the cold things out of the car, then get him to an emergency room."

On the way to the ER, I begin piecing together their take on yesterday. According to their version of events, we spent all day in the garage, storing whatever we couldn't find a space for inside the house. Then, an hour or so past midday, I told them I needed a break and made a roughly two hour round trip into Portland, after which I returned with Einstein's biography. At one point last night, just after we had decided to stop to eat dinner, I was trying to store a box somewhere near the garage's rafters when I leaned a little too far and the ladder I was standing on slipped out from under me. Mom and Dad were looking elsewhere when I landed. By the time they turned to see what had happened, I was picking myself up and brushing myself off, smiling and assuring them everything was fine. When I start giving them my version of events, they become silent.

Dad tells Mom, "I suspect he sustained a concussion

as well."

"I'm not crazy," I object.

"You did spend much of the night talking in your sleep," Mom replies. "You woke me a couple of times. I just wish we had taken your fall more seriously."

"But… "

They dismiss my objections as ridiculous, so I spend the rest of the ride to the hospital wondering whether they are just products of my imagination. I have to admit, my memories of all that has occurred until now, especially yesterday, do seem surreal. Were it not for the ache in my temples and the shimmer that continues to be laid over everything, I might be inclined to agree with them.

This visit to the ER goes much the same as the last one, by which I mean the first visit, the one that does not match my parents' recollections. This is a different hospital, but the CAT scan still shows nothing serious and again I end up wearing a plastic brace to protect my wrist and hand. Although I decide not to mention the visual effects, my parents tell the doctor how my memories don't match theirs, so I'm once again held overnight for observation. Just like the last time, the doctor prescribes something for me that's supposed to help with the headaches.

When I finally get home, I decide to conduct some online research and learn that many individuals who experience migraines describe a phenomenon that medical professionals term an aura. Their descriptions liken it to what I call a shimmer. Auras sometimes appear as a network of lines, like the ones I've been dealing with, although there is no reference to migraine victims finding them tangible the way I have. There is certainly no mention of anyone experiencing similar results.

When I shut down my computer, I spot a Post-it® with note I've left to myself, telling me my course advisor appointment, which I thought I already had, is scheduled for tomorrow!

... ...

The ride into town reminds me of Groundhog Day, a movie Dad and I watched together on cable a few years ago. It's about a weatherman who visits a small town and keeps waking up in the same hotel room at exactly the same time every morning with the same radio program playing, the same scene outside his hotel window, and he keeps living the same day over and over again. Although several things have changed since the first ride into town, just like that weatherman, I catch the same bus at about the same time and wonder what this trip has in store for me.

When I transfer from the bus to the Orange Line, I find myself drawn to the same seat as the first trip. And while a similar brunette is sitting across the aisle from me, a couple of things about her are different. Instead of that radical hairstyle, her hair is cut into something symmetrical. Instead of frizz, it falls into ringlets and her facial jewelry is gone. When she glances up, she gives me a smile, but doesn't cross over to sit next to me. I'm somewhat relieved, and at the same time find myself wondering what will happen if I am the one who takes the initiative. Deciding I have to give it a try, as the train pulls away from the next stop, I keep my eyes fixed on her as I rise out of my seat and take the one beside her.

"I... ," I begin, but when she glances over, I hesitate. She gives me a curious look, so, still feeling nervous, I try again. "Hi," I say, hoping it will sound close enough to what I started to say a second ago that she won't notice the misstep.

"Hi," she replies, still appearing uncertain, but with a hint of a smile.

"Do you mind if I sit next to you?"

"Looks like you already are," she says and chuckles.

I can't help but laugh and it seems to relieve any tension between us.

"My name's Eric."

"Erin," she replies. "Nice to meet you."

I explain that I'm new to Portland and that I have recently relocated from Santa Fe to attend Portland State University.

"I think you'll like it there," she says. "It's a good school and most of the students are easy to get along with."

I'm so relieved that she doesn't have the same attitude as the previous Erin and that the conversation seems to be flowing naturally. When she tells me she is a creative writing major, I'm pleasantly surprised that the person beside me is not the same radical individual I met on the last trip. Furthermore, her admission leads me to show her some of my attempts at writing poetry. When I hand over my paper notebook, she stares at it.

"You don't have a laptop?"

"I use it for most things. Somehow, though, I seem to be more comfortable writing this kind of stuff with a paper and pen."

She nods, as if understanding, then starts thumbing through, pausing from time to time, until she stops at "Reminder," the poem that attracted the previous Erin. She appears to read it a couple of times, then says, "I like this one."

So, they do have, at least, one thing in common. This pleases me and we spend the rest of the ride getting acquainted until we finally step off onto SW Sixth, where we agree to meet again this coming weekend. As I walk to the SRTC to reintroduce myself to my course advisor and Erin heads toward the student union, I glance back and wonder whatever happened to Alex.

It doesn't take me long to find out. She's standing at the train stop, clad in a T-shirt and jeans. Her arms are folded over her chest and the word HORROR, printed in black ink with red blood dripping from the H and each of the Rs, peeks out from under them. To make matters worse, this iteration of

45

Alex is scowling. Have we done a flip-flop? I don't know what to make of it. We haven't yet spoken, so perhaps I'm reading too much into this. Then again, so many things have changed recently, I suspect there may be more going on than I'm aware of. Everything that has happened since I woke up yesterday morning—Scratch that!—since the afternoon before in that alternate world, has my mind working overtime. I still don't understand what happened outside the library, despite my theories. To make matters worse, what happened last night at the dinner table comes rushing back and I recall experiencing a migraine and tearing away the resulting shimmer before I found myself upstairs. I return to thoughts of leaving one Eric's body and ending up in another as I peeled away one reality and replaced it with this one. This is craziness. This can't happen, can it? Then again, nothing else explains it and I'm growing seriously afraid. Although every part of my intellect cries out against it, the sensation I experienced when I folded aside the shimmering, crumpling world around me to expose each new one, felt tangible, as real as the concrete that's now underneath my feet.

Deciding the best thing I can do—for the moment, at least—is to simply ignore her, I turn toward the campus to keep my appointment.

Chapter
Five

Fortunately, this Basab Basu is the same as the last one and together we make the same decisions about my degree path as we did before. I find it encouraging, because I don't know how much more uncertainty I'm ready to take.

I'm about to exit the building when several objects in the lobby I failed to notice earlier capture my attention. This makes me wonder if I simply missed them, or if they hadn't been here the first time. There are skeletons on display and I wonder if they might be fossils of ancient animals. The fact I'm a physics major is probably why their presence surprises me. I've been so absorbed with organizing my major, which primarily deals with what most people would consider abstractions—although, in fact, they deal with the most fundamental realities, the stuff that underlies everything in the universe—that it never occurred to me this building would feature items such as these. I laugh to myself at my failure to think things through and stop to examine them.

Each of the display cases are walled with glass, providing an unobstructed view of their contents. They're arranged along one side the lobby, half of which has wooden tables flanked by uncomfortable looking black plastic chairs. The other half contains leather upholstered couches and chairs throughout. I find it oddly comical that all of the black plastic chairs are occupied, while the more comfortable upholstered furniture is completely empty.

Setting my amusement aside, I decide to examine these objects which seem to interest no one but me. The first case I approach, as I enter the foyer from the physics department, contains the remains of a California sea lion and a harbor porpoise. In addition to the bones, there are photographs of both creatures affixed to the glass, rather than drawings or digital likenesses, making it obvious that these are not fossils. So much for my preconceptions.

I spend a minute or two examining both, then move to the second display where a black spider monkey and a Sumatran orangutan stand side by side. I spot a notation on the orangutan's label that these skeletons were "articulated by BI 406 students"—a senior year biology class—and I'm impressed by how well they've been assembled. A tan business card beneath the spider monkey's photo tells me these artifacts are on loan from the Museum of Natural History. It also provides a URL that promises more information. Wondering if all of these skeletons are student projects, I return briefly to the sea lion and porpoise display and learn that the students who assembled these two are mentioned by name. The case nearest the street contains the remains of a sloth bear and a tiny red panda. All in all, there are three glass display cases mounted on light brown wooden pedestals.

"Interesting, aren't they?" asks a masculine voice next to me.

A glance to my right reveals a tall slender dude who appears to be somewhere around my age. The sides and back of his straight black hair have been buzzed to a fade, with a much longer top gelled back and trimmed neatly around its edges. He is studying the smaller of the two reconstructions, but even though his eyes, colored somewhere between blue and violet, are focused on the display cases, I can feel that his attention is squarely on me.

I nod.

"They're museum quality," he observes. Turning toward me and looking directly into my eyes, he smiles and adds, "The only way they could excite me more is if, say, they were a T-Rex or saber tooth tiger." Then to introduce himself, he extends a hand and says, "Dan Hastings."

I accept it and find he has a firm, sincere grip.

"Eric Folder," I reply.

"Are you setting up your course load?"

"Pretty much. I still have a few things to think about."

I'm about to inquire if he is a biology major, which would explain his interest, when he tilts his head and asks, "Are you a native Oregonian?"

Wondering what directed him onto that tangent, I shake my head and return a questioning look.

"Me neither," he replies, then goes on to explain, "I moved up here from California and I'm trying to decide if I want to take on more than eight hours per quarter and pay the non-resident tuition, or if I should just remain part-time until I qualify for residency." Then, smiling sheepishly, he adds, "I also have trouble making friends, so I'm feeling a bit isolated."

He seems friendly enough and not the least bit reserved, so deciding against pointing out the apparent contradiction between his statement and his outward openness, I return the conversation to his previous remark.

"Are you in a hurry to graduate?"

"Kinda. It seems like I've been in school for as long as I can remember."

"If I were in your situation, I'd wait. It's only one more year. After that, you can take as many units as you want."

Dan Hastings shrugs and says, "I guess so."

He appears to be considering my comment when a woman looks up from her laptop and asks, "Can you please keep it down?"

Even though this is not a library and there are a few

other audible conversations going on in other parts of the room, she is still glaring at us.

"Are you hungry?" Dan asks in a quieter voice. "The student union's food isn't half bad and I'm thinking lunch would be good right now."

Realizing that the interview with Professor Basu has left me hungry as well, I agree to join him. After exiting, we make our way down Montgomery and across the South Park blocks to the Smith Memorial Student Union. As we enter, I glance through a glass partition on our left and see what appear to be sound technicians setting up some kind of a musical event—a small concert perhaps, because there's not much room for a dance floor. There's a stage on the enclosure's far side, and several audio mixers and computer monitors spread throughout the space in between. Ordinarily, I would probably go inside and ask questions, but Dan appears to be on a mission, so we head straight up the double stairwell in front of us.

The food court is a large room filled, for the most part, by a dozen or so rows of tables and chairs. A quarter of its space is taken up by food service counters and some freestanding beverage coolers. After checking out what's available, we decide to pass on the Asian cuisine and burgers. We are commenting on the absence of pizza, when we notice a vendor serving burritos to a couple of other students. We nod to each other and walk toward him.

I settle on a cilantro chicken, carne asada mix served on a bed of brown Spanish rice with a sprinkling of black beans and hot salsa. Dan, on the other hand, keeps his burrito simpler, requesting only the carne with standard frijoles, adding Cheddar cheese and shredded lettuce, while keeping his salsa mild. After he picks up a coke and I select a bottle of yerba mate, we head to a checkstand. When Dan's eyes flick to the bright blue plastic encasing my left forearm and hand, he asks, "Do you need any help?"

"Naw. I'm fine. But thanks for the offer."

We spot an empty table in the middle of the dining area and head straight toward it. On the way, he asks, "Do you mind talking about it?" glancing toward the cast and the bandage on the back of my head. When I tell him about the fall from the ladder, he winces, then suggests with a grin, "Maybe you should tell people you're into MMA."

I shake my head. "Not a good idea. One, I don't lie, and two, once the cast comes off, someone is likely to make me prove it."

We laugh as we get down to the business of stuffing our faces. I must have been hungrier than I'd thought, because it's not long before I take a last swallow and wash it down with a swig of cold tea.

"Do you live here on campus?" he asks.

I shake my head and describe my situation. "What about you?" I ask.

"University Pointe. It's really nice and my aunt's paying for it."

His comment surprises me. "Not your parents?"

He shakes his head. "They can't afford it and probably wouldn't if they could." When I remain silent, waiting for him to elaborate, Dan compresses his lips and turns his head away. Eventually, he turns back to me and explains. "They drink too much and aren't interested in my situation." As I open my mouth to comment, he adds, "Aunt Enid has always been like a mother to me. When the fights between my parents get too loud and I can't take it anymore, I pack my clothes and spend the night at her place— sometimes a couple of nights—and my folks never seem to notice that I'm missing. It's been like that for as long as I can remember.

"When I told Aunt Enid that I intended to go to college, she suggested Portland State," he explains. Anticipating my next question, he adds, "She grew up and went to school here. She thought PSU would be perfect for me. They have a good science department, Portland is far enough away from home that my parents won't be on my back—that is, when they stop fighting long enough to even think about me—and the city's small enough that I won't need a car. Also, Portland has a great deal to offer whenever I need a break from my course load. Knowing how expensive housing can be, she decided to pay for my portion of the room at University Pointe."

"Your portion." Although I phrase it as a statement, it's clearly a question.

"It's a four bedroom suite with two baths. Two of my roommates have already moved in, and we're expecting the last one to arrive in another ten days."

"But you're paying your tuition."

Dan nods. "I have a small savings account that I set up while I was working."

I decide not to inquire about the details. Instead, I suggest, "But it's not enough to cover a full course load."

"Not nearly, although I might qualify for a Pell Grant and financial aid. I'm giving those possibilities some thought."

"Which means you'll have to start working to pay the non-resident tuition."

In response, he just nods.

"That's crazy. Why kill yourself when, in just one more year, your tuition will drop and you can spend all of your time focusing on your studies?"

"That's what Aunt Enid says."

"If I were you, I would listen. Look," I say. "If you're working full time and blow your GPA bad enough, won't you have go home?"

"I suppose."

"Sounds like a no-brainer to me." When Dan looks away scowling, I add, "Hey! I didn't mean to offend you. I'm just trying to help you think this thing through."

On one hand, I believe he has a right to feel offended. After all, we have just met and here I am telling him what to do with his life. On the other hand, since he brought up the subject without any prompting on my part, I have to wonder if I can take it as an unvoiced request for input. I'm relieved when he turns back again and says, "No prob, dude." He gives me a smile and asks, "Would you like to come over and check out the place?"

I had been planning to simply return home, but since I haven't made any friends yet—with the possible exception of Erin—I agree. Besides, I've been home almost all of the time since I got here, and I would like to expand my awareness of Portland and the University.

The building he lives in is a two minute walk from the student union. I'm impressed with how modern it looks, with its well-defined red brick facets and its laminated wood, glass and steel entranceway. I was expecting something older, like many of the buildings nearby that are labeled as campus housing. We step inside and its lobby makes me feel as if I'm entering a hotel, with its polished floor and glass walls. Before we take one of the elevators, Dan shows me the ground floor facilities. There is a reception desk, social rooms, a study retreat with computers and a printer, and a fully-equipped gym. He also explains that there's a walkway and something like a park on University Pointe's roof, giving anyone who cares to go up a view of the city and the surrounding hillsides. The only thing that turns me off is that the wall with the elevator doors and some of those in the lobby are the same lime green as SRTC's interior. I guess nothing is perfect. In fact, I want to live here and I haven't even been up to his room yet. All the time he's giving me this tour, the smile on his face shows how happy he is that he's living here. There are so many students from obviously diverse backgrounds that I don't think it will take him too long to make any number of friends

We leave the elevator on the building's tenth floor and he approaches a door and unlocks it. We enter a room that is outfitted with leather chairs and couches, not to mention artwork, and I pause in the entrance to admire it. It even has a small kitchenette with an eating counter and chairs. Just off the living room, there's an alcove with a small circular dining table, four chairs and a view.

"How much does this place set Aunt Enid back?" When he states the amount, I reply, "That's half of what I've seen landlords charging for similar apartments throughout Portland. The demand must be astronomical. How did you manage to get in?"

Dan shrugs and says, "Aunt Enid made the arrangements some time ago. You'll have to ask her."

Just then, a dark complexioned man with a backpack slung over his shoulder arrives from somewhere in the apartment's rear. He smiles and nods to us.

"Hi," he says. Then, to Dan he asks in an unfamiliar accent, "Made a new friend?"

Dan nods and says, "Juba, this is Eric. He moved here a few days ago from Santa Fe, New Mexico."

"*New* Mexico?" Juba asks.

"It's one of the fifty States," I explain. "It's the one between Arizona and Texas."

"Ah!" he says. "I've heard about Texas."

"What about you?" I ask, smiling to impart a friendly tone to my question. "You don't sound as if you're from around here either."

This elicits a laugh. "Hardly. I'm from Lagos, Nigeria," he says, then goes on to explain it's the country's largest city and, further, he belongs to the Yoruba, one of the country's two major ethic groups.

"He's a public health major," Dan adds.

We spend a while talking about our various backgrounds and what has brought us here. At one point, I glance over at Dan and notice his face has turned pale and he's starting to look faint. When he grips the back of a couch and clutches at his chest, I immediately panic.

"Are you all right?" I ask.

He shakes his head and gasps, "Heart."

Until now, Dan has made no mention of a health condition, so this comes as an unexpected surprise. Turning to Juba, I ask, "Can you do something to help him?"

Visibly as shaken as I am, Juba manages, "I'm not studying medicine. Just public… "

An audible gasp from Dan cuts him off. I reach for my phone and punch 9-1-1. When the voice at the other end asks, "What is your emergency?" I reply, "I think my friend is having a heart attack."

"What's your location?" she asks and I go blank, unaware of the street address and even unable to remember the name of the building we are in. "Here," I say and hand the cell phone to Juba. "Tell her where we are."

But as Juba begins providing the dispatcher with the necessary information, I tune him out when I begin to see how bad Dan's appearance has become. His knees start to buckle and I don't believe he will last until an ambulance arrives. As perspiration beads across his forehead and his skin begins to turn blue, my head starts to ache and the shimmering that I have completely forgotten begins obstructing Dan and Juba from view. Furious that I can no longer see them clearly, I reach out with my hands and try to tear away the obscuring white lines and flashes of light that hang like a glistening veil between us. There is a palpable sensation of my fingers becoming caught in a softly throbbing webwork. I start to pull it down in an attempt to tear it away and notice a clear space above it and what appears to be blue sky beyond. How can this be? We're in a room on the tenth floor of a sixteen story building, and yet I'm beginning to see sky.

Glancing back down through the shimmer, I can barely see, let alone hear Dan as he appears to drop to the floor. Looking at Juba is no better, because he has become a dark silhouette, almost invisible, behind the veil of light that surrounds me.

Desperate to see and to hear what is happening, I reach up toward the top of the veil and pull downward. The certain knowledge of how this action improved Joe Dexter's situation overrides any momentary concern over whether this is the right thing to do. As I continue to pull, the barrier that is between myself and these two appears to fold down on itself, revealing blue sky and the trees in the park that runs in front of the student union. All at once, I'm standing outside and looking at Dan Hastings. He is holding a paper cup emblazoned with the logo of a nationwide coffee chain.

"What's with you?" Dan asks. "You look like you've seen a ghost."

"I…"

My mouth has gone dry and I find speaking impossible. I look down at my hand and notice I'm holding a white paper cup that also bears the green coffeehouse emblem. This is just as bizarre as what happened after the dining room incident. I do the only thing I can think of and put the cup to my lips. Tasting chai mocha latte, I swallow and manage an uneasy laugh. For the moment, there is no easy response since, like my parents, he would consider me crazy if I were to tell him my take on what just happened. Still, I find myself wondering what actually occurred. How did we get to this outside location and what do I say next? Something like: How's your health? Are you feeling all right?

From the look of him, Dan Hastings has never felt better. There is color in his cheeks, his eyes are clear and focused, and he's standing strong and steady. Furthermore, he's dressed noticeably better than he had been earlier. Instead of a T-shirt and jeans, he is wearing slacks and a pressed, long sleeved white shirt with starched collar and cuff links. I, on the other hand, must look a mess from the way the man is staring.

I have to figure this thing out, assuming it's even possible. I can't deny that Dan's situation has obviously improved, just like Joe Dexter's. Aside from Alex's apparent change for the worse, I'm pleased how much good seems to have resulted from two of these… folds, I guess you could call them. Lacking a better name, I'll stick to it.

Ironically, Dan asks, "Are you feeling all right? Are the migraines getting any worse?"

I put my free hand to my head and start to refer to my recent head injury. But, once again, the bandage is gone. I glance at my wrist and so is the cast. This time, however, my wrist isn't swollen and the back of my head feels just fine.

It has finally dawned on me that, with each new fold, I have been entering separate realities in parallel universes. This explains why things become different after each new fold. While there are certain factors in common with each of them, I suspect that, because of how complex the world is, the number of possible decisions all of the individuals might make would lead to different outcomes in each of them. Some of the results might be exactly like the ones I'm familiar with. Others might be slightly different. While many will not resemble anything I've experienced before. This makes me very uneasy about the reality I've just folded into.

Unsure how much I might have already told him about my headaches, I change the subject by telling him about having met Erin, adding I have no idea where I should take her on Friday night. And, in fact, I really don't, assuming we are still going out in this reality. I decide to ask for his advice. When he pauses to consider, I suggest, "Maybe we could just hike over to your place and figure it out."

"Not likely," he says. "I live in the South Waterfront." I shoot him a questioning look, so he explains, "It's doable, but it would take us a good half hour or longer to walk there and I'm not into hiking.

"On the other hand, I'm not parked all that far from here and we can drive there in maybe ten minutes." He claps his hand on my shoulder, then wraps his arm around me.

Giving me a hug of sorts, he says, "Now that you mention it, I'd like to show off my crib."

I stare and try not to act confused, not only because of his change of residence, but also because he's acting as if we're much closer than two dudes who met less than an hour ago.

Chapter
Six

Dan leads me to where a shiny new black Camaro convertible is parked and I'm surprised when he opens the door to let me in.

"Is this a 1LT?" I ask as I run my fingertips along the passenger door's window molding. The model is not marked on the car's exterior and naturally I assume it's one of Camaro's lower end configurations.

Dan grins and shakes his head. "2SS," he replies and I'm dumbstruck. If I have the numbers right, this car costs fifty thousand dollars, give or take a few.

Naturally, the next question out of my mouth is, "Is this something your Aunt Enid gave you?"

"Hah! Aunt Enid? No. Whatever gave you that idea?" he says and throws me a curious grin. "This is a bit beyond her means."

If not Aunt Enid, then who? I wonder, as I ease myself into the car and reach for the seatbelt. How could Dan afford this car on his own, when he can't even come up with full-time tuition? I settle back into the passenger seat and decide to let matters unfold on their own.

True to his word, ten minutes after Dan fires up the engine, we are rolling between the cluster of towers on the Willamette River's west bank that mark the district known as

Portland's South Waterfront. Passing the Oregon Health & Science University hospital, which stands at the foot of a tram that connects the facility with part of the university campus on the hillside above, we turn onto Gaines Street where we arrive at the Atwater Place Condominiums. This high rise structure has a shiny, rectangular, green glass, four story base topped with what must be a twenty story green glass tower. Between the condos and the river beyond, I can just make out a grassy aquatic park. Holy crap! And I thought University Pointe was impressive. Is this where my impoverished friend lives?

We turn onto the building's southern side and Dan wheels his Camaro into the parking garage that takes up much of the Atwater's ground floor. He locates a vacant space, then punches the ignition button. When the engine's throaty rumble subsides, he leads me to an elevator where we ascend to the building's eighteenth floor.

"So, Aunt Enid's renting this place for you?" I volunteer hesitantly.

"What's with all these Aunt Enid questions?" I'm about to refer to our earlier conversation, when it occurs to me it may never have happened—not between me and this Dan Hastings. Instead, I take an alternate course. "Something you said earlier made me think that she might," I suggest, despite having no recollection of anything prior. "Obviously, I got the wrong impression," I add and my answer seems to satisfy him.

When the elevator door opens, Dan leads me down a multi-door corridor. When we are part way along, one of the doors opens and two men, who appear to be in their mid to late twenties, emerge, each one toting a pair of small aluminum suitcases. Well-dressed in the extreme—expensive suits, fashionable shoes and finely styled hair—they turn in our direction. Another man steps into the hallway behind them and says to their backs, "Nice doing business."

Neither of the pair acknowledges. Instead, they head

for the lift we just exited, passing by in single file. Dan's eyes flick toward them, then fix on the one still standing in the hallway. In contrast to Dan and the departing duo, this one is barefoot and shirtless and his body is covered with tattoos. His dark hair is uncombed and greasy, and looks as if it hasn't been washed for any number of days. When we arrive beside him, Dan studies the man for a second or two, then demands, "Is this how you present yourself to our clients? Is this how you walk around when I'm not here?"

"Yeah," the shirtless one replies, looking disgusted. "And 'what will the neighbors think?' is going to be your next question, isn't it, Mother?"

"Exactly," Dan snaps. "How our clients perceive us directly affects our business. More than that, look where we are." Dan gestures expansively with his arms. "Are you trying to draw attention? Because, if you are, this isn't going to last long." As if he suddenly remembers I'm with him, Dan glances at me, then back at the man he is addressing. He frowns, and in a quieter voice says, "Let's get out of the hallway."

He steps around the shirtless man and enters the apartment. I follow and the man cocks his head as he appraises me.

"New customer?" he asks.

When Dan glances back, mouth tight and the space between his eyebrows deeply furrowed, the man smiles. Extending his arms with his palms facing towards us, the shirtless man says, "Hey! I was just asking."

When we are inside and the door is shut, Dan whirls around and opens his mouth as if starting to speak. Once again noticing me, he pauses, then purses his lips as if he's considering what to say next. Dan smiles at me and says, "Eric, this is my roommate and business partner, Marco. Marco," he says to the shirtless man, "This is Eric, a friend from Portland State."

"Don't tell me you're still keeping up that charade,"

Marco replies as, with the back of his hand, he rubs a white powdery residue from his nostrils and sniffs.

Dan replies, "Someday I'm going to have to change occupations and I'm going to need something to fall back on. This can't go on forever."

"No? Why can't it?" Marco asks.

"Do I really have to explain?" Without waiting for Marco's response, Dan turns to me and says, "I have to apologize. Sometimes we get into arguments. Shit happens." He sighs and asks, "Would you like something to drink?"

Apparently deciding he ought to be sociable, Marco volunteers, "We've got a nice scotch. Or maybe you'd prefer beer."

Feeling awkward at having walked into a situation I would have preferred not to witness, I attempt to make the best of it.

"I'm sorry," I reply. "I don't drink. Do you have any iced tea?"

Marco hesitates a beat, then recovers. "I guess we could manage that. Never can tell what a client will ask for."

As Marco heads for the kitchen, visible across the unit's open floor plan—similar in many respects to the one we had back in Santa Fe—Dan turns to me and asks, "So what do you think of the place?"

I'm still feeling unbalanced, not only by the argument, but that my friend appears to be dealing drugs. I've never had anything to do with anyone who's even remotely criminal. Yet, here I am, standing between two of them and the thought makes me wonder if they're armed. What have I walked into? I hesitate, then start to examine my surroundings. From its polished wood floors and the crisp interior lines, broken by an occasional oval-shaped pillar, to the abundance of floor-to-ceiling windows, the entire condominium is a huge step up from the student accommodations I had visited only a few minutes earlier. As difficult as the concept may be for me to digest, this is clearly a different reality—the only explanation for all that occurred after I folded away each previous one.

I walk to a wall of windows to take in the view. To our north, between us and what I believe are the Ross Island Bridge and the Tilikum Crossing—the Orange Line's route across the Willamette—stand twin blue glass towers with yellow rectangular columns bookending each of them. Both are clearly taller than the one where I'm standing, and I can just make out the edge of another one off to my left, most of its bulk hidden behind the Atwater.

From there, I move to the river-facing windows where, out of the corner of my eye, I get a glimpse of the kitchen and Marco dropping ice cubes into a glass. When he steps out of my line of sight, their clinks are followed by the sound of liquid pouring and I return my gaze to the waterfront, shaking my head at how much it must cost Dan to live here. These are not student quarters by any stretch of the imagination and I wonder if both of my parents, with their incomes combined, could afford such a place.

Hearing Marco come up behind me, I turn to see him handing me a drink.

"Your iced tea," he says, forcing a smile. Then, adding a hint of sarcasm, he says, "Are you sure you wouldn't prefer an Arnold Palmer?"

"Too sweet," I reply. "Besides, I hate lemonade."

His smile disappears and I can see he didn't anticipate that I would understand that an Arnold Palmer—named after the legendary golfer who particularly enjoyed this beverage combination—is made of equal parts lemonade and iced tea. I accept the glass and thank him graciously. Just to rub it in, I smile as if to say, "I may be a teenage kid, but I'm not stupid."

When Marco turns away abruptly, I flash Dan a look that asks, "what's going on?" He shakes his head almost imperceptibly, as if to indicate this is not the time to discuss it.

"It's really great," I say, taking the conversation down a different track. When Dan raises his brows, I explain, "You asked what think." When he still appears not to understand, I add, "About this place." He nods in comprehension. "I think it's really great," I repeat. Then, in an attempt to satisfy my curiosity about the quality of his living quarters, while avoiding the obvious financial questions, I ask, "How did you find it?"

"I told the realtor I wanted a place that was centrally located and didn't require any outside maintenance. This is what she came up with."

Deciding not to ask why a student would be dealing with a real estate agent, let alone how he could have established enough credit at this point in his life to satisfy a bank, I turn the subject to how he likes living here and question him about the locale, wondering all the time if this had been an all-cash transaction and how many zeros were involved.

About twenty minutes into the discussion, Marco loses interest in playing the genial host. He disappears into the back of the unit and, after three minutes more, emerges in a sport shirt and… I think the hat on his head is called a fedora.

"I got some business to attend to," he says as he pulls a set of keys from his right front pants pocket.

Dan glances at him disapprovingly. "You could at least take the time to shower."

"The hell with you. There's half a pound of… " Marco notices me, drops the rest of the sentence and says instead, "I need to get going."

Once Marco has gone, Dan pours himself a drink from the wet bar, then pulls up a chair and asks me to join him.

"I can already hear all of your questions," he tells me.

He takes a sip of what I suspect is either bourbon or the scotch to which Marco had referred earlier, then sets down the glass and rubs his hands together. I can almost hear gears turning inside his head as I sit waiting for him to collect himself. And Dan is right. I do have lots of questions, ranging from the cost of this place and the drugs I expect paid for it, down to why an eighteen or nineteen year old kid is drinking hard liquor. Eventually, he comes up with a remark I would never have expected.

"Marco's not as bad as he looks."

I take a sip of tea and stare. Apparently sensing both my surprise and disbelief over his declaration, he takes another unanticipated course.

"I'll get around to Marco and how we hooked up later. Right now, I should get down to why I brought you here." I'm expecting him to say that he wants me to become a part of his operation or something similar, when he says instead, "I'm going to need some help fitting into school."

I can feel my jaw drop. At a complete loss as to how I should respond, I can only maintain my gaze and hope that somehow this will eventually come together in a way that makes sense.

"Eric," he says, "I'll be up front with you. I was actually being honest when I said that someday I'll need to change occupations. This... " He gestures at the space around us. " ...all came together much faster than I ever could have anticipated. It's too complicated to go into all of the details, so let's just say that, at first, I was dealing pot in high school before I met the right people, did some increasingly larger deals until, two years later, here I am. The thing is, this thing scares the shit out of me: the people I'm dealing with and the fact I have to carry a gun."

That grabs my attention and answers my earlier thought. Dan reaches into his jacket and pulls out a fancy-looking handgun and lays it between us on the table. I shove back my chair and start to stand.

"Don't," he says. When my eyes travel from the handgun to Dan, then back to the gun again, he smiles and says, "Please don't be afraid. I'm not going to hurt you." My eyes remain fixed on the weapon, so he adds, "I only brought it out to make a point. I wanted to show you that everything is not as smooth and easy as I make it appear." He sighs and says, "Will you please sit back down?" Then, glancing toward the pistol, he adds, "I'll put it in a drawer if that will make you more comfortable."

All I can do is nod, so Dan rises from his chair and picks up the piece, while making an obvious effort to keep his fingers away from the trigger. After crossing to the sideboard next to the wet bar, he opens a drawer, then tucks the gun inside and closes it. Turning to face me he asks, "Better?"

I nod and he returns to his chair.

"Please," he says and gestures to where I'd been sitting. "I'd like to finish."

Feeling easier, but still unsure if I should remain here, I retake my seat and look into his eyes, wondering how he intends to explain himself. After a moment of silence, during which we sit staring at one another, Dan resumes.

"This isn't at all what I want. I mean, sure, the car and crib are nice, but I would prefer to live without the constant fear of being busted or getting shot. Look what I came home to today: Marco looking like the drug dealer he is—running around looking like that is sure to alert the neighbors, especially when he has a noseful of powder—and two guys I've never seen before. They could be anybody. Organized crime, for all I know. Marco set it up and I used to have confidence in him. But now that he's started sampling the goods…

"Look," he says and spreads out his hands. "What I'm trying to say is I can't go on living like this. I want to study biology."

That's at least one thing that carries over, I tell myself.

"I graduated from high school with a good GPA and

decent SAT scores. The one thing I can't figure out is, after two years with this kind of lifestyle, how I can adapt myself to student living."

He stares at me, clearly waiting for me to respond and I wonder what I should tell him because I have no idea how he's going to fit in. How does a criminal suddenly change his ways and become Joe ordinary? How does a drug dealer find doing homework, researching a term paper, studying for a final exam in any way satisfying or even interesting?

When it appears he's not going to continue, and that it's my turn, I ask, "What do you want me to say? I've never been in your situation, but it seems to me that the solution is obvious." I have to admit, the next thing I'm going to say is a stretch, but it's the only way to get from where he is in life to where he says he would like to be. So when the questioning look on his face remains the same, I say, "Give it up. Just walk away from it."

"It's not that simple."

"Why not? Because you're addicted to the fancy lifestyle? If you're really serious, all this is going to have to go away sometime. If you ask me… I don't mean to offend you. But you've got to be pretty desperate to bring a complete stranger like me into all of this and expect me to… What? Wave a magic wand? Tell you something you don't already know? Because if that's what you're expecting, I'm going to disappoint you big time when I tell you that, except for maybe arrest and imprisonment, or getting shot, there's no other way out."

Dan just sits there breathing deeply. His chest continues to rise and fall a minute longer. Then suddenly he says, "I just can't."

"That's what I thought," I reply and push back the chair.

"Wait."

"Seriously? You've managed to accomplish all of this on your own. You don't need me to explain things."

67

"But… "

"You really want an explanation, don't you? All right. This is what you should do: Tell Marco, 'Nice knowing you,' or something like that. Pack your bags and rent a cheaper apartment. I'm sure that what's in those suitcases that just walked out of here can set you up nicely for the next four years of college, even if you split the amount between the two of you. You've already got everything you need to get started."

"I considered doing exactly that, but the truth is, I'm so deep into this that the people I've been dealing with probably won't let me."

Now it's my turn to stare.

"I know too much about them," Dan explains. "But I think I'd be too much of a threat to their operation for them allow me to just walk away."

His eyes plead for understanding, so I drop back down and pull my chair back to the table.

"I'm sorry. That never occurred to me." I may be smart in any number of ways, but I'm way over my head here. "Look, I'm more than willing to help you fit into school, but this," I say, spreading my arms to indicate the apartment and the lifestyle it represents, "is something I don't have any experience with.

"Maybe you could go to the police," I say, with a hopeful tone in my voice.

"And tell them what? That I've been a drug dealer and now I'd like to go straight? They'd lock me up in a heartbeat, and *then* demand my cooperation."

My mouth hangs open when I realize how stupid that was. I pull myself together and ask, "So what do you want me to tell you?"

Dan outlines his plan to gradually put Marco in charge as he phases himself out over the next six to eight months.

"By then, I should have fallen far enough into the

background that I'm actually no longer in touch with their current activities, no longer a threat. I will be able to step aside while Marco takes over. Hopefully, you'll have introduced me to enough of your classmates that I can start living as an actual student and no one will question it."

It sounds reasonable enough that we spend the next half hour discussing how to begin. When we feel we have enough of a plan in place, I head for the door.

"Don't worry," I add. "I won't tell anyone about your little operation."

"I know. I wouldn't have brought you here if I thought you would."

I raise my eyebrows in a quick 'see you later,' then shut the door behind me and head for the elevator. On my way down the corridor, I sigh, wondering briefly if I should return to PSU, or simply go home—that is, if my home is still where I remember it to be, or if that part of my reality has also changed. I decide on the second option.

During the ride's first ten minutes, I sit staring out the light rail's window, wondering what has been happening to me ever since the automobile accident… or the fall off the ladder. In Isaacson's book about Albert Einstein, the author states that the great physicist—originally no great mathematician, but who eventually learned how to express all his theories in numbers—believed it was more important to be able to visualize any concept before committing it to paper than to be able to express it in equations. In fact, that is how he first developed some of his most important theories. When my mind touches briefly on his theory of relativity, it strikes a chord and I wonder if Hugh Everett might have been right when he first postulated the original relative state formulation, which Bryce Seligman DeWitt later renamed "the many-worlds formulation" that sets forth the possibility of multiple parallel universes. Have I somehow found a way to cross between the multiverse's innumerable alternate realities the theory describes? Tearing away one to reveal

69

another would certainly go a long way toward explaining all that has happened until now. I find it both reassuring and frightening—reassuring in that it means I'm not going crazy, frightening because it raises the question of whether I can ever return to my original world. Since I don't have any idea how I've managed to do any of this and I'm not at all sure that returning will ever be possible, I pick up my feet, rest them on the seat and wrap my arms around my legs. For the rest of the ride home, I hold onto myself… for now the only constant in all of this.

Chapter
Seven

It's Friday and I'm wondering if Erin and I still have a date. We exchanged cell numbers and I'm debating texting her to see if, one, if she exists in this universe, two, if she knows me and, three, if she's still interested. I'm about to punch in a message when Trish calls me from her bedroom.

" 'Sup?" I ask as I peek through her doorway.

Trish is stretched out on her bedspread and staring at the ceiling. That surprises me because Trish is a neat freak to the extreme and never allows anyone or anything to disturb the bedding once she's arranged it. You may remember how concerned I was about disturbing her bathroom. She would have had a cow if I had done so. Yet here she is, creating an indentation like a meteor crater in what would otherwise have been a minor work of art. I have to ask myself if this is a remake, another iteration, a result of the folding, or just a momentary lapse in her behavior.

Without turning to face me, she asks, "Are you happy here?"

I find it a curious question, so I take a few seconds to think before answering. This is something I haven't given any thought to. Sure, a lot of bizarre things have happened since we arrived here in Portland, but I don't believe they've affected my overall mindset since, at my core, I remain an optimist. After a moment's consideration, I pull myself into the present and say, "Yes. I am. Why do you ask?"

"So am I."

"Really? I mean that's good, but it sounds as if you have something else on your mind."

She averts her eyes downward as if she's embarrassed.

"I guess so," she replies, sounding timid. All at once, she sits upright and, with a puzzled look on her face, and stares at me. "I thought I was happy back home," she says, then catches herself. "I mean back in Santa Fe. I had lots of friends. I was about to become an upper classman. So when Mom and Dad told me we were leaving, I totally freaked."

She pauses and I think she's expecting me to add something relevant. Unable to come up with anything better and wishing I could, I respond with a simple, "I know," then wait to hear what comes next.

She stares at me and asks, "Was I really that bad?"

I nod, trying not to appear judgmental. Still, there is no getting around it. "You were gruesome," I admit and watch as her body sags. Before she can break into tears, I give what I hope is an encouraging smile and ask, "What makes you so happy now?"

The question seems to calm her. As she gathers her thoughts, I gesture toward a place at the edge of the bed and tilt my head to ask if I can sit there. Trish nods and I join her.

She begins by discussing school. It's now late August and her high school's fall semester has already started, whereas classes at Portland State will not begin for another month. She spends the better part of the next twenty minutes enumerating the people who have already befriended her, boys and girls alike. She discusses the extracurricular activities she has begun taking part in, from the school play to the various clubs she's signed up for, again, largely out of fear she would have trouble meeting people.

"You? Having trouble meeting people? You're

always at the center of everything.”

"There's a reason," she admits, then returns her eyes downward.

"Such as?"

"*Such as…* ," she begins, returning my stare and sounding irritated. As fast as the old Trish appears, she flicks out of existence and the new Trish, sounding once again fragile, continues. "The same reason as in Santa Fe."

"And what was that?" I ask, trying to let her know by the tone of my voice that I'm truly interested. I could not be more pleased she's confiding in me. I hate to say it, but up until now, Trish has been my sister in name only. Now that she's starting to trust me, it's beginning to feel as if we're connecting the way siblings are supposed to.

She pats the bedspread beside her, indicating she would like me to sit next to her, rather than merely perch on the mattress's edge. I hesitate briefly. Then, before that can offend her and cause her to change her mind, I kick off my shoes and scoot beside her. She grabs a pillow from the headboard and wordlessly passes it over. I tuck it behind me, then sit back and wait for her next comment. After a moment of silence, she says, "I needed to fit in. All the time we were in Santa Fe, I felt as if I was on the outskirts—an outsider looking in. Our folks weren't the richest, but they weren't the poorest either. I know there wasn't any good reason for me to feel that way, but I did."

"And you *did* fit in. You were a cheerleader. You belonged to several clubs, you…"

"Also, you were Mom and Dad's firstborn and they love you best."

When I start to object, she cuts me off. "No. Seriously. They do and you know it."

When her irritation rises, I realize that if I don't want to turn this into an argument, I need to shut my mouth and agree with her. She pauses a moment, as if expecting an objection. I nod and, even though she keeps her eyes straight ahead, it's apparent, when her body relaxes and the tone of her voice softens, that she senses I am being sincere.

"It isn't their fault or yours. It's just the way things are. I've always suspected that, if I were in their place, I'd do the same and favor my firstborn as well." She sighs. "I know that they love me and that none of my friends has it any better than I do. Still… " Another awkward pause. "Eric," she says, and once again she has caught me off guard. Trish never calls me by name, except when we're fighting. "You've always been the brainy one, while I had to study extra hard just to get passing grades. I got decent grades. I'll admit it. And although I'm no scholarship winner, I never got anything lower than a B on my report cards."

She releases another sigh.

"So when we moved to Portland, into what I expected would be a far more competitive environment, I was scared I'd be the class dummy. And you know what? I'm not. Far from it. Not only that, I've made friends. I mean *real* friends. They've been inviting me over and we do lots of cool things together. The best part of all… " She pauses and I can almost hear her wondering if she should confide what's coming next. Abruptly, she decides in my favor. "There's this boy," she says and her face lights up. "Actually, he's more like a man." When I turn and stare in shocked disbelief, she modifies her statement. "Actually, he's about your age," she says and I start to relax. "He's really cute and… I won't tell you anything more about him, because for now we're just at the talking phase. But if it starts to get serious, I'd really like you to meet him." She turns to me and asks, "So what do you think?"

I have to admit I'm surprised. I find myself struggling to come to terms with this new degree of intimacy. Trying to avoid any lag in my response time, I decide less is more so I leave it at, "Cool."

Trish nods and returns a tight smile, probably as unsure and uncomfortable as I am. It's then I decide to reciprocate.

"Maybe you can help me," I offer and she cocks her head and furrows her eyebrows. Deciding to take a chance that Erin exists in this current reality, I say, "I've met someone too."

"Really?"

I nod.

"Tell me about her."

I begin by describing how the two of us met.

"She even likes my poetry," I conclude.

"Yeah. I like your stuff too. Some of it anyway."

Although I've never showed any of my writing to Trish, I refrain from calling her out on how she has managed to read it. No sense in undoing what is taking a positive turn. Instead, I reply, "So the thing is, now that we're getting along, I've decided to ask her out."

"And?"

I shake my head and run my fingers through my hair.

"And I don't have any idea where to take her."

"Why not Burgerville or a pizza place?"

"Really?"

"Why not? Look, you're not old enough to drink and you don't have a lot of money to spend. Do you?"

I shake my head.

"So, since this is just your first date, I'd think you'd just like to talk to her." She turns and looks me in the eyes as if to ask, "*Wouldn't you?*"

It takes me a second to get her meaning. Sometimes I'm smart, but sometimes I'm so dense it embarrasses me.

"Of course."

"All right then. Not rich. Not looking for… Anyhow, taking her someplace cheap for something to eat is better than going to see a movie. At least this way you both have plenty of time to talk instead of just sitting together, staring at a screen for a couple of hours with nothing to say until afterwards. Where does she live?"

"I… I'm not sure."

Trish turns to look at me and I suspect she is sizing me up.

"Let's see. You met on the train, so that makes me think that she lives on the East Side like we do. Where did you tell her you'd meet her?"

"On campus."

"Well, I guess that would work, but do you have to?"

"No," I reply, unsure what she's getting at.

"It strikes me as more than a little dumb for the two of you to ride all the way over to the West Side to go out, before climbing back on a train to return to the East Side. Sellwood's really walkable and there's lots you can do on this side of the river. I hear Oaks Park has a roller skating rink and an amusement park and it's not far from here."

"A skating rink?"

"Well, you don't have to go skating. You don't have to go to the amusement park either, but the days are still long enough… " She sighs and shrugs, as if dealing with someone who's obviously oblivious to the subtleties of a budding relationship is growing tedious. "My point is there's a lot you can do on this side of the river that can give both of you plenty of time to get to know one another without spending most of your time riding public transportation. If I were you, I'd text her and find out where she lives before making any plans. I'd keep my options open."

I lean over and give her a kiss on the cheek.

"Thanks," I say and she turns and stares back at me.

It's the first time I have ever done anything like that and I think I've surprised both of us. Before she has time to react, I leap out of bed, grab my shoes and rush out the door while reaching for my cell phone. I punch in Erin's number, then tap **R we still on?** Barely a minute passes when the word **Def** appears, followed by **Where? When?** I ask for her address. When I learn she lives almost to Wilsonville, my heart sinks. How can I possibly get there and still have enough of the day left afterwards to do anything? I wonder if it would it be OK to have her meet me. I'm pulling on my shoes at the top of the stairs, debating what to do next, when the front door opens and Dad enters, carrying his briefcase. He looks up and notices me.

"Eric? You look worried. Is anything wrong?"

When I tell him what's happening, he reaches into his pocket with his free hand, pulls out the car key and dangles it in front of him.

"Will this help?" he asks as I'm starting down the stairs.

I stop, caught off guard.

"Really? You're sure?" He nods and I ask, "What about Mom? Don't you have to pick her up from work or something?"

He chuckles. "She's taking the TriMet. She and Cat"—Cat's one of our neighbors—"have a similar commute. Cat picked her up this morning and took her to the TriMet parking lot over on East 99. Your mom's taken care of, so what do you say?"

"Sure. I mean thank you."

Dad laughs and delivers an underhand toss.

I catch it and ask, "When do you want it back?"

"It's the weekend. Enjoy yourself," he says, then adds, "On one condition."

I stop and stare.

He grins. "You'll have to tell me something about her afterward."

His expression assures me this is not an urgent concern, so I smile back and nod.

"One more thing," he says as I'm reaching for the door.

He sets down his briefcase, reaches into his hip pocket and takes out his wallet. He extracts a pair of twenties and extends them toward me.

"Dad," I object, "I have the credit card you and Mom

gave me."

He shakes his head. He comes close and presses the bills into my palm.

"I want you to enjoy yourselves," he says, then picks up his briefcase and heads toward his office.

Needless to say, I'm stunned. But I'm also chuffed. I text Erin about the car and she texts me back: Ur Dad is the coolest.

I agree. The car will give us hours more time and opens up all sorts of possibilities. I hate being broke and depending on my parents for money, but Mom and Dad insist that getting a job will make it harder for me to maintain a GPA that is high enough to qualify for grad school. Consequently, as much as I dislike being dependent, I realize that the sooner I can finish my studies and start a career, the sooner I can begin handling monetary matters on my own.

I shut the front door behind me and I'm turning toward the street when I stop dead in my tracks and stare at the blue Subaru Forester parked in our driveway. We own a silver Honda Pilot, or at least we used to. I glance at the key and notice it bears the Subaru emblem.

Chapter
Eight

While I can't begin to express how grateful I am that Dad loaned me his car, I take my time as I walk toward the Subaru Forester, staring at it, knowing it shouldn't be here. First, there was Joe Dexter. Next, my relocation to the upstairs hallway. Then, Dan's move into the criminal world accompanied by the disappearance of my cast and other injuries. And while Trish's transformation into a loving sister could be accounted for by any number of explanations, this sky blue hulk stands before me as further evidence that nothing is now what it used to be. Yes, it's only a car. But it also indicates how many other things might no longer be as I remember them. My sudden joy at being able to see Erin is instantly transformed into a growing fear of what might happen next, especially now that I notice the shimmer still lays across everything. Now that I stop to think about it, I realize it has always been there. Ever since the automobile accident, or since my fall from the ladder, depending on which reality's event set it into motion, it's always been there, even though most of the time I tend to forget about it.

Resigned to accept the phenomenon, I climb into the driver's seat, close my eyes for a minute and inhale. The momentary pause does nothing to relieve my apprehension over what might happen next. But since Dad always leaves a water bottle or two in the glove box, I reach inside and—yup—find one that's unopened. I reach into my pocket, take a tablet that the doctor prescribed from my shirt pocket and swallow it. Better not to leave anything to chance today, since it's only the thought of seeing Erin that makes me insert the key and fire up the engine.

… … … … …

If I had been forced to ask her to come see me while I waited at a bus stop, or worse yet, if I had tried to use mass transit to meet her before starting our date, most of the day would have vanished before we had any chance to enjoy ourselves. As it is, the drive to the intersection where she asked me to meet her takes roughly fifteen minutes and she is waiting there, smilingly broadly, the second I pull up to the curb.

"I'm so glad you decided to get together," Erin says as she piles onto the passenger seat and buckles her seatbelt. "It's such a beautiful day and I would have hated to spend it alone." Before I can comment, she asks, "What do you have in mind?"

"I was thinking maybe Oaks Park," I say, hoping the idea won't sound too lame.

She surprises me when she says, "Cool! I went there a couple of years ago to catch the Rose City Rollers." When I frown, her explanation, "Women's flat track roller derby," causes me to grin.

"Really?"

I'd heard about roller derby when I was in New Mexico, but Dad wasn't interested in driving all the way back to Albuquerque for a couple of hours' entertainment. I mean, who could blame him? He worked long hard days and was glad for whatever rest he could get in the evening. Since Trish found the entire concept boring, and I was unable to talk Mom into chauffeuring me while Trish stayed at home, I never got to see it. Although it sounds strange, when one of my friends told me about it, he made it sound totally extra.

"Do you think they'll be playing today?" I ask.

"I don't know," she says, "But I can Google it while you drive. I've always wanted to see them again. My friends weren't interested in going to an amusement park, so I had to go alone. I hated it. It's something I wanted to share with somebody else, so I've always been wondering if I'd ever get the chance to repeat it." She laughs and admits, "I guess the kid in me never grew up."

"Me too," I respond.

I'm glad when she grins back at me, then pulls out her phone and starts searching the internet. After a minute or two, however, she looks disappointed and tells me the Rollers aren't scheduled today, or any time soon. We're both disappointed, but when she suggests we might still check them out at some later date, I find it encouraging because, at least at some level, she envisions we might have some sort of a future together.

For the first several minutes, we talk about everyday things such as friends and how we've been spending our summer vacation. At one point, I'm running on about my meeting with Professor Basu when I realize Erin is no longer listening. Afraid I'm becoming a bore, I start to apologize when she turns and faces me.

"If you had a secret," she asks, "who would you tell?"

I'm not sure how to answer. I immediately begin thinking of any secrets I might have, so I can put her question into a context that would allow an intelligent response. Unable to come up with an example, I'm about to tell her as much, when Dan Hastings's face flashes in front of me. Realizing how hard it would be to trust anyone with that kind of information, I reply, "I don't know. It would depend on what kind of a secret, who I knew, and how sure I was they could keep it."

She nods, then sits back in her seat and stares at the

roadway. Her frown tells me something is burning inside of her and begging to get out. Realizing, however, that we've just met and she doesn't yet know me, I decide not to press. Instead of discussing what's troubling her, I make a few attempts at small talk, then spend most of the time riding in silence.

Oaks Amusement Park is located in Sellwood on the Willamette River's east bank. Shortly before we arrive at the Sellwood Bridge, my GPS diverts me onto a side street. When it takes me to a stop sign in front of some railroad tracks and the street that parallels them northward, I switch the device off, confident I can navigate the rest of way on my own. On the opposite side of the intersection, an arrow-shaped, multicolored sign points to the right and announces, **Oaks Park, where the fun never ends!** with depictions of Ferris wheels, roller coasters and other amusement park rides painted across the top of it. Hoping those attractions will brighten the darkening mood that is threatening to sabotage our first date, I turn as it indicates.

The road winds its way between a lush green park that borders the Willamette on our left and a bicycle-slash-jogging path on our right. At the roadway's end, I turn left, where I pass through a wrought iron gate bearing a sign that reads **Welcome!** When I pull into a parking space, we open our doors and are greeted by the joyous sounds of young girls screaming. A roller coaster has just ratcheted its way up to the ride's summit and is taking its initial plunge.

Erin laughs and exclaims, "This is so cool!"

I close the driver side door and take a moment to study her. Standing with her fists on her hips, eyes fixed on the amusement park, she's grinning like a little girl who has just seen Santa Claus. I begin thinking that maybe there is a chance this will be a good day after all. Erin's smile doesn't lessen when she notices me watching, although her chin does dip in a show of self-consciousness.

"You must think I'm the ultimate nerd," she

apologizes.

"Not really. In fact, I think people who can't let go and enjoy themselves are a little pretentious."

It's obvious I said something right, because she comes around the Forester and takes hold of my hand.

"What do you want to do first?" she asks as she studies the various rides.

Caught up by her skin's softness and warmth, I'm flooded with images of holding and kissing her as my thoughts grow far too inappropriate for a first date at an amusement park. Afraid she'll see how much I want her, I try to think of an intelligent response. Instead, what emerges is, "I… I don't know."

My face is burning and I want to kick myself at how lame I sound. Fortunately, Erin's too absorbed with our surroundings to notice my embarrassment, and we begin discussing the place as we try to gain our bearings.

Between us and the coaster is a huge blue and yellow U-shaped structure holding a giant blue and yellow dish. People are strapping themselves into orange chairs fitted with handlebars. The chairs are spaced evenly around the dish's perimeter. A cluster of yellow, pink and mint green buildings at the end of the driveway that brought us here obscures most of the other attractions, but I see a scarlet carousel peeking out from behind one of them. As we move to a spot where we can see things better, a star shaped device similar to the Ferris wheel comes into view. Its spokes are tipped with red and white cages that look as if they're intended to spin their occupants. Just as another group of girls scream with delight, Erin spots a tiny rust-colored house that looks like a ticket booth.

We're walking through Oaks Park's chain link and iron bar fences, discussing which rides would be likely candidates, when our eyes are drawn to a narrow asphalt road snaking between several islands of grass. Automobile tires, rather than curbs, line the roadway's edges and we notice three rows of vehicles, looking like bumper cars, parked underneath a large pillared roof. As people begin climbing into them, Erin, grinning ferociously, squeezes my hand and takes off running.

"This!" she shouts, pointing with her free hand as I hurry to keep up.

Before I can complain that we haven't bought any tickets yet, she points at a vending machine that accepts dollar bills. She releases her grip and I fumble for my wallet. Tucked next to Dad's twenties are a couple of singles and I hurry to feed them into its slot.

As I hand the ride's attendant our tickets, he asks, "Do you want a double or single cars?"

I slow myself down enough to notice that the cars in the nearest row are wider than those in the other two and can accommodate two riders side-by-side. Thinking how nice it would be to sit next to Erin, I'm starting to say "double" when Erin says, "You're not afraid of a little competition, are you?"

The look in her eyes tells me everything.

"Single cars, please."

"Take cars four and eight," the attendant replies.

Erin nods and makes a beeline for the race cars. Somehow in our excitement, Erin and I wind up in two different rows. Her pink car number eight is the last car in the first of three rows, while my blue number four is the second car in the second row. Clearly excited, she looks over her shoulder and flashes me a grin. Disappointed at not being next to her, I force a smile, then suddenly realize it doesn't matter. My grin grows larger when I remember I'll have the rest of day with her. Over the engines' rumbles, I hear someone on a microphone telling us not to go until the starting signal—mounted on a post to our left—changes from red to yellow to green. We secure our shoulder straps and lap belts while two Oaks Park employees walk from one car to the next, making sure each rider's harness is properly fastened. Erin is bouncing up and down in her seat, looking back and forth from me to the roadway ahead, and I'm starting to share her excitement.

And then, we're off. Erin's car leaves the gate a second or two before I get mine into gear, but that's enough to allow three other drivers to insert their cars between us. I'm not sure what I was expecting—whether these go carts would be disappointingly slow or way over-powered—but I'm happy to find they're set somewhere in between, with engines set just strong enough to make the ride exciting.

The fact they all are set with similar speeds makes it difficult to pass, but it soon becomes obvious my best chance to catch Erin will be on a turn. As we round the first one, she glances over her shoulder and shouts something back at me. But with everyone gunning their engines, I can't make out anything. When I cup a hand to my ear and shake my head, she laughs and returns her eyes to the race course.

Determined to catch her and pass, I begin watching for any opportunity to close the distance between us. Fortunately, the man who's in front of me, driving orange double car number ten, isn't paying as much attention as he should. As he points out something to his son, he takes the next turn wide. That allows me to slip by on the inside.

It's clear that no one is about to pass Erin and the next two laps leave me positioned solidly in fourth. A lapse in attention by the young girl ahead of me allows me to move into third on lap number four—where I remain for the next two circuits.

On lap number seven—I ask myself how many are there? Maybe ten?—the woman in the white car ahead nudges the steel rail that separates the perimeter tires from the race course. When the bump forces her wide, I press the accelerator, which is already floored, hoping I can manage a little extra. I'm still not sure if that additional millimeter is what makes my move possible. Maybe the jar from her collision causes the woman to lift her foot. Whatever it is, in only seconds I find myself a few feet behind Erin and gradually catching up.

She should be well ahead of me by now, I tell myself. *Is she easing off to make this race seem more competitive?*

Two more laps go by with Erin in the lead and me gradually closing in. When the man on the microphone announces, "This is the final lap," Erin looks over and grins and I realize that I've never been happier.

As we round the last turn, we are neck-and-neck on the last straightaway. I'm beginning to edge into the lead when the announcer says into the microphone, "Slow down as you enter the pit area." A red metal bar has been moved onto the track and it narrows the raceway down to a single lane. I ease off the gas, lean back into my seat and realize how hard I've been trying… especially when I didn't have to. I smile and exhale.

Erin and I meet outside the ride's fence where, yet again, Erin takes my hand into hers. I'm expecting her to make some sort of statement about who won and who lost. Instead, she kisses my cheek and asks, "So, what do you want to do next?"

Another anxiety shoved to the rear and I feel happier than I can remember.

We spend most of the afternoon enjoying the rides and eating junk food. Mostly, though, we just stroll and pass the time getting acquainted.

At one point she asks, "So how did a physics major start writing poetry?"

"Do you think that I'm odd?"

"I don't know. I've never met a physics major before." She pauses and looks uncertain. "Maybe I'm stuck on the stereotype."

"Someone with a pocket protector who doesn't have a life outside of his computer and textbooks?"

She nods and averts her eyes downward, looking embarrassed. "I'm sorry. I didn't mean… "

"Don't be. That's generally correct."

"But… "

"No really," I say. "It's just me. I guess I'm weird." She starts to say something else, but I continue. "A lot of physics majors are socially impaired. Many of us have ADD or Asperger's syndrome. Look it up online. It's pretty well documented. I don't mean to imply that Asperger's is necessarily a bad thing. It's an abnormality, but then again so is genius." She tries to interrupt again, but I'm persistent. "I'm not making a blanket statement when I say this. I don't think it's ever wise to make universal assumptions. But still, take a look at most of the socially active people you went to school with and I'll bet that your typical geek was rarely among them. I know I'd offend a number of people if I stated this publicly, but that's where stereotypes come from.

"Look, if we were to consider, say, construction workers, I don't think many of them participate in ballroom dancing."

Erin grins.

"See what I mean? That doesn't mean that none of them do, and that isn't a bad thing either. Certain pursuits attract certain types of people. Then again, certain pursuits don't attract very many people of any… " I search for a word. " …personality, maybe. Most people don't write poetry. Most people don't study physics. Among physics majors, that makes me the weirdest of the weird."

Then, realizing I haven't answered Erin's question, I inhale and say, "I went through a rough patch back in New Mexico and I needed to express what I was experiencing. Let's just say I needed to vent. Mathematical equations weren't going to describe my emotions and ordinary prose felt too analytical, too dry, almost scientific.

"Because of his occupation, my dad had introduced me to poetry several years earlier and I enjoyed reading and writing it. It resonated with a part of me that I couldn't reach in any other way. I can't describe it any better than that, but it seemed the best way to put my feelings into words without saying, 'A leads to B leads to C.' Poetry works for me because it's non-linear."

A chill runs through me when I remember the non-linear track my life has taken. It must be showing, because Erin squeezes my hand and asks, "Is something wrong?"

"Nothing. Really. I'm cool," I say, although I realize this particular secret is even bigger than the Dan Hastings one. Since she appears skeptical and frowns at my denial, I change the subject. "Do you want to go somewhere else and get something to eat?"

She studies me a second longer, then asks, "How about Chinese?"

I'd been thinking about pizza or burgers, but Chinese? I'm not sure the idea appeals to me because my family had found only two decent Chinese restaurants in Santa Fe and one was outrageously expensive. I apologize. "I don't have too much money left."

"What? Where do you come from?" she asks. The question is obviously rhetorical. "There's a nice place in Milwaukie and it's really inexpensive. Besides, I've brought some money of my own." Before I can object, she takes my hand and heads for the amusement park's exit saying, "Come on. I think you'll like it."

We've nearly reached the SUV, when I spot someone familiar out of the corner of my eye. It's Alex, and she's crossing the parking lot with her arm around the waist of a large, Goth-looking dude. He has multiple piercings through his nose, forehead, lip and ears and his arms display what appear to be recreations of Maori tattoos—thick black vine-like shapes running from shoulder to wrist.

At first, Alex doesn't spot us and I'm hopeful I can get Erin to the car unnoticed. I take her by the elbow and increase my pace before I realize what a mistake I've just made. Erin glances at me, then follows my gaze to see what I'm looking at. That's when Alex notices us. She comments to the one beside her and both of them glare at us an ominously.

"Don't worry about them," says Erin, turning to face me.

I'm not sure if it's the look in her eye or the fun we've been having, but I place a hand on her waist and wrap my other arm around her neck. Drawing her close, I lean toward her and find she isn't resisting. Our lips touch and I begin kissing her gently, feeling her lips against mine, delighted when she starts kissing me back. Being careful not to seem overly aggressive, I press my mouth against hers. When she opens her own in response, I wordlessly tell her how much she means to me.

Chapter Nine

The waitress brings us a dish the menu calls Happy Family. It's a combination of beef, pork, chicken and varieties of seafood—I recognize shrimp and scallops—mixed with vegetables and mushrooms. After asking if I appreciate food with a little bite to it, Erin requested that the chef make our meal spicy. Consequently, there are little red bits of chili pepper scattered throughout, as well as half a dozen or so whole pepper pods. At Erin's suggestion, I scoop a fair-sized portion of white rice onto my plate, then place half of the Happy Family on top of it. Since Erin dives into her dinner with a set of chop sticks, despite never having used them before, I decide to experiment. I remove mine from their paper sleeve, and stare at them. Now that I'm holding them, I'm not sure what to do with them.

Erin grins. "You don't have to use them."

"Really?"

She shakes her head. Relieved, I set them aside and start in with the fork. I take a tentative bite and Erin pauses. Suspending the next morsel in front of her mouth, she watches me, waiting for my reaction as I start to chew.

"Not bad," I say, once I've swallowed it. I pause for a moment to consider the combination of flavors. "Actually, it's really quite good."

"Not too hot?" she asks, as I take a sip of Jasmine tea.

"No. New Mexican food is often a great deal hotter. This is well within the range of what I can handle."

She smiles and consumes the scallop.

I pause for a minute, to consider how beautiful she is. From her sky blue eyes—unlike the amber of the earlier Erin—the rich gold of her hair—unlike her earlier brunette— to the blush of her cheeks and the deeper pink of her lips, I realize for the first time this is all natural. The light streaming through the window beside us reveals the nearly invisible down on her face. Her almost unnoticeable pores confirm she's not wearing any makeup. Unless she just colored her hair in the last day or two, the lack of apparent outgrowth tells me her hair is unaltered as well. Aside from Erin's physical beauty, her apparent love of life and her undeniable intelligence makes me stop and smile at how lucky I am to have found her.

In between bites, she looks up and catches me staring. "What?" she asks.

"Nothing."

"It's not nothing. You're watching me."

I can see she's not upset. Her expression suggests only amusement and curiosity. Still, I find myself apologizing. "I'm sorry. I… "

She puts down her chopsticks and folds her arms across the table in front of her, then says something I'm unprepared for. "I like you, too."

I'm at a complete loss for words.

"Look, Eric. I'm not spending the day with you because I have nothing better to do. And I'm not wasting my time with a geek, a nerd, or whatever other name you'd like to use to disparage yourself. I read your poetry and it gave me a glimpse of the kind of person you really are when you're not being so insecure. I don't know if we'll ever be anything more than friends, but I liked what I saw and I'd like to spend some quality time getting to know you."

I remain staring, because nobody, especially no girl as attractive as Erin, has ever spoken to me this directly.

"Is that all right with you?" she prods.

I nod dumbly, before I realize I need to put my answer into words and manage to gasp, "Yes."

"Fine." She smiles. "Now that we've got that out of the way, will you please lighten up?" I manage a smile of my own and she says in acknowledgement, "That's better."

Realizing this sudden bout of awkwardness is completely out of character, I remind myself that I had no such trouble expressing myself candidly to Dan. I understand that, in his case, it was because I wasn't worried about losing something. In the same instant, I understand that acting out of fear of losing Erin will result in exactly that.

"Yes, it is," I agree. "Sorry. I wasn't being myself."

Just then, the waitress stops by and asks, "Is everything all right?"

"It's fine," we reply simultaneously and burst into laughter.

The waitress's frown clearly shows she doesn't understand the humor behind it. Instead, she volunteers, "Can I bring you anything else?"

"We're fine," I repeat and Erin grins.

For the rest of the meal, our conversation flows naturally until I notice it has grown dark outside.

I ask, "Shall I take you home?"

Her face darkens and she looks away.

Puzzled by her abrupt change in mood, I inquire, "Did I say something wrong?"

With her eyes still averted, she mutters something inaudible.

"I'm sorry," I reply. "We can stay, if you want to. Maybe find something else to… "

"It's all right," she says turning back to me. "You're right. It's time to go."

93

I don't know what to make of her reaction. Still, we summon the waitress and ask for our check. On the way to the car, I keep my eyes fixed on her. Erin has changed from a bubbling girl to someone quiet and uncertain and I'm unable to draw her out of her shell, despite repeated attempts to elicit a smile.

After a half hour driving in silence, we park outside her home. Hands on her lap, eyes straight ahead, she sits motionless. For several more minutes, I wait patiently, hoping she will offer some explanation. Not wishing to force her, but finding her immobility disconcerting, at one point I open my door and offer, as gently as possible, "I'll walk you to the door." Her head comes up and turns toward me as I add with a smile, "I really enjoyed myself. We'll have to do this again sometime."

Halfway up the walk, Erin pauses and we turn to face one another. Unsure if I should kiss her because of the mood she is in, I'm starting to comment on our day when a loud, masculine voice, slurring his words, shouts through an open window.

"Erin! 'Zat you? It's about time you got home. Get in the house, goddamit!"

Her eyes open wide and her face fills with dread. "I'll call you," she says, barely louder than a whisper. Before I can reply, she calls back, "Yes, Daddy," then turns and runs toward the door.

I remain where I am for a minute, stunned by the unexpected drama and what it revealed. Then, deciding that Erin's father might not appreciate my continuing presence, I return to the Forester, start it up and, without any further delay, drive off, watching as her house recedes in the rear view mirror.

All the way home, I ask myself what happened. Is Erin safe? Is it likely her father would injure her? I hope that I'm not working myself up over nothing. One minute I'm asking if anything is wrong. In the next, I'm asking myself how I could be so stupid. Of course something is wrong. I pound the steering wheel with my fists. Her father was obviously drunk. Her face had spoken volumes about how she feared going inside. *How can someone be afraid to go home?* I ask myself. Yes, I've watched the news. Yes, I have heard stories about similar situations. But up until this very night, I have never seen anyone so afraid to simply walk through the front door.

My head spins through several possible courses of action, most of which involve turning around and forcing my way into Erin's house. Of course, none of them will work. Although the man may be physically abusive—I have to say "may," because I've seen no actual demonstration—until I see signs of an injury, there is nothing I can report to the police. On the other hand, if it all comes down to shouting, it's not illegal to raise one's voice, even if it does cause emotional distress.

Still fuming, I turn the corner onto my street and slow when I notice a black Camaro convertible parked at our curb. Two individuals, backlit by porch light, are embracing and kissing at our front door. Really? Are they who I think they are?

As if in answer, they separate and I see Trish retrieve a key from her purse, open the door and go inside. With her body no longer blocking my view, the light reveals the grinning face of Dan Hastings before he steps into the darkness and returns to his car. The engine fires up, the headlights come on, and the Camaro motors past before I can decide what to do to address this.

Is this the "man" Trish told me about? Is my sister dating Drug Dealer Dan? In addition to my having stumbled onto Erin's probable secret, this is one too many upsetting incidents to endure in one night.

As I park the SUV in the driveway, I debate confronting Trish before deciding against it. After having only recently gained her confidence, this would be a sure way to alienate her for years, if not forever. Instead, I decide that Dan and I need to have a heart-to-heart chat tomorrow morning… before I rip his heart out.

Chapter
Ten

I knock, and after a minute the door cracks open. I shove Marco aside as I force my way through.

"Where's Hastings?" I demand, just before Marco grabs my collar and slams me against a wall.

"What in Hell do you think you're doing barging in like this?" he asks as he reaches into his trousers, pulls out an automatic pistol and wedges the barrel into the crease under my jaw.

"That's not very smart," I manage, as he presses the barrel into my skin. "What will the neighbors think?" I ask, reminding him of an earlier conversation.

"What will… ?"

Marco jams the barrel harder, so I explain, "My parents have gone out for the day, but I've left them a note telling them where I've gone and who I've gone to see. If I don't get back home and shred it before they return, they have instructions to call the police." The pressure eases a little, so I add, "I've given them both of your names, your descriptions and your primary occupation. Besides, your roommate has been messing around with my sister and the note tells them as much. She's underage and messing around with her can land you in prison. So I have to ask, do you really want to be part of it?"

Marco backs off and stares, clearly debating how to handle this information. Abruptly, he returns the gun to his trousers.

"Be a good boy," I say, making a point of straightening my shirt and looking indignant, "and fix me an iced tea." My heart is pounding, but I'm determined not to lose the upper hand. Marco doesn't move, and frankly, I don't expect him to. Still, I return to my initial question. "Please don't make me ask you again. Where's Hastings?"

Footsteps to my right answer the question for him.

"Eric?" Dan asks as he enters the living room. "What's this about?"

"The name of the girl you've started dating is Trish," I say as I turn my head toward him. "And Trish is my sister."

His eyes open wide and he says, "I'm sorry. I had no idea."

"No? She's never spoken about me? Never mentioned me or my family?"

"Honestly, no."

"I don't believe you. What do the two of you talk about, assuming you're even thinking about conversation when you put an underaged girl into your Camaro? If you don't talk about her life or her family, maybe you spend your time teaching her about anatomy?"

"It's not like that. Ever since we met… I'm sorry. What I was starting to say isn't important."

I grab him by his collar and demand, "Why don't you let me decide what's important and what isn't?"

Marco grabs my wrists and pulls out his handgun, jamming it into the side of my neck again.

Dan gasps, "Marco, don't."

When the scumbag looks at him, Dan says, "It's all right. Put it down. I can handle it."

It takes him a second, but Marco tucks the gun back into his waistband. Before stepping away, he shoves me against the wall, warning, "Watch your ass, mother fucker."

He frowns at Dan, who says nothing in response, so Marco shakes his head in obvious disgust. Just as before, he snatches a suitcase that is standing beside the door. He turns the doorknob, shoves the door open, then, without looking back, slams it behind him. Returning my eyes from the doorway, I glare at the object of my anger.

"I'm sorry," Dan apologizes.

I look him in the eyes and say, "We were talking about my sister."

"I promise I won't see her again."

"Have you two *done* anything?" I ask.

"No," he says and it's clear he understands my meaning. "I've only seen her a couple of times, and they were in public places in broad daylight."

"Except for last night."

He stops cold, looking uncertain. "She told you about last night?"

"Should she?"

"Honest. I didn't touch her."

"Except on the porch."

"You said she didn't tell… "

"I *saw* you." Dan's eyes open wide and I add, "I watched until she went inside and you drove away."

"That was the extent of it. I took her to a movie and brought her home. I kissed her goodnight. That's it. I swear."

"That's good," I say, stepping close to him, until we're almost standing chest to chest. "Because, if you don't already know it, she just turned sixteen. So if I learn that she's pregnant… "

"She's not."

" …I'll see you do hard time."

Beads of sweat start forming across his forehead. He looks genuinely worried as the impact of the information hits him full in the face. I'm breathing hard now and my hands are balled into fists.

"*That*," I say, pointing to where the valise had been,

"is something else I don't want her involved in."

"Never. I would never involve your sister in our business." Dan's face takes on a painful expression. "Eric, you have to believe me. Until you told me just now, I had no idea Trish was your sister. Can we just sit down and talk for a minute?"

"We've already done that."

"Please," he says, gesturing toward two chairs in the living room standing beside one another.

I take a deep breath and exhale, wishing I could be done with this. "Just for a minute."

We seat ourselves and I wait for Dan to start talking. He sits staring through the windows at the view for several long minutes, biting his lip and probably pondering where to begin. Just as I'm about to stand up and leave, he says, "I've done it."

I tilt my head and examine him, wondering what he is talking about. Has he done something with Trish? I'm starting to ask when he explains, "I've severed the relationship. I've terminated my business with Marco. The reason he was in such a hurry to leave is that's it's just him now. He has to set up the connections. He has to deliver the goods. He has to make it all work if he doesn't want to lose this place." Dan spreads his arms, indicating the condominium. "I've forced him to buy me out. With the prices of Portland real estate skyrocketing, he knows he can't afford any other location that's nearly as nice or as centrally located. Fortunately, he has almost enough cash to do it, and he'll have the rest of what he needs by this afternoon."

I'm stunned. His whole explanation sounds too easy and I have a hard time believing him. "Why?" I ask, leaving the question unfinished, certain he understands me.

"I'm going to attend college." Dan smiles and adds, "Thanks to you."

"Really? I didn't do anything."

"Oh! But you did. I couldn't ignore our last

conversation." Dan puts his weight on the armrests and leans toward me. "Have you ever noticed that, when something is right, all of the pieces fall into place?"

I nod, too fascinated to interrupt.

"An opening unexpectedly came up in student housing, right next to PSU." When I give him a questioning look, he explains, "Something happened to one of the resident's roommates. The student who's living there couldn't handle the expense on his own, so he posted a notice on Craig's List and I answered it."

"University Pointe," I venture.

"Did you see the ad too?"

I shake my head, only slightly surprised that I had guessed correctly. Instead, I answer, "No," adding, "Just something I heard." This, of course, is a lie and I remind myself that these parallel universes, despite all their differences, have many similarities. I'm about to ask Dan if his future roommate is a public health major who comes from Nigeria, then decide against it.

It's only now that I notice the ever-present shimmer. It has become a fascinating phenomenon since most of the time it seems benign. At other times, it seems to be somewhat beneficial, or at least it's landed me in largely improved circumstances. I doubt that it helped Joe Dexter after I left him there, winding up in a place where the thugs had gone elsewhere. I suspect he's still homeless. And while the original Dan Hastings might still have died from his heart attack, this one is alive and… should I say prospering? It depends how you look at it. One question presents itself: Can I remain in my present reality without being forced to fold again? While I don't believe I can figure out how to return to the world where I started, I think this one might work out for me.

"Is something wrong?" asks Dan.

His question makes me realize I've become lost in thought, so I change the subject. "It's nothing. How did you sign up for classes?"

Dan looks embarrassed. "I applied a while ago. I had almost changed my mind, until you made me see what a fool I'd be if I didn't follow through. I have to admit that you're right. Sooner or later the game will catch up with me. And then where would I be?" Dan chuckles, then answers his own question. "State prison most likely.

"I really have to thank you. Even now I'm wondering if Marco will get arrested before I can transfer the deed and remove my name from the title. That would be great, wouldn't it? Just as I'm making a fresh start, I get busted because of his carelessness."

"What do you think you will tell her?"

"You mean Trish?"

I nod.

He wrinkles his face and says, "I haven't had time to think about it. I'm kind of a coward, so I'll probably just not ask her out again."

"What if she texts you?"

"I'll make up excuses."

"Better be ready for some tears."

"I know. She's really nice and I don't want to hurt her."

"Which you inevitably will," I say.

Dan nods and looks out the window. "That really sucks," he says. "There really isn't any easy way out of this." After a pause, he adds, "But I don't want to lose your friendship." He gives me a smile with a sad edge to it. "You're really the only friend I have."

If that's true, it's a pitiful admission considering I never spend time with him. His statement makes me ask myself how we became such good friends, at least in his eyes. In the previous reality, we had just become acquainted. Now it seems we have a history together.

"Maybe your new roommate… " I leave the thought unfinished, but Dan understands.

"Yeah. My new roommate. Maybe," he says, and his smile brightens a bit.

"Do you need any help moving?" I ask, starting to feel sorry for him.

"Thanks, but I've that taken care of. I'm leaving Marco most of the furniture. There are a few things I don't want to part with, so whatever won't fit into my room at University Pointe is going into storage."

"Great," I reply and start to rise.

"You're leaving?"

"I have to get home soon," I answer without offering an explanation. If Marco thought I was bluffing about the note and had acted unwisely, he would have found he was terribly wrong.

As I head for the door, I hear Dan gasp. Fearing this might be the start of another heart attack, I turn to see him standing with his hands pressed against his cheeks. He looks at me and explains, "I have a date with Trish. It's set for tomorrow afternoon."

"And… ?"

"I don't know. I'm torn between calling to cancel and just… "

He pauses and I throw him a questioning look.

Dan shrugs and suggests, "Maybe just not show up?"

I'm glad that I told him to end it. If this is the kind of coward he is, aside from the fact Trish is a minor, she is much better off without him. It's better he hurts her now, before she becomes too emotionally attached, than later, when his fear of explaining himself crushes her.

Chapter
Eleven

It's Sunday and I've spent the entire morning texting Erin without a response. I wanted to phone her yesterday, but decided against it in case her father was still angry. But now I'm worried. Why won't she text me back? What could be wrong? I understand what could be wrong. Her father's a drunk, or at least gets drunk on occasion and then becomes violent, so I am worried about her safety. In that case, has he hurt her? Is she afraid that continuing to see me will give him enough reason to blow up again?

The rational scientist in me says to back off. Raising one's voice does not necessarily translate to physical violence. Dad has shouted at me on numerous occasions and usually I deserved it. He never hit me, though. Has her father struck her? Is this the secret she was hinting at? I'm driving myself crazy. I've been pacing back and forth for almost an hour, but my room is too small for this kind of activity and I decide to step outside.

"Eric!" Dad calls as I hit the bottom of the stairs and make for the front door.

"Yes, Dad?"

"Your mother needs help in the backyard and I can't leave this paperwork."

"I'm on it," I say.

He gives me a satisfied nod through his office door, and I make an abrupt U-turn in the living room. I head toward the kitchen, then hurry through the laundry room on my way to the back door… only to run into a wall of heat as I step into the open. It's one of those late summer days that either drives people inside, or else sends them into the nearest body of water.

From the tiny back porch, I stop to study the yard, trying to locate Mom. After a minute, I see one of the bushes near the back fence shaking. The leaves rustle a moment, then stop, and she emerges. She's wearing a cloth bandana, a dirty white T-shirt, blue jeans, gloves and green plastic gardening shoes. She shoves the clippers she is holding into her trousers' back pocket, then starts brushing leaves and bits of debris from her head, arms and shoulders. After wiping her eyes with the backs of her hands, she blinks a few times, then notices me.

"Eric, I'm so glad you're here. Can you give me a hand?"

I bounce down the stairs and trot over to join her. Normally, I'm not much into gardening, but since I need something to take my mind off of Erin and her father, this seems like the perfect solution.

According to Dad, when the developer remodeled our house, he was forced to tear out most of the surrounding garden to give his workmen room to work before he eventually replanted it. He left the bushes at the rear of the lot untouched, though, and for some time afterward, no one looked after them. Since the day we arrived, Mom's been complaining that those bushes resemble a jungle. Now that the house's interior is largely to her satisfaction, she has decided that this is the perfect time to put the back lot in order. This is the project I'm to help her with and there is a great deal waiting for us to take care of. With so many weeds having sprouted and filled in the area, it will be hard at first to determine what we want to keep and what we need to get rid of. We give each other a look.

"Ready?" asks Mom. "There's a lot of work that needs to get done."

I nod and smile, as much to myself as to her, knowing it's not going to be easy. I reply, "Let's get to work."

By mid-afternoon we are drenched with perspiration and covered with fragments of the bushes we've been trimming and the weeds we've been tearing out. We fill the entire green waste container, despite cutting up the branches into lots of little pieces. Only a chipper would have done the job better and possibly have left room in the bin for more.

Once we have raked up the waste and deposited it, Mom turns to me and says, "You're quite the handyman." Then, eyeing me carefully, she laughs. "You should take a look at yourself."

"Yeah? Well Dad's going to really love getting close to you," I say as I begin pulling twigs from my hair. Still panting from the exertion, I ask "Do you mind if we call it quits? I need to get something to drink."

"That's not a bad idea. How about some ice cold lemonade?"

Just for a second, my thoughts flash to Dan, the South Waterfront condominiums and the lie I told Marco about hating lemonade.

"Sounds great."

Just then my hip pocket pings. It's my cell phone signaling it has received a text message. It reads,

c u tomorrow?

It's from Erin and I hope she's all right. I text her back.

definitely! where?

She replies,

PSU

We decide that meeting at the bookstore at noon will work, since we need to start purchasing supplies for the coming term. Still, I wonder why school? Why not someplace closer? So many possible explanations come to mind that I can't decide which ones are plausible and which ones are going to drive me crazy if I let them. I set my concerns aside and follow Mom to the kitchen.

"Do I look as bad as you do?" she asks as she reaches into the refrigerator.

"Worse," I say, although neither of us has had time to examine ourselves in a mirror.

She is covered with pieces of debris. Strands of her hair are poking from under the scarf she is wearing. Her clothes, like mine, are so dirty that, under normal circumstances, if I came in looking like this, she would order me to strip, leave them in a pile in the laundry room, and go to my bathroom and shower. I'm sure I'll have to do so pretty soon, and she will probably strip down as well, after I've headed upstairs. Right now, though, we are craving refreshment.

"What happened to you guys?" I hear Trish ask as we are downing our drinks.

I swallow the last gulp and it goes down hard. I gasp as the cold fills my mouth and ices my throat and I get an immediate brain freeze. I peer at her over the frosted rim of my glass. She is wearing a new summer dress I've never seen before. She has obviously spent a lot of time fixing her hair and makeup and she is almost bouncing with excitement.

"Wow! You look great," I tell her.

Of course, I know she's all dressed up for her date with Dan, but I don't dare let on. If she gets even a hint that I know Hastings, that I know they are dating and, further, that I want to end their relationship, she'll go out of her way to make sure I won't have even a chance at success.

"Trish has a new boyfriend," Mom explains.

"Oh?" I say, raising my eyebrows. "When did this happen?"

"He's the one I told you about," Trish reminds me.

I nod appreciatively, remembering our discussion in

her bedroom and Mom asks, "What have you two planned?"

"He won't say." Trish smiles. "It's a surprise."

It'll be a surprise, all right, I tell myself, feeling guilty that I am responsible for ruining her day. I really love her and hate to hurt her, but I'm certain that, if she continues dating this criminal, worse things could happen. Telling myself a ruined afternoon is better than a ruined life, I wait to see how matters unfold.

An hour later, she is pacing in the living room and texting. The joy has gone out of her face and I really wish it didn't have to be this way. However, I only have Dan's word that he is going to get out of the drug dealing business. He might as well be a total stranger in view of how little time I have known him, not to mention that someone who carries a gun is completely unacceptable for a teenage girl to date. Since Trish has never been one to forgive and forget—the Trish in my original universe—I'm hoping this episode will kill their relationship.

All of a sudden, I see Dad entering the dining room from the kitchen. He's carrying a plate with a sandwich in one hand and a soft drink in the other, probably to tide him over till dinner while he works in his office. His eyes come up as he passes the dining room table and he stops when he notices Trish. While Mom might have asked what the matter was, Dad has learned, over the course of many similar incidents, not to disturb her until her temper has cooled. His eyes shift away from her as he evaluates what course of action to take next. Abruptly, he changes direction and takes the longer way around so he can get to his office without running into her.

Yeah. Same old Trish. Same old Dad. This much, at least, remains the same and Dan is now history. I smile, hoping the next guy she sees will be a little more normal. I'm also relieved because I notice that, after taking my medicine this morning, the ever-present shimmer has faded almost to the point of invisibility. Since it seems to increase as a crisis approaches, then fade when the episode has passed, I cautiously accept this as a sign of reassurance.

I also remember the second fold: the one that occurred after I came home from the library. Nothing stressful precipitated it. The shimmer increased on its own without any prompting. Even so, I remain hopeful that the medication has controlled it.

… … … … …

I'm in the university's bookstore, in the process of picking out whatever books I will need for the coming quarter, when I hear Erin's voice behind me.

"Hi," she says, almost in a whisper.

"Hi," I reply as I turn to look at her. Understating how strongly I've felt, I add, "I missed you."

Her arrival puts a smile on my face until I actually see her. She's wearing a torn pair of jeans, an old T-shirt and sunglasses, and she's not standing fully upright. Her shoulders are hunched and she tilts her head downward, as if she's either afraid to look at me, or else she's afraid for me to see her. Needing to get even the barest glimpse of the face I've been longing to see all weekend, I reach out and, with my fingers, I tip her chin upward. I nearly drop all the books I am holding when I notice a rim of purple peeking out from behind one of the lenses.

"My God! What happened?"

"I can't go back home," she says and her voice cracks.

"What happened?" I repeat.

Abruptly, Erin breaks down and cries. I place my books on the floor, wrap my arms around her and draw her against me as she shudders and starts sobbing. She doesn't resist. Instead, she collapses into me and bawls like a baby. I'm sure people are watching, but I don't bother to check. Her warmth and her frailty are all that concern me. Minutes pass. Time no longer matters, only that I'm holding her and

110

that this wonderful, loving girl needs me. I run my fingers through her hair, stroking her head and muttering meaningless assurances—meaningless, because how do I know how everything will work out? I'm pretty sure I know what has happened, at least in general terms, but I have no idea what I can do about it.

After a while, she begins to calm and her wails become sniffles. Without letting go of me, Erin takes a half step back and asks, "What am I going to do? I can't go back home." Her voice becomes desperate when the realization strikes. "I have *nowhere* to go," she gasps, and places a hand over her mouth.

"You can stay with me."

I have no idea where that came from, and I'm sure it surprises Erin as well, because she tilts back her head and asks a reasonable question.

"What will your parents say? I can't stay in your room."

That does pose a problem, I must admit. It's a tiny house and all of the bedrooms are occupied. Still, there has to be a way, so I try to sound reassuring.

"We'll work something out." When she starts to object, I tell her, "Let's talk to my parents. Between the four of us… "

"What about your sister?"

"Between the *five* of us," I amend, "I'm sure we can solve this."

We arrive at my house shortly before dinnertime and the place is filled with aroma of Mom's cooking. We decided against arriving earlier in order to avoid telling, then retelling the same tale over again, first to Mom, then to Dad and Trish when each of them comes home.

"You're late," Mom says as I poke my head into the kitchen. "I was afraid you'd miss dinner."

There's no edge to her voice, no irritation. She's just making an observation and I'm relieved because the

111

conversation is going to be difficult enough without adding anger to the mix.

"Oh!" she exclaims when Erin, who has been hanging back, steps inside and joins us. "You've brought a guest. Trish, will you please set another place at the table?"

It's then that she notices Erin's black eye and drops the spoon she is holding. It clatters on the floor as she asks, "Oh dear! What happened?" Her eyes dart back and forth between Erin's shiner and the mess the fallen utensil has made.

"Can it wait until Dad's in the room?" I ask.

Mom hesitates, then stoops to retrieve it.

"Of course," she says as she wipes up the mess with a paper towel, unable to keep from glancing at Erin.

As Trish moves to the cupboard to get a plate and utensils, she looks as if she wants to ask that as well. I'm thankful when she refrains from doing so.

"I thought I heard you come in," Dad remarks as he steps in behind us. "Who is this?" he asks. Our backs are toward him and Erin squeezes my hand.

"Hi, Dad," I say, trying to sound cheerful. "This is Erin. She's the girl I saw on Saturday."

"That's wonderful!" he exclaims. "I'm so glad to meet you."

As we turn to face him, he is extending his hand and Erin responds by grasping it and completing the handshake.

"I'm happy to meet you, too, Mr. Folder," she says, shaking his hand vigorously.

But as Dad notices her face, his smile evaporates and his eyes shift toward me.

"It's a long story," I explain. "Maybe we can discuss it over dinner."

He gives me a series of small, quick nods and replies, "Of course," then, "Certainly," he adds with emphasis, returning his eyes to Erin, while attempting to muster a smile. "Let's move into the dining room. It's a little crowded in here. Let's give your mother some room."

During dinner, we all mystically land on the same page, deliberately avoiding Erin's injury. Trish tells us about the clubs she has joined: Cosplay and Lacrosse. Lacrosse? I can understand the costume thing, but my sister's never been the least bit athletic… not my previous sister. Erin tells us a bit about her interest in creative writing and that draws in Dad. He gives her insights into PSU's faculty: specifically, which instructors would most appreciate her propensity for memoir. Finally, Mom, who never—and I mean absolutely never—discusses her work, goes into great detail about the new line of sports gear her employer has just launched. It's obvious what we are avoiding. I mean it's great that we can have a lengthy conversation. It's a strong indicator that we can all live together. But this is too much. It's going on far too long. Finally, in my most diplomatic tone I say, "Erin's father got drunk and slugged her."

Silence. The sound of jaws dropping.

As Mom opens her mouth, perhaps to ask a question, I add, "This is not the first time."

I know because Erin filled me in on her father's behavior over the course of the afternoon. Today was not the first time he had injured her. He has a long history of abuse that extends all the way back to her childhood. She told me about the many times her mother had taken her to the ER and the multiple injuries he had caused, things like unexplained bruises, broken bones, even a concussion.

Before anyone has time to speak, I add, "She's wondering if she can stay with us."

If their silence could increase, it would, as Mom, Dad and Trish exchange glances.

"What does your mother have to say about this?" Mom asks. "Have you talked to her about it?"

Erin shakes her head and lowers it. "She's dead."

"Dead?" Dad asks as he lowers his own, trying to peer into Erin's eyes. "How long ago was that?"

"Two years ago last April."

"What about family?" asks Mom.

"I don't have any," answers Erin. Then she raises her head and explains, "Mom used to talk about some of them, but Dad usually cut those conversations short. He never wanted to have anything to do with them, so I don't know their names or how to get in touch with them."

In a quiet voice, Dad asks, "Has he ever done anything else?"

Erin lowers her head again and nods, but offers nothing further.

"How old are you?" he asks.

"Eighteen."

"Do you have a photo ID?"

I interrupt with, "What does that have to do with anything?"

Dad explains, "It's of legal importance." Mom nods.

Erin fishes a plastic card from her hip pocket explaining, "I don't drive," as she hands over the Oregon State identification card.

Dad studies it a moment, holding it up to the light, examining both sides before he returns it. Mom and Dad look at one another, apparently considering what to do next. Then, before either of them can speak, Trish offers, "She can stay in my room."

"Trish," says Mom. "We're not talking about a weekend visit. If we do as Erin is requesting… " She turns and asks Erin, "Is this something you want? It's not just Eric who's asking, is it?" When Erin affirms that this is indeed her desire, Mom looks back at Trish and says, "This could be permanent."

Trish swallows hard and says, "I know."

Dad looks at her and says, "Your room is too small for the two of you." When Trish starts to object, he raises a hand to silence her and says, "If we decide to go through with this, I'll buy a queen size fold-out couch and put it in the living room." He turns to Erin and says, "You won't have very much privacy."

When Erin nods, Trish volunteers, "You can use my bathroom."

When Mom nods at this, Dad asks, "What about your things?"

When Erin returns an uncomprehending stare, Dad runs his fingers through his hair and explains, "Your things. Your clothes. Makeup. Did you bring any of that with you?"

"No," Erin replies. "I didn't think. I just had to get out."

"Well, you're going to need them," says Mom. "You're going to have to go back to your house and get them. We'll go with you. That is, we can ride there together. Now, where do you live?" When Erin says Wilsonville and gives them an address, Dad turns to Mom and says, "I'm going to phone the police and ask them to meet us there."

"Why the police?" asks Erin.

"I want to avoid trouble. There's something I believe they call a civil escort. I don't know if they can do it without a court being involved, but basically, they merely show up and make sure everyone remains on good terms: no aggression, no weapons and no violence. Does your father own a gun?" he asks. When Erin nods, he says, "Then I'm definitely going to arrange for an escort."

Erin appears to be verging onto tears, but nods in agreement. "Then I can stay with you?"

Dad inhales deeply, then sighs. "For the moment, at least. We'll have to take this one day at a time. But, yes, you can stay with us."

Chapter
Twelve

By the time we are underway, it has grown dark. Dad's in the driver's seat, while Mom rides shotgun and Erin and I are riding in the seat behind them. Meanwhile, back at the ranch, Trish has elected to stay home in order to have enough time to create space in her closet, her chest of drawers, as well as her bathroom. For that simple act of selflessness, I cannot begin to express how much I admire my new sister.

It would be an understatement to say that we're nervous. When Dad contacted the Wilsonville police at their non-emergency number and explained our situation, they agreed with him, calling his request for a civil escort wise. Only Erin knows what her father might do, and even she admits he's unpredictable.

As we pull up to the curb, two white police cars, each with one thick black stripe and two thinner ones beneath it, are already waiting. Dad parks behind one of them and kills the ignition.

Sighing deeply he asks, "Is everybody ready?"

"I'm scared, Mr. Folder," says Erin. "I'm not sure I can go through with this."

Dad turns in his seat and faces her.

"I understand," he tells her. "I'd be afraid, too, if I

were in your position. But this is something you have to do. You're going to need your clothes and some of your other things if you're not going to go back."

"It's not too late to change your mind," Mom adds, but Erin shakes her head.

Dad says, "You're not alone in this. We'll all be there with you—me, Eric, Bea, and don't forget about the police. Your father is going to have to think twice before he tries anything stupid."

"You're right, but I'm still scared."

I lean over and take her arm. "Come on. You can do this."

Erin takes a deep breath and I can tell she's trying not to cry. She looks at me and forces a smile. "All right. Let's go before I change my mind."

We open the doors and step out to meet the police who are already standing beside their vehicles. A man and woman police officer, dressed in short sleeved black uniforms with gold stars on their chests, approach. The male officer introduces himself as Sergeant Robert Miller and his female companion as Corporal Marie Davis. We introduce ourselves as well. Dad explains why he requested their presence. He had spoken with the dispatcher, but these two were not given all of the information, only that they needed to meet us here. When he informs them Erin's father owns a handgun, the male officer tells Erin, "I would suggest you knock before entering and identify yourself. We don't want to startle him and we need time to explain the situation."

Corporal Davis asks, "Do you plan to go inside alone, or are any of these people going to assist you?"

Erin begins, "There is a lot I need to get."

Sergeant Miller replies, "I'd suggest that you take only the bare minimum: a few outfits, some underwear, and a few keepsakes you can't replace if your father won't give you a second opportunity." Glancing our way, she says, "It's probably best to have everyone help."

"Take what's most important," the male officer adds, "and maybe you'll have a chance sometime later to go back and get more.

"Let's get started," he says. Repeating his previous instruction, he tells Erin, "Knock on the door to announce your presence and the rest of us will wait there with you. Once we determine it's safe to go inside, I'll enter first, then my partner will escort the rest of you." Turning to Erin, he emphasizes, "This needs to happen fast."

"I put a couple of suitcases in the trunk of the car," offers Dad.

"You won't have time to pack things. Just take what you can carry. While nothing bad may occur, sometimes things happen unexpectedly."

Erin replies, "I understand," then nods and heads for the door.

At this point, my new danger alert system is starting to become more evident. I don't know if some all-knowing force in the universe is alerting me, or something that's within, some part of my brain reacting to possibilities. Whichever it is, the shimmer is transforming from a dimly perceived, almost unnoticeable presence, into a glowing gossamer web that is overlaying itself across everything around me. Also, my head is throbbing and I realize I'd forgotten to take my medicine. It's too late to do anything about it now. Whatever happens, I hope I can retain enough presence to avoid doing anything like the earlier incidents.

Erin arrives on the porch and knocks, with the male officer positioning himself immediately beside her. His partner is standing with rest of us, a few feet behind Erin and the other officer. The porch light is on, as are most of the houselights, but for more than a minute, no one answers. Erin raises her hand again and is starting to knock when the door opens and a barefoot man, who easily weighs three hundred pounds and stands over six feet tall, appears in the doorway. His uncut hair is a mess and only the bottom two buttons of

119

his shirt are fastened, revealing a broad hairy chest. When his eyes move from Erin to the policeman beside her, the officer asks, "Mr. Jowalski?"

Erin's father nods and asks, "What's this about?"

His words are somewhat slurred and he looks as if he's trying to focus.

"I'm Sergeant Miller of the Wilsonville Police," the officer explains. Erin's father moves his head an inch or so backward and furrows his eyebrows, as if the explanation startles him. With his eyes on Mr. Jowalski, the officer adds, "This is my partner, Corporal Davis. Your daughter would like to retrieve some of her belongings and she has brought some friends to assist her. May we come in?"

For the first time, Erin's father notices the rest of us. He studies us for a moment, then growls, "When that little bitch walked out, she walked away for good."

He is reaching for the door when Sergeant Miller explains, "We can come back with a warrant, or you can make this simple." He pauses, then repeats, "May we come in?"

I'm not sure if the officer is bluffing. As little as I know about police procedure—since no crime has been committed aside from his punching his daughter—I suspect this is just a ruse. Still, Erin's father appraises the size of the group, then regards the two from Wilsonville.

He steps aside and growls, "Make it quick."

Sergeant Miller turns to Erin and says, "Remember, just take what you need."

Erin leads us through the cluttered interior and into her bedroom. While the officers stand guard in the hallway, she opens her wardrobe and, at her direction, Dad grabs an armful of blouses and dresses. Moving to her bureau, Erin pulls the top drawer open. It's full of socks and underwear and it's clear that only a few items can be carried by hand. Corporal Davis is standing near the door, so Erin calls to her.

"Can I take the whole drawer?"

When the officer nods, I grab it by the knobs and remove it, gripping it on either end once it comes free. Erin is instructing Mom to fill a wastebasket with perfume bottles and certain other personal items as I'm heading for the door. I'm just entering the hallway, where Sergeant Miller is keeping Mr. Jowalski at its opposite end, when her father breaks away and dashes through a door. Sergeant Miller is unholstering his gun when Erin's father emerges with a pistol. He fires two bullets into Sergeant Miller as he's raising his weapon.

As the sergeant collapses, I hear Corporal Davis, who is standing behind me, shout, "Get down!"

I don't know if she's ordering me, because I'm now in the line of fire, or Erin's father, but it's suddenly hard to see as the shimmer intensifies. Afraid I'll get shot, I drop to the floor with the drawer underneath me.

"Father, no!" cries Erin.

Her voice is right behind me and I'm afraid she'll get hurt or even killed. Two more shots are fired and someone lands on top of me. An edge of the drawer digs into my chest, and I struggle to pull myself to one side, as much to slide off as to extract myself from under the person on top of me.

Down on the floor, my head begins pounding and the shimmer increases. Unable to see what is happening, I claw at the webwork in a desperate attempt to regain an unobstructed view. In all of the confusion, I'm not thinking clearly. I ask myself is it Erin who's fallen or Corporal Davis? As more shots explode, I'm establishing finger holds and feel myself seizing the obstructing phenomenon. Two arms wrap around me and I hear Erin cry, "Eric! What's happening?" as gunfire increases and this world begins to disappear. Her shout is right in my ear and I understand it's she who's holding onto me. *Will she come with me?* I wonder.

Afraid I'll get shot and needing to see clearly, I continue to tear at the webwork. Too late, I'm aware of my

actions' consequences as, abruptly, the obscuring filaments
are gone, along with the gunfire.

... ...

In the next instant, I find myself in a place that's gray
and without definition. I'm not standing on anything solid.
There are no houses or people, or anything else here. I'm
trying to figure out where I might be when someone starts
materializing in front of me, as if stepping through a fog in
the distance. The person begins approaching and, after a
moment, I can see it's a woman. She's trying to speak to me,
but I can neither make out her words nor hear any footsteps,
as if I'm in a vacuum where sound doesn't carry. As she
starts drawing nearer, I become aware of her vaguely familiar
emerald green eyes. Unsure of her intentions, I begin backing
away, trying to recall where I might have seen them.
Abruptly, my mind goes back to the dream I had before
waking in the hospital. I was afraid of her then, but I'm less
so now because she smiles and does not appear threatening.
She continues speaking, but I can't hear what she's saying.
When I try to tell her, I feel my vocal chords vibrate, but no
sound emerges. Frustrated, I cup my hand to my ear, shake
my head and she appears disappointed. Hoping we can
somehow communicate, perhaps with hand signs, maybe by
reading each other's lips, I try again but the scene begins
fading.

... ...

Abruptly, I find myself standing on the sidewalk in
front of Erin's home. The Forester is still parked at the curb
and a car I don't recognized is directly behind it. In place of
patrol cars, a fire department ambulance is parked in the
driveway with its red lights flashing. The houselights are on,
the door is wide open and Erin is standing next to me. One
minute, we were lying on the floor, and the next, we're
standing outside. My mouth is open, my heart is pumping

122

from adrenaline and I find myself wondering if she came along with me.

"Thanks for coming," she tells me, making me doubt that she folded as I did. Her comment and tone of voice indicate no surprise whatsoever in finding herself here, only a reassurance that I am here with her.

People in paramedics' uniforms coming through the doorway, transporting someone on a stretcher, catch our eye. From the individual's size, I can only assume that the person they're carrying is Erin's father. When a woman appears behind them, Erin squeezes my arm, digging her nails into it, and calls, "Mother? What happened?"

She releases me, pauses a second, then runs to where her mother is standing. I follow as Erin bounds up the stairs and embraces her. As I draw near, Erin and her mother begin talking with great animation. Her mother is shifting her attention from her daughter to the stretcher and back again, looking distraught and confused. When I arrive, standing at the foot of the steps, I hear her mother explain, "Your father had a heart attack."

I remain in the yard looking up at them as a whole raft of questions tumble down on me. What was my relationship to this universe's Erin before I arrived? We obviously knew one another, but for how long? Had we just met? Are we a couple, or are we just friends? Has Erin already introduced me to her mother, or am I here to be introduced? I'm not sure how to proceed, but I have no other choice. This is not like the previous times I folded away one world and stepped into the next. While those prior instances presented a few awkward instances, once everything here settles down, the questions that will certainly arise will be difficult, if not impossible, for me to answer without sounding like an idiot. I can't simply leave, so I stand here hoping to learn why I've come here.

In the moments before the ambulance pulls away, during which I wait while mother and daughter embrace and exchange comments, a few questions arise that I believe will never be answered, most pertaining to the gunfight and which of us survived. I set them aside for the moment and focus on my present situation. I decide to give Erin and her mother a few private moments and remain where I'm standing. At one point, Erin turns to me and gestures for me to join them.

"Eric," she says when I'm standing beside them. "This is my mother, Christina. Mother, this is the friend I've been telling you about."

Well, this answers some of what I've been wondering. Her mother tries to muster a smile. She extends her hand and I accept it.

"I'm sorry we're forced to meet like this," she apologizes, her eyes flicking from me to the ambulance that's leaving, then back again.

"Perhaps I should go," I suggest, "and leave you two alone."

"Nonsense," Christina says. "Come inside with me while I get my car keys."

On the way to the hospital, Mrs. Jowalski makes a few attempts at polite conversation, despite how worried she is. I expect it's because she's trying distract herself from her worries about her husband's condition.

"Erin tells me you're a budding scientist," she says. *Hopefully, I'm still a physics major.* "And that you've moved here from Arizona."

Just as I'm becoming alarmed that my family may have moved from an entirely different State, Erin corrects her. "New Mexico."

"Ah! Excuse me. From New Mexico. How do you like it here?"

"I like it a lot," I say as I notice Erin's increasing distress. In an attempt to move the conversation to the core of what's troubling them, I ask, "Do you mind if I ask what happened to your husband?"

The question seems to put Christina off balance. For a

second, she appears to be uncertain and I wonder if it's because she considers the question inappropriate. I'm about to apologize when she answers, "No. Not at all." Glancing between the two of us, she explains, "He hadn't been feeling well all day. He'd been sweating. He complained he felt dizzy and had trouble breathing." She looks at her daughter. "I kept telling him to go see a doctor, but he wouldn't listen. You know how stubborn he can be," she says to Erin. "Then, all of a sudden, he grabbed his chest and dropped to his knees. I called 911 and they sent an ambulance."

She stops abruptly and I can see that we've arrived at the hospital's emergency room parking. After Christina locks the car, we spend an hour or so in the waiting room. When a nurse comes to see her, he informs Erin's mother that it will be a while longer before she and Erin can see him. In turn, Mrs. Jowalski suggests that Erin take me home.

"I need to see him," Erin protests.

"I understand. But your father will certainly spend the night here and I'm sure Eric has other things he needs to do. In the time it will take you to drop him off and return, the doctors will probably still be looking after him." She turns to me and says, "It was nice meeting you, Eric. I'm sorry it had to be under these circumstances.

"No problem," I answer. "These things happen. Maybe we can meet again when your husband's feeling better."

You might think I'd be happy with the way things worked out. Erin and I are alive and her mother is still alive in this world. Erin's father doesn't seem to be a threat like he was in the last one, although I'll have to determine whether that's true through future conversations with Erin. I hate to admit it, but I'm more than a little glad to leave. I'm certainly concerned about Erin and her parents, but I'm suddenly exhausted. All of this folding back and forth between realities is starting to take its toll. I'm overwhelmed by all of the uncertain outcomes and their emotional consequences. In one

125

of those realities, my parents are dead, shot down and murdered in cold blood. While in many others, there are various alternate resolutions. In one of them, I, or else my father—Erin, perhaps—turned out to be a hero. He, she or I found our way through the bullets, then tackled and subdued Mr. Jowalski. In the one we just left, Erin and I, as well as my parents, along with two well-meaning police officers, are in a house with a madman who is trying to kill them and they are trying to stay alive. The thing I'm trying to get at is there are likely to be countless possibilities in countless alternate realities. If an event could turn out one way in one reality, it could turn out in as many other ways as one can imagine in other realities. The possibilities are endless and the thoughts of them are exhausting.

What happened tonight is similar to what happened when Dan had his heart attack and I moved into a different situation from the one before. This compels me to ask what happens when I move into a parallel universe. Clearly, when I fold, I occupy a different body, as evidenced the time I woke up and my cast was gone and my injuries had changed. And when I say "I," I mean the conscious entity who has been watching all these events transpire since before the original accident. What happens, then, to the Eric Folder I displace? I assume that the awareness inside me is not comprised of matter. I base this assumption on the fact that when someone dies and the consciousness departs, there is no measurable loss in weight, no detectable loss of mass. Therefore, it's not unreasonable to assume that the being I call "me" is some form of energy.

Since the law of conservation of energy, also called the first law of thermodynamics, states that a universe's energy must remain constant—it can neither increase nor decrease—when I move into an alternate universe, what happens to the entity I displace: the second universe's Eric Folder? Clearly, he cannot remain, otherwise the second universe's energy would be increased by my insertion. Logic tells me that he must then be thrust abruptly into the universe I just left, into the body I just departed, or else that universe's energy would be diminished by my absence. What must he be thinking when that transition occurs? I, at least, have some sort of clue to what just happened. But does he? Does he think he's going insane when he abruptly finds himself being shot at?

Another thought occurs. What happens if I move into another Eric Folder at the moment he gets killed? I must certainly die. If I get killed, what does it matter if Eric's still alive in any of a hundred thousand alternate universes? The Eric I displace moves into my previous body—assuming that's what happens—and goes on living while I die in the one he just left. Dead is dead. I disappear. Is anyone aware of their million other instances? Of course not. It doesn't matter if they are well or injured, happy or sad or disease-ridden. I'm the only one this consciousness is aware of. The same goes for Erin. Whether she is alive or dead in the place I just left is irrelevant. She is with her mother in this reality and, hopefully, the two of them will live happily ever after.

Paraphrasing the words of Shakespeare, "Prick me. Do I not bleed?" Prick the other me. Sure, he bleeds, but I don't feel it and I don't give a damn either. Stab them. Shoot them. To hell with all my other instances. I know I sound crass and insensitive, but there's only so much anyone can take. *This* Eric Folder is the only one who matters to me and I'm growing bitter. There is nothing for me to do now but sit back and go home while Erin drives me there.

Chapter Thirteen

I didn't sleep well last night. How could I? How well does anyone sleep in a strange bed or in an unfamiliar house? It isn't any easier to fall asleep in a strange body. Yes, it's Eric Folder's body all right, but not the same Eric Folder's body I started out in. Just as one reality differs from the next in countless ways, some of them almost unnoticeable, others overwhelming, each Eric I fold into differs from all of the previous ones. Last night, when I got ready to crawl into bed, I realized this Eric Folder is left handed. I've always been a righty, so this is a little disconcerting. When I tried to get ready in the way I'm used to—brushing my teeth right handed for example—things suddenly became awkward, totally uncoordinated. When I eventually realized that the best way for me to do things was not to think about them, but go on autopilot, letting this body do what felt natural, things started to come together.

Sheesh! I've always tried to be flexible in the way I approach things, but this is starting to stretch my adaptability to the limit. Then again, what choice do I have? Now that the truth has sunk in, I'm trying to live with it, and I have to say it isn't easy. The more I've been thinking about it, the more differences I sense. Some of them are almost imperceptible. Is my vision the same? Is my hearing or the rest of my senses? With many aspects, there's nothing I can put my finger on, nothing I can point to with certainty, but this body perceives things slightly differently. I'm sure of it. It's something I'm going to have to live with from this point forward, if not in this Eric Folder's body, then in another's when I'm forced to fold yet again… and another's… and yet another's. I laugh at the irony and climb out of bed, wondering what the day holds.

It doesn't take long to begin spotting other differences. On my desk, instead of a Mac there is now a PC. My Xbox is gone, as are my books on physics and mathematics. Also missing is Isaacson's biography of Albert Einstein. In their place, I see books about botany and zoology and I suddenly wonder if it might be too late to change Eric's course load. If Professor Basu exists in this world, I need to drop by and talk to him. What will I tell him? After a life spent pursuing biological sciences, I've suddenly decided to study quantum physics. Yeah. Right. Like, that's going to be easy to sell.

These changes are killing me. I want to find a way to get back to my original self, but I don't see how that might be possible. I wound up here by chance. And I expect that if I could initiate another fold on my own, without remaining a victim of circumstance, wherever I might end up next would be the result of rolling the good old cosmic dice again. This would be worse than D&D, where rolling a twenty sided die would represent the most complex change possible. The one I would roll here would have a million, billion, *TRILLION* sides… so how could anyone control that outcome. I sigh and begin my day.

After showering and dressing, I head downstairs to the kitchen. Last night has left me hungry and I know I'm going to need to eat something if I'm going to think clearly. I stop at the top of the stairs and stare at the wheelchair someone has left standing there.

This is unexpected. Who does it belong to? It's then

that I notice the rail running down the wall opposite the bannister and the seat affixed to it at the rail's lower end. This appears to be a mechanical device to help someone either climb or descend. Why didn't I notice it last night? I suspect it's because I came home exhausted and didn't bother turning on the lights. Also, the seat is folded to vertical so that it's next to the wall and I could have easily climbed to the top without running into it.

I'm halfway down when Trish rolls out at the bottom on a second wheelchair and stops in front of the stairway. Clearly, this is not some temporary condition or my parents would never have resorted to such an expensive solution. It also becomes obvious that, in this reality, Trish does not play Lacrosse and I wonder how she became disabled. I'm not going to ask, but it breaks my heart to see her like this. I'll just have to allow this information to emerge on its own— depending on how long I remain here.

"Hi!" she says when she notices me. She smiles broadly and asks, "How did your date go?"

"Fine," I reply, trying to sound as if I mean it.

I'm reluctant to get into what happened to Erin's father. It's a small lie, like all of us tell at one time or another to avoid discussing something unpleasant… like a heart attack. The fact is, the drive home with Erin really worked out well, including the long, extended kiss when she dropped me off at the curb. I'm sure the smile that's spreading across my face, as a result of that memory, backs up what I told her.

"You're off to a late start."

"Why?" I ask in a panic. "Am I supposed to be somewhere?"

She shakes her head, and I'm relieved that I'm not missing anything of importance.

"It's just not like you to sleep in like this," she replies.

At least this is unchanged.

"What's up for you?" I ask, trying to sound casual as

I attempt to unearth something informative. The last thing I need is another surprise, although I have a feeling there are an abundance of unexpected events out there waiting for me to step into them… kinda like stepping in dog shit.

After setting the chair's handbrakes, Trish starts to transfer herself onto the railing's seat. "Gotta get ready for school before the shuttle arrives."

As the chair ascends toward me, Trish leans forward a bit, puckers her lips for a kiss and I lean toward her to reciprocate. We each mange to plant one next to each other's mouth before she rides past me.

Looking back downward, she says, "Go get some breakfast. You don't seem like yourself."

"I've been thinking about changing majors," I call back.

"Do you think Parker will let you? You've already hinted at what a bitch she is."

Parker and not Basu? Now I know I need to eat something. And after I've done that, I need to get online and see who this Parker is and where her office is located.

"I'm going to give it a try since I'm just starting out. Besides, first year courses are pretty much the same for everyone."

I hope I'm just starting out. I could be a sophomore. This morning, anything is possible. I'm relieved when Trish returns a smile and a nod as she arrives at the stairwell's summit.

Turning toward the kitchen, I begin to notice our house's interior and wonder what other misfortunes have befallen us. Our furniture was never remarkable, but it was reasonably new and well taken care of. It all now appears to have been purchased from a secondhand store and the house smells, well… I think the word for it is "musty." More details to acquire over time.

… … … … …

Doctor Parker's office, like Professor Basu's, is in the SRTC near where his was located. While many of the walls are still painted the same brilliant lime green as they were in previous iterations, I begin heading up the entrance stairs on the lookout for more of the unexpected.

It doesn't take me long to spot some of them. The display cases in the lobby are in different locations and their contents appear to have changed. I approach the one in the lobby's center, eyeing a rather large and unusual specimen. Is this what I think it is? When I'm only halfway there, I halt, shaken by what I believe I've identified. This is not an orangutan or a sea lion, or any other modern day creature. Instead, it appears to be a genuine saber tooth tiger. How can this be? Drawing closer, I see that the brown colored skeleton appears to be roughly four feet in height and almost twice that in length. In its skull are two yellow canines almost twelve inches each. When I'm standing beside it, I read the identification tag. It tells me the bones belonged to a creature named *Smilodon populator* and goes on to state that the animal goes by the common name "saber tooth cat."

Not only is this specimen "museum quality," as the initial Dan Hastings appraised the original displays, it's undoubtedly priceless. How an institution like Portland State could acquire such a piece is beyond my ability to speculate.

"I knew I would run into you eventually," says a feminine voice directly behind me.

I turn and say, "Alex?" surprised when I see her.

"Damn right it's Alex," she replies, loud enough to draw a few students' attention. "What are you and your slutty friend up to these days?"

Holy crap! What's going on? At least the Groundhog Day weatherman had the benefit of events repeating themselves. I, on the other hand, am treading on alien soil.

"Wh… what do you mean?"

I'm sure Alex is referring to Erin, but I have no idea what I've done to offend her. I feel as if I'm navigating a minefield, first with encountering my sister's unexpected disability, now Alex, and probably, a few minutes from now, with my course advisor.

"I don't like being dumped, is what I mean," she says in a voice seething with anger.

"I… "

"Don't even try to defend yourself. Now that I know you're still on campus, I'm going to get even."

She spins around and leaves me with my mouth hanging open, before she storms through the doors and into the street. Glancing around, I see several women casting disapproving looks. Great! This is going to leave me in a wonderful state of mind when I meet Doctor Parker… assuming she has time enough to see me.

I locate my course advisor's office on SRTC's second floor. The door has been left slightly ajar, so that when I knock it swings on its hinges and opens. The woman at the desk is facing to my left and poring over a small stack of papers. She is thin, almost gaunt, and her dark hair, streaked with gray, has been put up into something like a bun. However, it looks as if she had spent only seconds attempting it before giving up. Several strands are hanging down behind it, trailing over the collar of her rumpled, cream color blouse, while others dangle over her forehead. She turns to look at me. Pulling her glasses down over her nose, she frowns.

"What is it this time?" she asks.

"Pardon?" I reply, unsure what I'm walking into.

"Don't you remember when I said that you need to make an appointment?"

I nod. "I'm sorry."

She places her glasses on top of her desk, then puffs air through her nostrils to blow away some of the strands. Rotating her chair toward me, she says, "All right, Mister… Folder is it? Now that you have my attention, what is it this time?"

The exchange does not go well. I won't bother you

with all of the details, but it seems my counterpart has been coming to her office several times weekly asking to change majors, increase or decrease his course load, or return to an earlier choice. He is a total mess and I'm ashamed to be him. In the end, I simply tell her I have come to apologize and that I won't bother her again.

"You could have sent me an email, if that's all you wanted."

I agree, then step back into the hallway and ease the door shut behind me. I lean against it, exhale, and wonder what other wonders this new life holds in store.

Chapter
Fourteen

I spend the rest of the afternoon texting Erin, but it's not until almost dinnertime that I hear back from her.

Sup?

Now that I have her attention, I'm not sure how to respond. There is simply too much to fit into a text message, so I decide just to ask,

How's it going?

I'm expecting her to say, "super," or "great," or something of that nature. I'm surprised, then, when she replies,

Not sure

Has ur dad gotten sicker? I text.

Worse.

This is a stunner. We both decide that we need to talk in person. She tells me about a burger place located on Main Street in Wilsonville, and we agree to meet there at eight o'clock this evening.

When I arrive, Erin is standing near the front door with her arms wrapped around herself. She looks worried and appears to be verging onto tears. Today is Monday, so several tables are available. When I tilt my head toward one in a corner, she gives several quick nods and we make our way toward it, not bothering to check if we should wait to be seated.

Almost at once, a server appears and deposits menus in front of us. The time we spend studying them gives us room to think before starting our conversation. Mom and Dad weren't home by the time I left to come here. But even though I haven't had dinner, I'm not really hungry and end up ordering fries and a cola. Erin, less enthusiastic about food than I am, requests a glass of water with ice. I'm sure our server expects that the tip will be miniscule at best. Nonetheless, she musters a smile and disappears into the kitchen.

"Father's not doing well and Mother isn't either."

"How so?"

"They sent him in for a quadruple bypass, but he's not responding."

I tilt my head to the side and frown to indicate I need more details.

"I'm not sure what's happening, but I'm afraid he's not going to make it." She pauses a moment, then adds, "Mother won't leave the hospital. I spent most of the day with her, but I finally had to leave and find some room to breathe. There's nothing I can do to help, but staying home was driving me crazy too." She reaches across the table and takes my hand into both of hers. "I hope you don't mind, but I need to be with you."

Why would I mind? I'm happy to sit here all night with her if she wants me to. I ask, "Is there anything I can do?"

"Just be with me."

"No problem."

We spend the next hour holding hands and looking into each other's eyes, mostly in silence. During that time, our server drops by periodically. When it becomes obvious we're not interested in ordering anything else, she eventually leaves us alone.

At one point, Erin asks, "How did your day go?"

"Mixed bag. I decided to drop by Parker's and apologize for being a nuisance." I chuckle.

"And?"

"She thought I was being a nuisance."

"Don't worry about it. She has a reputation for being hard on students."

I decide to avoid telling Erin about my thought on changing majors, for the time being at least. Taking a chance I've already told her about my newest enemy, I say, "And I ran into Alex."

Erin's eyebrows go up and I wonder if I've screwed up.

"How did that go?" she asks.

Her otherwise lack of surprise when I bring up my former girlfriend indicates that creepy Eric at least had the decency to be honest about her. This is one point in his favor. When I tell her what happened, she crunches a piece of ice between her teeth and asks, "What exactly happened when you broke up that made her so mad at you?"

"I'm not exactly sure," I say, which is not a lie. Needing to say something that sounds like an explanation, I add, "It just wasn't working out. You know how it goes. So I just moved on."

Erin nods. "Maybe I can learn something about her take on what happened and get a clue about what's bothering her."

"I don't think that's necessary. Besides, considering what you're dealing with… "

Erin touches her finger to my lips to silence me, then smiles as she places her hand back over mine. I'm blown away that this girl, who is facing life and death issues with her father, would even consider dealing with this. To my amazement, she adds, "I have some friends who know her. Maybe they can get inside her head."

"Seriously?"

She nods.

139

"Thank you. That would help out a lot. She totally freaks me out. From the minute she walked up to me, she was in my face. She was aggressive. She threatened me… "

"Threatened you?"

I nod. "She told me she was going to get even with me for dumping her."

"Did she say how?"

When I shake my head, Erin says, "Give me a day or two. I'll get to the bottom of it." All of a sudden, she giggles. "Maybe you really were a jerk and totally deserve it."

"Great. Really great," I say, then cringe as she erupts into laughter. I look around and see several people staring.

"I'm sorry," she says and tries to contain herself.

Erin probably is right. Doctor Parker indicated I had been close to intolerable. Maybe my advisor was being polite, as her position requires, and I'd been over the top. If I had been the same toward Alex, that might go a long way toward explaining her attitude.

Unless circumstances force me to fold this current reality aside and dive into another, I'm going to have to start remaking myself. Certainly, if the shimmer begins to present itself, I'll do my best to avoid folding. I touch my shirt pocket and am relieved to find a bottle of headache medicine. I mouth the words, "Excuse me," and retrieve it. After downing two tablets with the last of my cola, I put it back and take Erin's hands into mine.

"Still having headaches?" she asks.

I nod and say, "They're manageable."

I really like this Erin and I'd like to maintain this relationship. The fact that she's sticking with me is a good indicator that maybe I'm not quite as bad as Alex and Parker have indicated. I'm glad, because I really like this Erin and hope our relationship can continue. That said, how long, I wonder, does it take a creep to start changing other people's opinion about him once he alters his behavior? I suspect much longer than I care to consider. I sigh, guessing only time will tell.

"In view of Father's heart attack, I'm starting to wonder," she says, "do you think we should still go ahead with our plan?"

"What do you mean?"

I have no clue what she's talking about and I'm hoping the question will be ambiguous enough to unearth enough useful information to help me answer without revealing the extent of my ignorance.

"If we move in together, Mother will be on her own."

That much is obvious… but *we're moving in together?* Holy crap! I mean, I do find Erin attractive. In fact, she's downright beautiful. So beautiful, in fact, that everything inside me insists I want to get close to her. However, aside from the fact that she's my walking, talking fantasy, this is a huge, *huge* step and I'm speechless that we're even considering it. I pull myself together enough to say, "I know. I mean, I understand. What are your thoughts about it?"

"Well, it doesn't resolve the abuse in your house, but I'm worrying if Father… " She pauses and appears as if she is holding back tears. "If Father dies," she manages, "I'm worrying how Mother will handle things if she's left on her own. Our house is so small that clearly you can't move in with us. But you can't go on staying with your father either. I'm worried what will happen if he injures you again, but worse this time, not just a blow to your head, but something worse like he did to your sister."

Whoa! Injures me *again*? Like he did to my sister? These are two serious issues. I thought either Trish was born with a disability in this reality, or else had been injured in an automobile accident or something similar. To learn that this world's Dad had been the cause of it makes me wonder if it's even safe to return home. So maybe our decision to move in together was based on more than mutual attraction… more like mutual necessity. My mind is trying to unearth memories of what happened when Dad injured me, when Erin explains without any prompting, "Your headaches started right after it, and as long as your mother enables the son of a bitch by refusing to report him, you're still in jeopardy."

This is another startling revelation and raises several questions such as is Dad intimidating Mom as well? Has he injured her in the past? I can't believe that someone so inclined to violence would draw a line and not injure her if she angered him. Does this also extend to his job, and is this the reason our house is so shabby? What kind of family have I folded into this time?

My mind shifts to thoughts about folding.

I began doing so after my initial head injury, as did my third iteration—the one who woke up with the missing cast. I never questioned why the fourth Eric, the one who lived in the world of Drug Dealer Dan, was able to fold. If Eric number four had indeed suffered something similar, or else had grown up experiencing migraines, it was something I had not been around long enough to determine. Erin said I've been having headaches, which are not the same as migraines, so would this Eric Folder be able to fold as well? I will have to learn if this is a misstatement, or something close to the truth. Now that I know he had suffered a head injury like the previous Erics, it's something worth considering. If I have that ability in this world, I'll have to be careful not to use it and fold away from her.

A thought occurs to me. Am I destined to move into only Eric Folders who have migraine headaches and will, therefore, be prone to an endless progression of altered realities? On the other hand, if the ability to fold is tied directly to a head injury or related condition, but I'm *not* destined to only inhabit similarly afflicted Erics, will I at some point end up being stuck in a reality with no way out if I need one? This is a little unnerving, so I climb out of my head and return my attention to Erin.

"I'll understand if you decide you need to look after

your mother and cancel our plans. I'll be fine. Don't worry about me." When Erin scowls, I add, "I really will. Please believe me and do what you need to."

She screws up her mouth and says, "You know, the more I think about it, Mother will be fine on her own. She's always talking about how much she misses the independence she had when she was younger. I think it will be good for her, once she's gotten over losing Father, if that even happens, so I think we should go on with our plan. We will each drop some of our classes and change to part-time." She firms up her mouth and nods, looking determined. "I like the idea more than ever. I'm starting to feel hungry," she says, so we flag down our server.

Once again my head starts spinning through the possibilities and I have the distinct feeling I'm not going to get much sleep tonight.

Chapter
Fifteen

I check the clock on my nightstand almost as soon as my eyes crack open. The digital readout says six-thirty-two and the dim light filtering through the blinds confirms that it's morning. My stomach grumbles, so I head downstairs to grab something for breakfast. On my way, I hear voices, sounding like Mom and Dad, coming up from the kitchen. I'm halfway down when I realize that I've not really spoken to either of them—except last night when I asked if I could borrow their car to meet up with Erin—and I wonder what kind of people they are in this world. Yes, I know this Dad's an abuser and Mom's an enabler, if not a possible victim. When I think about it, that sounds a little unnerving because I have no idea what I'll be facing when I actually meet them. When I arrive in the kitchen, wearing something between a smile and a frown, I notice that Dad hasn't shaved yet and Mom's wearing a faded flannel nightgown. Dad sounds irate.

"That jerk Morgan wants me to also offer two undergraduate lectures… without any additional compensation, no less."

"Isn't that unusual?"

Dad raises his voice, almost to a shout. "Unusual? My schedule is full—almost too full—and now, here we are, two weeks before classes begin and he expects me create two entire courses from scratch: a two hundred series and a three hundred series."

"How does he expect to fill them? Wasn't the deadline for signup a week ago?"

"They're already filled."

"What?" says Mom.

"That's right. Already filled. I'm to be presenting the two hundred course in a lecture hall packed with one hundred twenty sophomores. And the *third* year course consists of a weekly lecture on Tuesdays, broken down into three separate, but smaller, Thursday classes. Is he out of his mind?"

"But how did that happen? I mean courses that are already filled."

"Some schmuck got a better offer from a larger university in Chicago. He didn't even have the decency to leave me his course notes when he decided to bail. He just vanished and now I'm expected to take up the slack."

I decide not to engage and glance at each of them as I head toward the refrigerator. "Good morning," I say quietly, in order not to seem rude.

"You were out awfully late," Dad snaps.

"Erin was trying to deal with a problem and asked for my advice."

"And it took until almost one in the morning to give it to her?"

"I'm sorry. I… "

"You bet your sweet ass you're sorry. That's the last time I'm going to let you use my car."

I turn to stare at him. He has never acted like this before. My original Dad was understanding, so I'm hoping this is just a side effect, brought about by the issues he's discussing with Mom, and not a reflection of his normal personality—although Erin's comments last night suggest otherwise. Even worse: it could be a result of a bunch of things jerky old Eric did before I took over his body.

"It won't happen again," I reply.

"I'm thinking I should ground you."

"Really? Dad, I'm eighteen years old. I'm starting college. Grounding is something you do to… "

"I *know* what it's for." His voice lowers a few decibels and adds, "Just watch yourself."

"I'm sorry. I will." I look around and notice neither of them has started fixing breakfast. "I'm going to put together a scramble. Are either of you hungry?"

At first, neither of them seems to have heard. Then, as I take out the carton of eggs, Mom says, "No, thank you. We'll take care of ourselves."

I take down a bowl and remove a wire whisk from one of the drawers. I turn on a burner and am about to pull out a skillet when Dad says, "I've contacted Doctor Ramirez and asked if he'll consider taking me back in the Spring."

Doctor Ramirez was the head of Dad's department in Albuquerque. Dad hated him. I'm about to voice the obvious when Mom does it for me.

"Is that a wise thing to do? You and he were always fighting. Actually, from the way you put it, you were always at each other's throats. That doesn't sound much better than what's happening here."

"But I was always in control of my schedule. He never blindsided me with something like this. Maybe there's another university… " Mom starts to interrupt but Dad cuts her off. "I've made up my mind."

"If we go back, I won't have a job."

"We'll think of something," he says.

"What about the children? Do you think that it's fair to yank them both out of school when they're just starting to acclimate?"

"Goddam it, Bea. How many times have I told you not to contradict me when I make a decision?"

147

He raises a hand, palm open, as if he is about to slap her and Mom cringes. This does not happen in our house, so I tense myself, preparing to protect her if he does what he seems to be threatening. Fortunately, he lowers his hand and Mom relaxes, though the look of dread on her face still remains. I'm breathing hard now, so I try to calm myself. I had envisioned launching myself at him, pummeling him with my fists if he decided to follow through and actually strike her. My mind leaps to Trish and her wheelchair. Was this what Erin had alluded to, the result of a push down the stairs? I don't dare ask either of them, or even Trish, but now I'm suspecting that I should do what Erin suggested: namely, change to part-time status, then see what kind of job I can find. The possibility of leaving Trish and Mom with this monster worries me, but I'm not sure how I can save them. I decide to talk to Mom about this later. Hopefully, she'll use the income from her job to keep this house and demand that Dad returns to New Mexico on his own. If this is a realistic possibility, it leaves Erin and me with a workable solution. If it isn't and Dad takes her and Trish with him, Erin and I will definitely have to find a place of our own. Maybe, with the two of us working we can rent something small—if not a one-bedroom apartment, then maybe a studio.

I take a mental step back to consider. Erin and I have only held hands and exchanged a few kisses, at least in our last iteration. Although this world's Erin and Eric might have gotten far more intimate, for me, sharing a bed is a tremendous leap forward. I like Erin a lot, but I don't know if I want to initiate something so intimate. I mean, sure I've had my fantasies. What healthy guy wouldn't? She's beautiful and extremely well-endowed. She's loving and intelligent. But would I want to take the chance of ruining our friendship if it didn't work out? This is something we need to discuss, and probably sooner than later. I certainly need to find a way to learn the extent of our relationship. That part will be difficult at best.

I begin replacing the utensils and eggs now that Mom and Dad are returning to their argument. I need to get outside where it's quieter and I'm thinking the bakery on the corner a few blocks away will be the perfect location. I can grab one of the quiches they make and a nice cup of tea, then text Erin from a place where I can think clearly.

I slip out the front door and make my way on foot. As I walk down the street, I notice the neighborhood has changed. It was dark when I left last night, so none of this was apparent. What had been a modest district, made up of generally well-kept houses, now seems to have fallen into widespread disrepair. Our own exterior, originally a recent remodel as Dad once called it, has changed from newly painted wood slats to deteriorating shingles, many of which are in the process of peeling away from the underlying plywood. The lawn is in the process of dying, having neither been mowed nor watered, and it's filled with weeds, a few of which have grown to the size of bushes. Most of our neighbors' homes are in similar condition, but some also have cans and bottles littering their property. A rusted bicycle lies on the lawn of the house next door.

I'm still puzzling over how all of this might have happened when I arrive at the bakery. I'm feeling a little less hungry than I had been a few moments before. Still, I decide I ought to eat something in order to get my head straight.

There are several homeless individuals panhandling out front and along either side of the street. The outside tables are empty, in contrast with the times before when they had been filled with couples and families enjoying themselves. Inside, the situation is similar. A solitary man, bearded and grimy, is reading a newspaper and a half empty cup of coffee is on the table before him. The display cases next to the cash register contain only a few trays of doughnuts, but no croissants, quiches or danishes, and the writing on the chalkboards on the wall behind the cashier is faded, some of it partially wiped away.

149

My stomach is grumbling, so against my better judgment, I buy a glazed doughnut and a cup of tea, and carry them to a table outside. A few minutes pass before I bring myself to sample them, during which I study my surroundings and wonder what my chances are of finding some kind of decent job in this environment. Portland seemed to be flourishing when I visited PSU in previous realities. If that's still the case, maybe Erin and I will have to relocate.

I text her to see if we can get together and plan. While I'm waiting for her to respond, I find that, as I suspected, the doughnut is stale and the tea is weak and, because I'd left it standing so long, it's now tepid.

... ...

"You're kidding," says Erin when I tell her what Dad is considering.

It's late morning and we're sitting in the coffee shop in the middle of campus, across from the Alumni Center. Even though classes have not yet started, the coffee shop is full and we manage to snag the last remaining table. That this place is so busy, compared to the bakery in Sellwood, indicates my suspicion about our need to relocate was accurate.

"What about us? Do you want me to start looking for an apartment?" she asks when I explain we are probably moving.

I nod and say, "You were right. I think we could manage if we both found jobs."

"I'll get on it at once."

She reaches across the table and takes both of my hands into hers. Their warmth and softness fill me with a flood of sensations, bringing on some embarrassment but, at the same time, making me confident that I've made the right choice.

After a moment, she says, "Meanwhile, I've learned

something about Alex."

I take a sip of my chai, glad it's noticeably better than what I had earlier.

"And… ?"

"Rumor also has it she has a few male friends who have agreed to get you."

"Get me?"

Erin nods. "It seems you need to be careful."

I'm alarmed. "But who should I look for?"

"I have no idea." She grimaces, then adds, "But I am a little worried."

"Great. Just great. Now I'll have to be looking over my shoulder whenever I'm on campus."

Her frown turns into a smile when she adds something unexpected. "Apparently you two were into something very passionate. At one point, she claimed you had gotten her pregnant." My jaw drops. "Really, Eric Folder, this is not something I'd expected to hear about you. Apparently, you're quite the lover."

I'm about to defend my innocence, when the ridiculousness of her explanation starts us both laughing.

"It's not something I would expect of me either. Was I really that good?"

She pauses, as if debating how to reply. Then she winks and says, "Only time will tell. You've now got a reputation to maintain."

Her response tells me that physical intimacy is uncharted territory and I feel myself blushing.

"Anyhow," she says, taking on a more serious tone. "Word has it that you suddenly broke off the relationship when she told you about the pregnancy."

"I broke it off, but she never told me about being pregnant."

I stop when I realize this is a genuine memory, not something I'm making up. Memories are hardwired into the brain. So am I beginning to access the previous Eric's thoughts? If so, spending enough time in this new body may eliminate some of the uncertainty as I acquire more of his history.

"Maybe she invented it to justify her position. Anyway, the girls I was talking to said she was trying to get you to marry her. She figured if she could talk you to into it before she should have been showing, she could claim a miscarriage once you both were married and, by then, it would have been too late."

I sigh. "So, Alex is something of a monster."

"So it would seem."

Chapter
Sixteen

It has become obvious that if we don't find an apartment soon, or jobs for that matter, the house will have been put on the market and sold and my family will be relocating to New Mexico while Erin and I are still trying to resolve our situation. Even though we no longer live in one of the more desirable neighborhoods, word has it that real estate prices are skyrocketing and out-of-state buyers are looking for anything cheap. Since that would make our house a perfect quick sale candidate. I need to solve my employment situation at once if Erin and I are going to make our plan work.

After confirming that, even in this universe, I have a full-ride scholarship, changing from fulltime to part-time is only a matter of dropping a few classes after school has begun. If worse comes to worst and the scholarship committee decides to drop me because of my part-time status when the first quarter ends, I can drop out temporarily. Then, once I have lived here a year, I will be an Oregon resident and classes will become affordable enough I can probably handle the cost on my own… or so I tell myself. At any rate, this is something I'll deal with when the time comes. However it works out, it makes finding a job the first order of business since the rising cost of property is driving the price of rentals skyward as well, and making it likely that a part time job won't work for me. On-campus jobs only pay minimum wage, so I need to find something that pays better and I start by searching online. Several boards are posting numerous positions, but all of the ones that pay anything decent require varying degrees of experience, which is something I don't have. I have barely begun searching, but things are already looking bleak.

… … … … …

I'm sitting on a bench in the parkway across from the trolley stop near where Park and Mill come together when I hear a voice that sounds familiar.

"Eric? Eric Folder?"

I glance around, but all I can see are students strolling either individually or in groups across the grass beneath the parkway's elder trees. Several others are sitting inside the bus stop's glass enclosure.

When someone who is now beginning to sound like Dan Hastings once again calls me by name, I look around as he separates himself from one of the clusters of students and begins walking toward me, increasing his pace to a trot as he draws near.

"Dan!" I call back when I spot him.

"Where have you been keeping yourself?" he asks as he slows to a walk before coming to a halt directly in front of me.

I am at a loss how to answer, since Eric's memories are slow to emerge. I have only a second or two to feel any guilt for failing to keep in touch while Dan embraces me.

He steps back and observes, "Your hair's different. I like the way you're wearing it."

"It's the one thing I seem to have any control over these days. So, why not?"

"I know, right?" he declares, breaking into a smile.

This Dan Hastings is dressed closer to the one I first

met in the SRTC. He's not wearing a T-shirt, but neither is he dressed in designer clothes. Rather, he's somewhere in between, wearing a sports shirt, Dockers and a pair of—I think Dad called them loafers—casual slip-on unlaced leather shoes, rather than the running or athletic shoes most kids seem to prefer.

"What happened to what's-her-name?"

"Alex?" I venture.

Dan nods. "Yeah. That one. She sorta freaked me out."

"She freaked me even worse. I have to admit she still does."

Dan tilts his head and frowns. "Really? What's she up to now? Don't tell me she's trying to fake another pregnancy."

"No. Worse." When he gives a still harder look, I reply, "I heard she has a couple of friends who are looking to get me."

"And do what?"

"I don't know. I'm not sure. I think Alex is looking to take some kind of revenge for my ending the relationship."

Dan wraps an arm around me and draws me down onto the wooden bench beside us. "Do you remember what I told you the last time something like this happened?"

I don't know how to answer, so I just shake my head.

"I have a number of friends who can take care of you. Just let me know who's out to get you and we'll deal with them."

I know Dan is attempting to reassure me, but I have to wonder if he's connected to another group of unsavory characters.

"Like criminals?" I ask.

Dan laughs. "Nothing like that. My friends are into MMA."

"Really?"

Dan nods. "A few of them work in various bars or

strip clubs as bouncers. They're not really violent, except maybe when they're cage fighting, or when some drunk tries to give the bartender or stripper a hard time." When my eyebrows go up, he adds, "If you encounter any sort of problem—someone threatens you, someone actually assaults you—just text me and I'll have one of my friends… How shall I say?… advise them why their strategy is a bad idea. Got me?"

This isn't the way I'm accustomed to handling my problems. On the other hand, this is not my usual world either. I pull out my cell phone and say, "Let me make sure I have your number."

Once he has given it, I make sure it's listed among my Favorites. And now I know it will only take a few key strokes to send the word "help" and get a phone call in response. I'm not sure if that makes me feel any better. Anything could happen before help arrives. But it's better than having no one at all to turn to.

Before I can slip the phone into my pocket, Dan asks, "What else is bothering you?"

Although I'm surprised he can read me this well, I answer, "I need to find a job that pays better than minimum wage, but I'm not having any success."

"I thought your parents were supporting you."

"Dad's got a bug up his ass. His department is messing with him, so he's decided to move us back to New Mexico."

"You're not going with him, I hope."

I shake my head. "Nope. I don't want to leave Erin."

Dan raises his brows and asks, "Is this something new?"

"Kinda." Although he doesn't press for additional information, his face indicates that he's considering this development. I decide to save him the trouble and explain, "We're going to try to find an apartment together, although to do that, I'm going to have to find a fulltime job."

"How are you going to manage that on a fulltime course load and maintain your GPA?"

"I'm planning on dropping some classes."

"Like you advised me to do," he suggests.

Like many other similarities between parallel realities, this particular detail carries over to this one. We discuss my failed attempts at trying to find gainful employment. At one point, Dan mentions the name of a big box store located near the Clackamas Town Center.

"A couple of weeks ago, I ran into a student who works there," he tells me. "Several other PSU students are working there as well. The best part is that they start you out at fifteen bucks an hour."

"Seriously? That won't make me rich, but it's way better than minimum wage." On further consideration I add, "They must have hundreds of applicants. I don't think I'd stand much of a chance."

"The dude I talked to said he'd put together a resumé, then dropped it off every week until he was finally on their radar. Apparently, that's the best way to stand out from the crowd. If I remember correctly, he also said they'd be hiring right about now, since a number of their student employees are returning to school."

"Yeah," I say. "With zero work experience, how am I going to put together a resumé?"

Dan spends some time assuring me he will advise me how to describe my real world experiences so that I can demonstrate that I have a good work ethic and that I would be good with customers.

"In the end," he says, "that's all that they're really looking for. There are enough students already working there that I'd set that worry aside."

I decide to take him at his word and see how things develop. When I express my concern about where I'll live if my family leaves town before I've found a job, Dan claps me on the shoulder and says, "No problem. You can bunk with me till you find something."

A part of me says this Dan is safe, and not a drug dealer, so I let out a sigh and turn my thoughts to less stressful matters.

Chapter
Seventeen

Fall Quarter started a week ago and I have already withdrawn from all my chemistry courses. I believe I can maintain the Freshman Inquiry and Math classes while holding down a job, although, since I've never had a job before, that remains to be seen. I'm on my way to Math 251 when my phone rings. I don't recognize the number, but I decide to answer anyway.

"Hello?"

"Eric Folder?"

"Yes?"

"This is Cathy from HR. I have received your resumé and I'm wondering if you can come in for an interview on Thursday morning at ten."

I've only submitted one resumé to anyone, but just to be sure, I ask if this is the box store in Clackamas. When she confirms that it is, I reply, "Of course. Do I need to bring anything with me?"

"Yes," she says. "You will need to bring a photo I. D. and a birth certificate—a passport will satisfy both those requirements—and something that verifies where you live."

I still have my passport. I came across it while I was going through this Eric's possessions to see what I could learn about him. I ask if correspondence from the university

will satisfy the last part. When she says that it will, I confirm
that I'll be there. I'm eager to tell Erin that our plan may now
be possible.

"That's wonderful!" she exclaims when I call.
"Yesterday, I found a lovely little studio. Can I pick you up
and show it to you?"

"I don't have the job yet."

"I'm sure you will get it. They only have to meet
you."

"And then what?" Realizing how rude this sounds, I
backtrack. "I'm sorry. I understand how important this is. But
even if I get hired, it'll be weeks before I get my first
paycheck. So if we like it and the landlord asks us to sign a
rental agreement, we'll need to give him the first and last
months' rent and probably a security deposit. That means
we'll have to pass until we have enough money and the place
will be gone by then."

"I've got that all worked out," she says and I fall
silent. After a pause, Erin explains, "I have a savings
account."

"What?"

"For years I've been putting money into a bank
account my grandmother set up for me and I've already
saved a few thousand dollars. Besides that, the burger place
where we ate is looking for servers. It's a bit far from where
we'll be living, so I'll have to take mass transit until I can
find something closer, but Portland's a big enough city that
I'm sure I'll find something that's better in no time at all. So,
Mister Pessimist, between my savings account and both of us
working, I think we can manage it.

"Come on, Eric. Mom's letting me borrow her car. I
can pick you up in twenty or thirty minutes. *Please*?"

I'm speechless. Everything is moving so fast it's
making me nervous. Still, I know Erin is right. If we don't
act at once, someone will grab it before we get there.

"And you're sure we can afford it."

"Yes!"

"All right. I'll be waiting in front of Neuberger Hall, near the sign that says, 'Let Knowledge Serve the City'."

"Great! I'll be there as soon as I can."

"Drive carefully."

"Of course I'll be careful. Do you think I want to spoil everything when we're this close to realizing our dreams?"

Our dreams? Clearly Erin has been having her own brand of fantasies and I'm as nervous as I am excited.

... ...

"You're the first ones to see it," the landlord declares as he unlocks the front door. He smiles and adds, "I hope you understand how lucky you are, considering the market and all." Still smiling, he says as he turns the doorknob, "I have several interested parties scheduled to see it after you."

He is insinuating—and not at all subtly—that if we fail to sign on the dotted line before we leave, we will in all probability lose it. As he swings the door open and ushers us inside, Erin takes me by the arm and pulls me close to her. We are barely through the door when she squeezes my hand and smiles broadly at the apartment's interior.

The unit is a furnished studio with sliding glass doors that open onto a tiny garden patio. Aside from the half-bath with shower, it's essentially one medium-sized room. It has a small kitchenette—similar to the one in Dan's place at University Pointe—that comes with a bar and barstools, where I guess we can eat. There is a couch and coffee table in the part of the room that is intended to serve as a living room. A built-in table on one of the walls is long enough for Erin and me to share as our desk. And while the closet, which has mirrored sliding doors—I suspect to make the room appear larger—is not exactly huge, it will probably do if we work to accommodate each other. The bureau will have to do as well. The one feature I'm having trouble removing my eyes from is the queen-sized bed that takes up a significant portion of whatever space is left. Erin tries to suppress a grin when she notices it too. She leans close and whispers, "I love it," into my ear.

We are not exactly honest when we fill in the rental agreement, since we state we have already been hired but have not started working yet. It's a partial truth at best. I hope if our landlord decides to phone and verify, it will be after my impending interview and Erin's hopefully eventual hiring. I suspect that the only reason he accepted us at all was that the balance in Erin's savings account—which she is able to verify using her smartphone—is large enough to cover our rent and living expenses for seven or eight months, in the event we both find ourselves still unemployed.

For the moment, I'm reluctant to tell my parents, since our tenancy is still unconfirmed and it will be two weeks before we can move in. But Erin intends to inform her mother this evening. She needs to confirm that we can use the family car to transport our belonging when the time comes, or else to determine if we need to make alternate arrangements. I'm hoping my explosive father will allow me to use his, but I'm not counting on it. In the meanwhile, I plan to spend part of the evening identifying which bus or train lines will get us either to work or to school, as well as transport us between them.

Even before I reach my family's front porch, I can hear my parents arguing. As I ease the door open, they are trying to shout over one another so that, other than my name and Trish's, not much else is distinguishable except for a reference to New Mexico. Clearly, this is not the best time to engage them, so I close the door, take off my shoes and tread softly upstairs. I would really like to learn what's happening, and an idea as to how I can do surfaces so as I'm walking past Trish's room. I rap softly and the door, which is standing ajar, swings open a couple of inches from the impact.

"Trish?" I whisper.

I am greeted by silence and I wonder if she's either sleeping or simply doesn't wish to be disturbed. An explosion of shouts from the kitchen kills the first idea. After all, how could anyone sleep through all that? Something made of glass shatters downstairs and the noise snaps my head around. What will it take before one of the neighbors phones the police? I almost miss it when Trish responds with, "Eric? Is that you?"

"Can I come in?"

"Sure."

I step inside and all of the lights are off. Except for half a dozen candles, Trish is sitting in total darkness. Having propped herself against the bed's headboard, she's sitting with her legs extended and she's using her iPad.

"Do you mind if I sit next to you?" I ask.

"What's up?"

I incline my head toward the ruckus downstairs. She pauses a moment to consider, then smiles and pats the spot next to her. I join her and she scoots over to make room, adjusting the position of her legs with her hands.

"Dad just told Mom that he's ordered a moving van," she says.

Stunned by the revelation, I reply, "But the house isn't sold yet."

"He says he's hired a realtor to handle it."

I remain quiet while I digest this. Then I ask, "How soon?"

"Two and a half weeks. Mom's blown away. She complained she hasn't even started looking for work, but Dad doesn't seem to care."

"This is crazy."

Trish nods. "When Mom told him it's so late into summer you might not be able to start school when we get there, he blew up. I couldn't make out what he said to her, but this... " She indicates by gesturing with her hand toward the uproar. " ...has been going on ever since. They started into it about fifteen minutes before you got here. It's a pretty nice mess we're in, wouldn't you say?"

The truth is, I don't know how to respond. I hope Erin and I can move into the apartment before the movers arrive. Even though I'm not sure how well Trish can keep a secret, I tell her about my own proposed move. When I tell her about what we're planning, she grins. Then, the smile evaporates. She turns to stare and says, "Let's hope Dad doesn't throw you down the stairs too."

This confirms what Erin had alluded to and what I'd suspected. Nonetheless, the admission startles me.

"I know you thought it was an accident. That's what they told me to say. Mom and Dad ordered me to tell everyone I injured myself falling."

"When, in reality… "

"Dad threw me down the stairs in one of his fits."

I have no words to express how shocked I am.

"Why did Mom… ?"

"She was afraid if I told anyone the truth, he'd do something worse."

"They would have put him in jail. You and Mom would be safe."

"Until he got out. Even murderers don't serve life sentences, and this was far less serious than taking someone's life."

"But… "

"You just don't get it, do you?"

The thing is, I do understand. It's Mom and Trish's understanding of this flaw in our legal system that drove them to conspire to protect Dad that leaves me speechless. Trish is right. If they had put the bastard away, once he got out, anything would have been possible. He clearly didn't care enough about the consequences—either to himself or to his daughter… Mom or me for that matter—to restrain himself.

I'm suddenly aware of the shimmer that remains

overlaid across the upper portion of my vision. I'm considering whether to employ it to try to alter this situation, when I remind myself that doing so would not help this particular iteration of either Trish or Mom. It would only move me into another reality where things would be different for me, while they would be left to deal with this situation on their own. Things would certainly be different for the Eric Folder whose body I moved into if he were, as I now suspect, displaced into this one. After all, he has to go somewhere. How would he react when he arrived here, clueless to all that is happening? Would that be fair to him either?

"I do get it," I insist. "Your explanation was just so sudden."

Trish clenches her lips. Nodding slightly, she reaches out and takes my hand.

"We couldn't even tell you. If you had told anyone… "

"Yeah. I really do get it."

Any way I look at it, the situation is awful. Trish can't move in with us and I can't stay here. Or rather, I will not allow Dad to force me to go with him.

"There is a bright side," she tells me. I turn to stare and she explains. "I haven't told Mom yet, but one of my friends at school says her mom owns an apartment building and a unit has just become available."

"Really? How soon could the two of you move in?"

"Just before the movers come."

"Dad isn't going to like it."

"I know," she says and flashes me a smile. "We're hoping to move while he's at work. She's planning to leave him a note not to come looking." Her expression turns into a frown. "I'm not sure if that's such a good idea." She pauses a moment, looking as if she's thinking it over, then manages a thinner smile this time. "Anyway. We'll be gone and he won't have our address. With the movers about to arrive, as Mom explained it, he'll have to start packing his clothes and

165

stuff. So she's hoping he'll simply give up on us and get on with his plans."

This makes me feel better about moving in with Erin.

"I hope she's right," I tell my sister. "Good luck to both of you."

I lean over, give her a kiss and head for my room.

Chapter
Eighteen

"Wow!" exclaims Erin. "That was easy… at least it was easier than I thought it would be."

We have just hung the last of our clothes in the closet and put whatever socks and underwear we will need tomorrow morning into the bureau. We've also unpacked most of our other things and even made the bed.

"Do you want to get something to eat?" I ask.

She shakes her head. Then, as she reaches up to take down her hair, she explains, "No appetite," and gives me a grin. She runs her fingers through her honey-colored locks and they cascade over her shoulders. "Besides, we both have a busy day tomorrow." With these words, she starts unbuttoning her blouse. "Come on," she says, her voice growing softer. "Get out of your clothes and let's get into bed."

For a second, I'm caught off guard. This is the moment I've been worrying about. But as Erin tosses aside her top and begins unfastening her bra, whatever doubts I've been harboring about what I would feel, or how I might perform, dissolve in the instant she is standing before me, naked to the waist. I feel myself growing hard, and now I can't undo my shirt buttons fast enough. It's almost comical how quickly we both undress, and we grin at each other as we toss our things onto the floor.

And then it's not. The humor evaporates as we come together fully naked. Our bodies touch and the sensation is almost electric. I wrap my arms around her and feel the warm mounds of her breasts press against me. As she pushes herself against my already firm cock, I press my lips against hers. Our mouths open and our tongues meet, desperately trying to find a way to go deeper.

All at once, I don't want to be standing upright. I step back just far enough to slide my left arm around and behind her knees, then lift her into my arms. Except for that brief moment, our mouths never lose contact. I carry her to the bed—the only piece of furniture in our apartment that now matters—and place her on top of it. The second I lay her down, Erin's hands are all over me, running across my shoulders and back, then tracing the contours of my backside. Using my mouth, I begin exploring her entire body, running my lips down her neck, across the top of her chest, then onto each of her breasts. I begin kissing the right one, cupping it with my left hand so that I can better feel its shape and I find that its density excites me. Neither soft nor flabby, its firmness within my grasp arouses me even more. I bring her nipple into my mouth and begin to suck. She gasps when I press it between my lips, toying with it before I lick it, running my tongue around it before I fill my mouth once again.

Erin shifts her body and runs her hand down my chest, trying to find me. I feel her fingers run through the rough patch of pubic hair. Then suddenly she is holding onto me. She shifts her body again, and now I feel myself slide against the shaved mound between her legs. She maneuvers me down and through the folds between her lips. All at once, I am surrounded the moist heat of her.

••• ••• ••• ••• •••

"That was even better than last night," she sighs, wrapping a leg around me.

It's morning and we are lying blissfully in each other's arms. We've just spent the better part of the last hour or so making love again.

"As much as I loved last night's passion, this showed a gentler side of you I can learn to appreciate," she adds.

I gaze into her eyes and the delight I see makes me smile. I study her face and run my upper lip across the almost unnoticeable down above her own. We kiss and I realize I've never communicated with anyone so intimately. She slides out from under me, sits upright, and a beam of sunlight streaming through the window blinds illuminates all of the stray strands of her hair so that they appear to be a halo. I tell myself I'm witnessing an angel. Erin bends down to kiss me, then swings her legs over the side of the bed and onto the floor. Looking back, she asks, "Would you like a cup of tea?"

"I thought you drink coffee."

"I do. But you prefer tea."

My smile grows even broader.

We spend the rest of the morning unpacking. By eleven o'clock, we're in her family's car and she's driving me to my parents' place. Our lovemaking has caused us to run late and she doesn't want to walk into class after it has started. So, after Erin leaves me at my place, she'll drive directly to school and I'll take the bus to the university. We would have gone there together, but while I was packing, I forgot to grab the identification badge I will need to clock in to my first day of work later this afternoon. My plan is to drop by just long enough to recover it and leave.

"Where the hell have you been?" Dad barks before I'm halfway through the front door.

"I have an apartment. Don't you remember?"

"You'd better enjoy it while it lasts. The movers will be here by the middle of next week."

"I'm not going."

"Like hell you won't."

"Dad, I'm not a kid any more. I just dropped by to pick up something I forgot, then I'm out of here."

He rises from his chair, and I debate whether I can make it up the stairs and back again without him touching me. I decide against it when he curls his hands into fists. Without looking back, I step back outside and slam the door behind me. "Eric!" he shouts, and I hope that is the last word I will ever hear from him. With any luck, the box store will issue me a new identification badge, because I can never go back to retrieve the old one. I'm afraid for my sister and I'm afraid for Mom. I can only hope they will get out safely. I certainly miss the loving home where I lived before this whole thing started, although I can say with almost certainty I'll never see it again.

Suddenly, I'm filled with dread. I sort through my memories, wondering if I have left anything behind that will give away my new address. When I remember packing my copy of the rental agreement, then unpacking it and tucking it into the bureau's drawer, I know that I'm safe… for the moment, at least.

On my way to the bus stop, I take a last look at our rundown neighborhood and tell it good-bye. I avoid the bakery, another part of this life gone wrong that I hope I'll never see again. That last fold was disastrous enough that I resolve never again to change my reality. I need to appreciate where I am and what I have, so I decide it's better not to mess with it. I'm starting a new life with Erin and, for now at least, I have a chance to improve my circumstances. I have a job that, although it does not pay as much as I would like, will help cover our expenses. In less than a year, I will have lived in Oregon long enough for the State to consider me a resident and allow me a resident's tuition. All in all, things are not so bad.

… … … … …

Erin and I have decided to meet at the university during the hour between when one of her classes ends and one of mine begins. I step off the train at College and Sixth and am about to turn toward the campus when I'm abruptly halted. College Street does not continue through as it once did. I find that odd. Why wouldn't it, considering how it's named? It's only then that I notice the street sign now reads Ondine Court. So, of course, since it no longer goes to the university, its name would not reference it.

I walk to the next intersection and turn left on Hall, then head toward the student union to wait for her. As I'm standing outside, enjoying the scenery, it becomes clear that autumn is approaching. Although the leaves have not yet started changing color, the summer heat has subsided. And while a number of the students making their way through the parkway are still dressed in T-shirts and shorts, long sleeves and pants are becoming more prevalent.

I glance to my right and notice Erin approaching. I'm starting to wave when the expression on her face changes from a smile to one of alarm. Someone grabs me by the shoulder, spins me around, and I find myself face-to-face with a guy I've never seen before.

"Eric, my boy," he says, "you've done something bad and now you need to be punished."

"What?"

The word slips from my mouth and, simultaneously, I understand who he is and what he is referring to. I realize this must be one of Alex's friends and notice two more dudes standing together beside of him. Just like the trio's leader outside the library, he turns to them and grins.

"This is that Folder dude," he asks, "isn't it?"

"It's him all right," says the second one. He nods and adds, "Alex pointed him out to me yesterday."

The leader grabs my shirt by the collar and pulls my face right up to his.

"You shouldn't have treated Alex like that."

171

"Like what?" I snap. Yes, they outnumber me, but I'm enraged that they think they can treat me like this. If I'm going to go down, it's not going to be without a fight. "If Alex wants to tell me something, have her say it to my face."

Just then, I hear Erin calling, "What are you doing? Leave him alone."

She tries to pull the leader away from me, but he reaches out and shoves her aside. This distracts him long enough for me to punch him in the face. Knocked back a step or two, he grabs his face and releases her.

"What the fuck!" he cries, taking a look at his hands, now covered with the blood that is streaming from his nose and into his mouth. His eyes open wide and he stares at me.

Before he can speak, I shout, "Keep your hands off of her. Don't touch her again."

Normally, I wouldn't be the one to throw the first punch, but he assaulted Erin when all she was trying to do was make him release me. Also, since I'm outnumbered, if I allow these guys to get the upper hand—which they are likely to do anyway—I'm done for. Better to cause some damage now while I still have a chance, than not at all, while I'm helpless and at their mercy.

Looking around, I can see we are drawing a crowd. Students with backpacks full of books or laptops are gathering into a circle around us, pointing and making comments. While some look concerned, others are laughing and, from some of the comments I hear, a few of the students are actually making bets on the outcome. Is this what reality TV has brought us to? Someone—meaning me—is apt to get hurt and they're finding it entertaining.

I wish there was a professor among them who might intercede, who might bring this fiasco an end to. Sadly, that's not my luck. I do have a moment's reprieve, however. The leader's friends, whom I suspect are either too stupid or insecure to make a decision on their own, are staring at their friend's bloody nose, looking like they're waiting for him to direct them. Their hesitation keeps me safe for the moment, but once the dude in charge gathers enough presence to decide what to do and orders them to attack—is there any other logical possibility?—I'm sure I'm dead meat.

Added to that, it's becoming difficult for me to see clearly as the ever-present shimmer begins to intensify. No longer a soft aberration of light, it's transforming into the usual luminous network of lines that resemble creases in a crumpled sheet of clear plastic. As my fear intensifies, so do the creases. The webwork begins to multiply and grow in intensity, so that it becomes increasingly difficult to make out my surroundings.

"Who is that?" the first one asks, gesturing toward Erin.

"It's his slut girlfriend," one of his friends replies.

The leader pauses a minute, probably to consider what to do next. Then, he turns to his friends and says, "Let's do him."

"Leave him alone!" shouts someone whose voice sounds familiar.

I look in that direction and can just make out Dan Hastings striding past Erin and heading toward me.

"Whatever happens, don't let them hurt her," I call to him. I point at Erin to help him understand. When he glances back to where I'm pointing, I tell him, "Please take care of her."

He looks back and replies, "No prob, dude. I've got it."

I don't know how much he can do to help her, but with so many onlookers watching, I suspect she'll be safe if I'm unable to handle whatever Alex's friends throw at me. Wishing we had some of his MMA buddies to help, I start backing away as the three start coming toward me. Straining to see through the growing luminosity, I see that Dan, Erin and I have become encircled by the crowd of onlookers, leaving us with no easy avenue of escape. Three forms move

173

toward me and there is a blow to my face, followed by two more in rapid succession. I'm raising my arms in an effort to defend myself when I see Dan grab one of them and spin him around to face him. He reacts faster than Dan probably expected and delivers a punch that knocks Dan's head back.

It would be nice if some of those watching would step forward to assist us, but it looks like it's going to be just Dan and me. I would actually prefer it if Dan would take Erin away from here and maybe I could go with them. But that's unlikely to happen since it's becoming almost impossible to see anything other than the network of lines. Even so, when one of the three grabs Erin by the hair and attempts to drag her away for some unknown purpose, I run after them and throw myself on top of him. My weight is too much for him and he collapses onto his knees, almost dragging Erin onto the ground with him. Somehow, she manages to shake herself free. When he lands on his face, she turns and begins kicking him, screaming things I wouldn't have thought possible from someone so sweet. I'm as angry as she is and I grab the hair at the back of his head. I lift it and bang his face against the concrete before I climb off, look around, and try to determine our situation.

"Let's get out of here," Erin begs. She takes my hand and starts pulling me through the students who are surrounding us.

"I can't," I say, planting my feet. As far as I can tell, two of the dudes are beating up Dan and I can't just leave him to fend for himself. "My friend needs me," I tell her. "Take care of yourself and get out here."

"Be careful," she says, sounding worried.

"I love you," I reply and both of us stop. The words slipped from my lips before I knew it and I think we're both surprised. Until this very moment, the thought never crossed my mind. I mean, I always knew that I liked her, that she attracted me. But that I love her?

"Really?" she asks, sounding startled. There is

happiness in her voice.

In the same instant, I know that I do and I nod. "I have to go."

I can just make out Erin nodding. If it weren't for these damned glowing lines in the air, I could see her expression. But since I cannot, I try to believe that she's smiling. The ache in my head is growing stronger as I turn to help Dan and find someone is standing in front of me.

"You really are stupid, aren't you?" he says and I recognize the leader. "You almost got away." He pauses and laughs. "But here you are."

A punch lands on my cheek and grazes my nose. Unable to see clearly, I try to land a counterpunch, but he dodges and I miss. He hits me in the gut and doubles me over.

"You're going to have to do better than that," he says as a blow from the side snaps my head to the right.

I stagger back. As each second passes, seeing becomes increasingly difficult. By now, the students around us are no more than a blur and I can barely see the one in standing in front of me. When I try moving away, someone in the crowd pushes me back. As more punches land on my stomach and face and I'm helpless to stop them. I realized that, if I'm going to survive, I have no other choice but to fold the lines away… even if it means leaving Dan at the mercy of his attackers. Unable to defend myself and left with no other choice than to be beaten mercilessly, I reach up and tear at the luminous network. As an entirely different scene from that of the university begins to present itself, something wraps around me and I wonder if it's Erin or one of my assailants. As I topple to the ground, I am able to maintain my grip on the webwork. Almost at once, I find myself standing upright in the new reality.

175

Chapter
Nineteen

"Grab the bucket, goddammit!" shouts a man to my right, even as someone on my left yanks something out of my left hand, splashing water as he does so.

Not knowing what else to say and still unaware of what's happening, I reply, "Sorry."

"Sorry won't cut it, kid. How many more gallons do you think the water tower holds?"

Is that some kind of riddle? Before I have time to consider, the man on my right shouts, "Here's another one. Don't drop it."

I look down and see he is handing me a wooden bucket that is filled to the brim. It has a metal handle whose handgrip is also made out of wood.

"Grab it!" he shouts. "It's going to burn down if we don't get enough water on it."

With no time to think, I reach with my right hand and take what he has given me. When its weight surprises me, threatening to slip from my hand, I also grab hold with my left.

"What's the matter with you?" shouts the man on my left. "Quick! Hand it over."

I feel him starting to tug, so I pass it to him.

"Here," shouts the man on my right.

I turn and he is handing me yet another one. This time, without further prompting, I pass it to my left. Seconds later, he hands me one more. I look up and see that I'm part of a chain—a line of men on my right passing me buckets of water which I, in turn, pass to the line of men on my left. Only then do I smell burning wood.

A quick glance up, when I hand the next one to the man on my left, reveals a nearby building in flames. I start putting the pieces together as I turn to my right and accept the next in what appears to be an endless line of water buckets coming toward me. I'm part of something I heard about years ago called a bucket brigade. The phrase did not hold much meaning then, but now I get the sense of it.

Where are the fire trucks, I wonder, and why are we not using a hose? It's only now that I notice the boys who are running in the opposite direction, returning the now-empty buckets to the place where the line begins.

My hands, arms, and shoulders are starting to ache, since each bucket seems to weigh twenty pounds or more. I also notice my pants and my shoes are becoming thoroughly drenched. Yet, no matter how much I hurt, no matter how uncomfortable I am, this is not something I can walk away from. It's obvious that if we were to stop now, the building would burn to the ground.

We continue like this for several minutes longer, when all at once, the process comes to a halt. I reach to my right, but instead of handing me the one he is holding, the man on my right just stands there, staring at the fire. He waits another second, then throws down his bucket, sending its contents onto the mud beneath us.

"Goddamn it!" he shouts. "It's a goner." He turns to the man who is ready to hand him the next one and says, "It's no use."

The entire line appears to have come to the same conclusion, because they have halted and now all of them are staring as he had. Some are watching the flames. Some are keeping a grip on the bucket they're holding while others let their buckets fall from their hands. I turn to my left and see the ones ahead of me are doing likewise, since the fire has grown into an inferno no mere bucket brigade could possibly extinguish. Like many of the others, I set my bucket down and rub my hands together, then massage my wrists and forearms. I begin wondering, now that I have the time to do so, how this line of men came to be and, for that matter, where I have landed.

As the line grows increasingly disorganized, then breaks up completely, I notice a bearded man dressed in blue denim overalls walking toward me. There is a familiar look about him, and I stare at him, trying to figure out who he might be. Could this be Dad? It sorta looks like him. But since he would never dress like this, it takes me a second to put his features together. Some of them are altered. His hair is darker and thicker than before, and his face, largely concealed beneath the growth of facial hair, appears somewhat gaunt, but after a moment I can see he is indeed Dad. Fighting the fire appears to have been harder on him than it was on me. His back is bent, his shoulders droop and his arms hang limp at his sides, hands open, fingers dangling as he walks toward me.

When he is standing beside me, he claps me on the shoulder and says, "We did the best that we could, Son, but sometimes even our best isn't good enough." His breaths come in long, drawn out gasps that make his chest rise and fall as he talks to me. "Still, I'm proud of you. You did a man's job like I've always taught you."

He has a strange way of speaking, uncharacteristic of what I'm accustomed to. Trying to think of an appropriate response, I attempt to mimic him. The best I can come up with is, "I tried to act like you'd expect me to."

As lame as it sounds, it brings a smile to his face.

"You did, Son. And for now, that's all that matters."

Glancing down to assess myself, I see the style of my clothing is similar to Dad's. I'm wearing dark woolen pants—possibly black, but they are too wet for me to be certain. My long sleeved shirt is made of heavy white cotton and I have on a pair of black leather lace-up shoes that come up over my ankles.

The place we are standing is equally strange. The streets are unpaved dirt and the buildings are one and two storied wooden structures for the most part, broken by a three story one constructed of brick. A sign on it reads **Stump Town Hotel** and confirms I'm still in Portland, although clearly not the Portland I'm familiar with. A street sign shows we are at the intersection of Sixth Street and School— not Sixth Street and College Avenue—and I'm wondering where all the automobiles are when a horse drawn carriage rolls by.

"Ma will be wondering where we've disappeared to," says Dad. Appraising the state of our clothing, he adds, "I'm pretty sure your trousers'll shrink. Couldn't be helped, though. Good thing we left our coats in the buggy. Once we've helped these good men tidy things up, we'll meet there."

The *buggy*? We have a buggy? As best as I can recall, a buggy is a form of horse drawn carriage, something with a convertible top, nothing motor powered. And what's this about… "Ma"?

"I'm sorry. I'm still a little confused," I say. "Remind me where it is."

He smiles understandingly, then squeezes my shoulder and indicates with his thumb the brick building across from us. "It's tied up behind the hotel."

We spend most of the day helping the rest of the men clean up the mess that we and the fire had created. All the time I'm working, I'm wondering about Erin and if I will ever see her again. In view of the odd situations most of the folds have put me in, I suspect that the two of us winding up together after leaving her father's house was just a coincidence. After each of these occurrences, the people I knew and their relation to me have altered. Since this situation is so much over the top, when compared with all the others, it's obvious I will have to wait to see what this dimension has in store for me and hope I can manage to fit in.

It's late afternoon when Dad tells me, "If we're going to get home before nightfall, we should be leaving." He begins to turn and walk toward the hotel, when he halts abruptly. Turning back to me, he says, "I almost forgot. I promised your Ma I wouldn't forget to pick up the items on her shopping list."

He withdraws a damp sheet of paper from his shirt pocket, then carefully unfolds and studies it.

"Come on. We have to purchase some canned and dry goods."

I accompany him and notice we're walking toward a building with a sign that reads **Boone's Mercantile & Dry Goods**. As we cross the street, I get a better idea of this universe's Portland. Horses and wagons are secured to hitching posts that stand in front of raised wooden sidewalks. Not a car, nor any other motor driven vehicle is anywhere to be seen. Most of the men I see are dressed as I am, or else in work shirts and either denim pants or overalls like Dad. All of the women are wearing ankle length dresses and bonnets. Is this another century? That question is answered soon enough. As we pass the hotel's entrance, Dad spots a newspaper stand. He reaches into his pocket, then flips me a nickel.

"Son, get us a copy of The Oregonian."

Once I have purchased a copy from the vendor, I'm surprised to see the front page is dated Tuesday, September 1, 2020. How can this be? From the look of things, I have landed squarely in the nineteenth century, but the paper argues this is the twenty-first century. Its headline story refs to a gang of bank robbers who seem to have arrived here after hitting a bank in Salem, Oregon a few days ago. Another front page article discusses whether Oregon should become part of the United States of America. Holy crap!

The sidewalk ends at the building's corner, but I'm too absorbed with the newspaper articles to notice and step into empty space. I drop a foot or so before my shoes make contact, and I nearly tumble face first onto the ground before Dad grabs me and pulls me upright.

"Are you all right?" he asks and I look at him embarrassed.

"Sorry."

"No need to apologize. That fall you took yesterday must have hurt you worse than I thought." He turns me around to face him and peers into my eyes. "How does your head feel?"

I pause a minute to assess myself. Suspecting this Eric Folder might have suffered a similar fate to those alternate ones, I put a hand to the back of my head and find a lump that feels recent. It's extremely sensitive.

"I'm all right. I'm just tired from all of today's work."

"You sure?"

I nod and say, "Yes."

"All right, then. Let's finish our shopping, then head on home."

After loading up the buggy with an assortment of canned vegetables, sacks of beans, rice, sugar and flour, I climb aboard while Dad unhitches Sal, as he calls the large, dark brown mare harnessed in front of it. Once he is seated beside me, he makes a couple of clucking sounds and flicks the reins across her... I seem to remember they are called hindquarters... and Sal breaks into a trot.

I'm glad he didn't ask me to drive because, even after seeing how easy it seems for Dad, I'm certain I couldn't have managed it. How many other tasks, that are everyday occurrences for this world's inhabitants, am I going to be expected to perform before people start questioning what's wrong with me? I'm suddenly terrified. I'm fighting to hold back tears because I realize that I might either be stuck here, or else wind up somewhere even stranger if I find myself forced to fold again.

Dad glances at me and observes, "You don't seem yourself today. Are you sure you're all right?"

I mutter, "I'm fine," but can't manage to give him a reassuring look, let alone a smile.

Even worse than being stuck here is the pain I feel knowing I have probably lost Erin for good. She is the best thing that ever happened to me and I don't know what I'm going to do without her. I was starting to fall in love with her, and now it feels like there's a hole in my heart. On top of that, everything familiar has vanished and I suspect it might be gone forever. Since I'm unable to control where I land after I fold, with countless universes to end up in, the chance that I will ever return to the place where I started is impossibly small. I suddenly start sobbing uncontrollably and give out a wail that causes Dad to rein the carriage to a halt.

He places a hand on my shoulder and asks, "Care to talk about it?"

I can only imagine how confused he must be by this behavior and I struggle to answer him.

"Maybe later."

He remains silent a moment, then replies, "All right," in a tone that sounds uncertain. After another pause, he adds, "Maybe some dinner and a good night's sleep will help."

I manage to nod and he flicks the reins again. Sal resumes her course.

I wish it were that simple. As I continue to cry, I wonder what I can tell him and "Ma" that will explain my strange behavior. Will they think I'm crazy? If so, how will they react? Do people in this world commit loved ones to insane asylums? The thought immediately sobers me and I pull myself together. I wipe my eyes with my sleeve and pull myself upright.

"I'm sorry," I say. "I don't know what came over me. Maybe it was a combination of hitting my head and the strain of trying to put out the fire. I think I'm simply exhausted."

He glances over, frowns for a moment, then nods.

"It's been a long hard day, the worst we've had since we left Prescott. That much is sure." He tosses me a smile and squeezes my shoulder again. "Combined with the move, a new school, then all this that happened today, I'm not at all surprised you broke down. I'm feeling pretty strained at the edges myself."

I hold my breath. Did he say we moved here from Prescott? Prescott, Arizona? In order to fit in, in order not to take another misstep—perhaps several missteps—I'm going to need to find ways to learn about our history without giving away the fact that I'm completely ignorant about any of it. After previous folds, I was in familiar enough surroundings that I could fake my way through most situations without seeming a complete idiot. But here?

Looking around, I see nothing familiar. Not only do I have no idea where our house is, I'm not even sure if I could find my way back into town if I were to jump out of the buggy right now. Forests cover the hillsides around us. The land we are passing through is interspersed with either isolated residences, fields of crops and farm houses, or else large expanses of open countryside. The road on which we are travelling is intersected by occasional smaller dirt trails, when not crossed by other roads rutted by wagon wheels. The one familiar landmark is the Willamette River lying off to our left.

"On a brighter note," Dad interjects into my reverie, "we won't have to take the ferry home today." To my inquiring look, he explains, "They just completed the Sellwood Bridge. I expect we'll have missed the celebration, but maybe that's a good thing. All of the whoopdedoo would probably have slowed us down."

His comments puzzle me. Even before we moved to Portland, I conducted as much research as I could to learn something about its history. For example, anything bearing the name Boone, such as Boone's Ferry, was either built or owned by a cousin of the legendary Daniel Boone right after the Civil War. I also studied the Sellwood bridge because I knew I would be crossing it on a regular basis. The first version, a trestle bridge, much like the span we might be crossing today, was completed in 1925. A more recent version, an arched design built to replace the dilapidated original that had grown dangerously precarious by the early 2000s, was finished in 2016. Clearly, this world only vaguely mirrors my own.

Chapter
Twenty

During the ride home, I come to understand why Dad wanted us to leave Portland as early as we did. Aside from a few street lamps in town—I cannot say if they were gas or electric—there are none of them elsewhere, making after-dark travel dangerous, if not impossible.

Dusk is approaching as we roll through a housing development on the Willamette River's east bank. Their roofs appear new and the paint on all their exteriors appears bright, so I suspect this housing development is newly constructed.

As Dad and I converse, I learn that the locals call the neighborhood Sellwood, just as they did back home. And while the finished homes are numerous, here and there is an occasional one in the process of being framed while a number of lots still remain vacant. The trees lining the streets, aside from the numerous, scattered conifers that were left standing while the houses were built, are small and immature. It will be years before they grow large enough to provide any useful shade along the streets where they have been planted.

Dad turns into one street that seems vaguely familiar and I'm only slightly surprised when he halts the buggy in front of a house that looks exactly like mine in all of the previous dimensions. He hands me the reins and climbs down.

"Hold her steady," he says, "while I carry in the groceries."

Unsure what to do with the lengths of leather he has given me, I inadvertently apply a slight tug rearward and Sal takes a step back.

"I said, hold her steady," Dad snaps.

"Sorry."

I ease my grip and the mare halts, snorts and tosses her head. I suspect this is because my touch on the reins is unfamiliar. In order to insure I do not make any further mistakes, I wrap the leads around the buggy whip's handle in an attempt to duplicate their arrangement when we first climbed aboard.

"Easy, girl. Easy," I say, and she looks over her shoulder, appraising me while flicking her tail.

In all probability, she senses something is wrong, but because my appearance and the sound of my voice are what they should be, Sal snorts again, then lowers her head and begins grazing.

After half a dozen trips, Dad tells me, "Go inside, Son, and I'll take care of the rest."

"Yes, sir," I reply, hoping a formal response is appropriate. I've seen a few movies that pretend to depict life in early America and I try to duplicate their presentation.

Wondering what I will find when I enter, I open the door and, at once, I feel as if I'm an intruder. I take off my cap and notice it's made of heavy gray wool, with a button on top and a tiny visor. I hold it uncomfortably, gripping it with both hands as I gaze around the living room.

The floor is exposed wood, instead of wall-to-wall carpet. A few area rugs are scattered around it. The furniture has a distinctly old-fashioned, rural appearance. The chair and table legs were obviously turned on a lathe and crocheted cushions are everywhere. My eyes travel to a pair of rocking chairs, then to the oil lamps positioned on most of the tables. A girl who resembles my sister, no longer paraplegic and with a couple of altered features to boot—turned-up nose, thinner lips—is in the process of lighting one of them.

She glances up when I enter and tells me, "Dinner will be ready soon. Can you help Ma in the kitchen?"

She eyes me uncertainly when I'm still caught up by the strangeness and fail to respond.

"Sure," I reply after a pause, realizing, as I stare back at her, what an idiot I must seem.

I throw her a nod and head to where the kitchen should be. So many things about this world are different, some of them minor, while most are major alterations. I can't afford to take anything for granted, not even something so apparently simple as where a room is located.

And, in fact, this kitchen is not at all like the former ones. There's no breakfast bar and, obviously, no major appliances. At the cast iron stove, Ma—I cringe when I call her that—is stirring a pot whose contents smell like they might be some sort of stew. Her light brown hair is tied in a bun at the back of her head and she's wearing a white, long-sleeved blouse tucked into a floor length flowered skirt. She turns to look when I enter, my shoes having announced my arrival on the bare wooden floor.

Frowning, she asks, "How many times do I have to remind you to leave your cap on the hat rack?"

"Sorry," I reply and I wonder how much longer I'm going to find myself apologizing for missteps. "I'll be right back," I add, then return to the living room.

Sure enough, there is a rack beside the front door and a circular receptacle standing next to it with handles protruding that I expect belong to umbrellas. I hurry to hang my cap before returning to learn what Ma requires of me.

"What do you need me to do?" I ask.

"Will you please set the table? Patricia's busy and dinner's almost ready."

189

Naturally, no one in a culture like this would refer to my sister as Trish, and this world's parents would not have christened her as such.

"Yes, Ma'am," I reply, glad when she turns back to her cooking, acting as if what I had said was perfectly natural.

With no idea which cabinet holds the dishes, I act on instinct and am pleased to find them behind the first door I open.

"Should I set any bowls?"

"Yes, please. And don't forget to place saucers underneath them."

"Plates as well?"

She turns back and gives me a smile.

"It's nice you're thinking for a change. I've been wondering how long it would take that boy of mine to start acting like a grownup. Now, if only you'll start taking care of your room and tending to all of your chores without my having to remind you, I can have a little more time for myself. And, yes," she confirms, "Plates as well.

"Wait!" she says when I turn toward the dining room. "Are those pants wet?"

"Yes, Ma'am."

Her face grows angry as she demands, "Do you have any idea how much your father and I paid for them?"

"No, Ma'am."

"Don't you have any regard for… ?"

"Bea," Dad interrupts as he enters the kitchen. "It's not the boy's fault. Eric and I spent the afternoon trying to help put out a fire."

Ma falls silent, then glances from me to him, then back to me again. "A fire? What kind of fire?"

"This can wait till we've sat down to dinner," he tells her.

Ma stops and studies him. "Your pants look ruined, as well."

"I suppose they are."

Appraising both of us more carefully, she observes, "Now that I look at you, you're both filthy as bird dogs." She shakes her head. "I guess it couldn't be helped, but I don't want the two of you ruining our furniture. Go upstairs and put on something dry." She pauses, then adds, "I suspect you'll both be needing a bath. There's no sense waiting till Saturday. Can't have you ruining the bedding.

"Patricia," she calls. "Will you add some wood to the stove, please? I need you to start heating up water for both our boys to bathe in. Walter, Eric, dinner's going to get cold if you two don't help. Grab some buckets from the shed and start filling them."

No sense waiting till Saturday? By now, I'm seriously puzzled, but I follow Dad outside to where he gets two buckets. Seeing two others standing beside them, I follow his example. He leads me to a well and starts pumping water into them.

"Tonight, I'll let you go first."

"Sir?"

"I don't mind a little secondhand wash water. You did what you had to without complaining, so you're entitled to bathe first for a change."

Wait! I'm going to bathe first? Is this all the water we'll use? Four buckets? How big is the bathtub anyway?

We lug them back into the kitchen and set them down on the floor next to the stove. By now, the metal lids that had covered three of the four burners have been removed and all of them glow from the fire burning beneath them. Four large pots are waiting on the countertop, and Dad sets the first of them next to the buckets while Ma removes the fourth lid, picking it up by its handle with a pot holder. Lifting a bucket, and nodding to me to assist him, Dad begins pouring.

"Tip 'er gently," he says. "We don't want to risk spilling and dousing the fire."

Once all of the pots on the stove have been filled, Ma

191

orders us upstairs.

"And don't leave those wet things lying about. Bring them back down with you. I'll have a clothes rack ready in the laundry room. Hurry up now, so we can start eating."

I find Eric's bedroom where mine was. As I sort through his clothing, trying to find something suitable, I stop for a minute, unable to move, holding the pair of pants in my hand. Every previous fold put me in another version of modern day Portland and I could take each one of those in stride because the world where I landed was recognizable. But the result of this fold terrifies me, not because the reality where I've landed is in any way threatening or dangerous. It's because this world is so different from the world I grew up in, that it indicates how radically different the next reality might turn out to be. Although I never imagined I would wind up in a real life version of Little House on the Prairie, not at all unlike the 2005 TV miniseries, these people are not so strange that I can't continue living with them. As for the state of this reality's culture, people existed for decades, millennia even, without electronics or modern technology, so I suppose I can learn to adapt. Maybe it will do me good to live more simply.

As I finish setting the table, my mind returns to Erin, the second girl that I've lost, the first lover I've lost. With no way to return to a particular reality, I know I'll never see her again. I choke back the sob that is forming and force myself to smile, then join my new family over dinner, hoping the conversation will yield hints that will help me adapt to my new world, hoping I won't make another serious mistake. After Dad says grace, we pass our bowls to Patricia, and she spoons beef stew into them while Ma slices what appears to be freshly baked bread.

"So," Ma says when our dinner is in front of us all, "what's this about a fire?"

Patricia, who is holding a spoon in front of her mouth, pauses.

Dad answers, "A new building that was just put up near the Simon Benson residence caught fire this morning. There's been talk of arson."

"Who'd want to do something like that?" asks Ma.

"Folks say the man who built it got in over his head."

"If that's the case, he's a fool. He's the first one the authorities will investigate."

"On the other hand, some of the men suspect it was burned down by the gang of outlaws who have moved into this part of the Territory: the bank robbers the Jacobsons told us about a few days back. It's the opinion of some of the men we fought beside today that the crooks tried to extort him. When he refused, they set the building on fire."

"Why would they try to do that? Extort him, I mean," asks Patricia.

"He's an easy target with deep enough pockets to interest them. He can't protect himself any better than we could," Dad explains.

Patricia appears confused. "Deep enough… ?"

"What I'm trying to say is that he has an awful lot of money. At least he did before the construction started. Assuming the men's theory is correct, when the crooks burned down his building, they shot themselves in the foot. Can't squeeze blood from a stone, as the saying goes."

Dad's mixing metaphors. My original Dad taught me that. And while I would like to explain to Patricia what Dad is trying to express, I don't dare open my mouth in case doing that might be uncharacteristic of the one whose skin I now occupy. It really doesn't matter, though, since Dad does it for me.

"What I'm trying to say is that a three story building, with so much square footage, costs so much to build that it probably drained the man's bank account. They can pressure him all they want, but if he hasn't got the wherewithal to pay them, they'll get nothing for their trouble."

"Isn't the Simon Benson house where the school is?"

asks Ma.

Dad nods and says, "It's about fifty yards from the nearest building."

Ma explains, "I was just worried about damage to the school or whether the cleanup will affect it. The fire won't interfere with your schedule, will it?"

"I expect they'll have most of the debris cleared by Monday morning. Classes will go on as usual."

"Thank God. After all that we went through to move here, the thought made me skittish."

Dad nudges me with his knee. "Bet you two thought you'd earned yourself a holiday," he says, looking at my sister and giving me a wink.

Again I'm confused. Clearly, she is still young enough to be in high school, so he is teasing her while bringing me in as part of the joke, hinting at some kind of conspiracy. The humor eludes me, but I chuckle at it anyway.

That said, the proximity between the school and what, in my universe, was Portland State University's Alma Mater Center, originally the Simon Benson house, and what these people call the "school," make me wonder if I'm attending college here. If that is the case, where would it be? On the other hand, if I'm not, how do I spend my days?

Each passing second makes me increasingly nervous. I can fake my way through dinner and probably my chores, but what will I do Monday morning? After I get dressed and eat my breakfast, what happens then? I can only hope I can unearth enough of what is expected before my cover is blown and they realize that their son or brother has completely lost his mind. I can't imagine how they will react then, but I expect it's not going to be pretty.

Then the hammer falls.

"How is your school project coming?" asks Ma.

What do I say now? With no time to react, I have to fake it.

"I'm thinking I may want to start over again. What

did you think of it so far?"

This is the best ploy I can think of to acquire necessary information.

"I thought it was pretty imaginative," Patricia volunteers.

"Really?" I ask. "Please tell me why."

"The way you made a straight metal bar pass semi-vertically through two curved slots in a flat wood panel is amazing," she says, "If you had told me about it before you showed it to me, I would have thought you were teasing."

Now I am a little relieved, because I'm certain I know what Patricia is describing. I don't know whether the thing I created is motor-driven or turned by hand, but I'm pretty sure I can envision it. I believe Eric mounted a crossbar atop a vertical axis. Next, he would have soldered or welded a diagonal shaft onto it, angled at probably forty-five degrees to vertical, while also angling it at another forty-five degrees to horizontal. As the axis spins, the angled shaft would conscribe what geometers refer to as a hyperbolic parabola—a concave three dimensional shape which, if you could see what the diagonal bar traces as it passes through the air, looks like the letter C attached to a rotating letter T. It's the rotation that allows the rod to create the shape's curvature. And now I have a basis on which I can build an understanding of how Eric has spent some of his days.

"Let's look at it together in the morning," I suggest. "Maybe I can get excited about it all over again."

I can't begin tell you how relieved I am when Patricia agrees. I'll let her lead me there. Then, while we discuss what I have built and the circumstances that required me to create it, there is a fair chance that I can wheedle enough additional information about which class the project is for and whether or not I'm in college.

After dinner, while the women gather the dishes and start washing them, Dad goes to the shed and returns with a large galvanized steel tub. Perhaps the word "large" isn't

195

really all that appropriate when I stop to consider I will soon be bathing in it. The tub is oval in shape, less than four feet in length, maybe two feet wide and again as many deep—just big enough to either squat or kneel in. I can't imagine sitting down in it, since doing so wouldn't leave much room for the water.

Dad sets it down in the laundry room's center, once again making it clear we don't have separate bathrooms or bathtubs. The thought suddenly stops me. If we don't have separate bathrooms, it would also indicate we don't have indoor plumbing. It occurs to me that Ma and Patricia went outside to pump water into another and smaller tub in order to do the dishes. Holy crap! That means we don't have indoor toilets either. If we do have an outhouse, I will never find it on my own once it grows dark. A glance through the window shows there is barely enough light outside for me to find it if I go look for it now. I give Dad a hurried apology and rush out.

Success! It's just as foul smelling and unpleasant as I had expected, but at least they won't catch me doing my business in the bushes. What a fine mess that would be.

When I return, Dad has emptied the contents of the first three buckets and has set the fourth one aside for rinsing. Handing me a scrub brush and a large bar of white lye soap, he instructs, "Don't dawdle. I don't want the water to grow cold by the time it's my turn."

Chapter
Twenty One

Patricia leads me to a shed I'd failed to notice yesterday and a workbench inside. In its center is a construction similar to the thing I'd envisioned over dinner.

"I wish you would reconsider," she says. "So many people build ant farms and other mundane things for their science projects. This," she says, gesturing with a sweep of her arm, "is a step apart. It shows real imagination, real originality."

"You don't think it's a little simplistic? I mean, it doesn't take a real world problem and present a solution. It just shows a geometric phenomenon."

"But very few are perceptive enough to understand the elegance the equations describe, let alone build a practical demonstration. That's what sets it apart. In fact, this is what sets you apart. For a mathematician, you are a very unusual creature. How many scientists also possess artistic vision?"

"That's not art. It's… "

"Yes, it is!" she counters. "I mean it's not oil on canvas, but it's a non-verbal demonstration of what, until you created it, was only explained by equations. Look at it. It has form. It has structure. It's rather beautiful, if I do say so."

I have to say, I enjoy this iteration of my sister the most. Her previous versions were not nearly as passionate.

Certainly, the fact that she's praising me contributes to my bias, but setting that point aside, I admire her thoughtful way of expressing herself and forcing me to reconsider my objection. She is certainly causing me to reexamine who I am in any of these dimensions. Frankly, I like what I see. Up until now, I've been regarding each of these Erics as someone separate and apart, someone who's not really me. I've considered each one to be somewhat like an apartment I've moved into, but without claiming ownership. This time, however, something feels different. Instead of viewing this mathematician country boy the way an outside observer might, I'm beginning to see myself as him and him as me. It's as if the previous occupant, who has been hardwired into this brain and nervous system I'm now required to use, is beginning to affect my inner consciousness, beginning to affect my identity, beginning to affect not only how I see myself, but also the way I think and how I understand things. I'm no longer only a budding physicist, but also a mathematician. Because I'm beginning to comprehend this one's views of geometry and mathematics, instead of regarding numbers merely as tools, I'm beginning to see them as ways to perceive the universe, the way I do the theories of physics. As I say that, I realize I'm also beginning to access this Eric's memories more than I have those of the others, all of which are, of course, stored inside his… that is to say *my*… brain.

"Thank you," I tell her.

She pauses, about to add something further. After a second she says, "I wish you would reconsider."

"I already have."

"And?"

"I'm going to keep it."

She smiles, nods her head for emphasis. "Good. I get so frustrated with you sometimes. You can go on to college and make something more of yourself, yet you take so many things you're entitled to for granted, simply because you're a man. If women could continue onward after high school, I surely would."

Women can't go on to college in this world? As I access Eric's memories, I understand she is right. In this universe, women must marry in order to secure their future. That's why Ma stays home and Patricia helps with the housekeeping. It's not because these are tasks they share with Dad and me, as was the case in my original world. They do so because this is their role as women. They live, in each and every regard, the way an indentured servant would. They're confined to cleaning and maintaining the house while Dad heads off to bring in the money.

Patricia sighs. Biting her lip, she looks away and I can see her frustration. She is intelligent, yet she is required to subordinate her desires and conform to what I hope were long-discarded standards in my original world—although some of the comments female students were making back there make me question even that assumption.

I would like to say something reassuring. But now, as I see this world through the earlier Eric's eyes, I realize there is nothing I could say that wouldn't sound condescending. Instead, I reply, "I'm sure you would," and I realize this is still an impotent response.

It occurs to me I must be evolving, accessing ever more of the previous Eric's memories because, all at once, I know that tomorrow morning I will go to an annex that serves as temporary housing for the first university courses ever offered here. Like the building that had burned down yesterday, the structures that are intended to house them are still being built and lie in the direction of what, in my world, would be the student union. The science department will just be forming—no physics department yet, but with a department of mathematics that will, for now, offer only a bachelor's degree. Dad, I now understand, is to head the budding university's English department. Prior to our arrival, he served as a professor at a college in Prescott, Arizona.

199

When I comment on the state of its construction, she replies, "It's about time someone decided to build one here. Just think. You will be part of its first class of graduates."

And then what? How much opportunity will there be for anyone who is not trained in, say, forestry or agriculture in a frontier town such as this? In some ways, my chances to express myself may be almost as limited as Patricia's are. Although notable mathematicians were accomplishing great things during my original reality's nineteenth and early twentieth centuries, it's almost certain I would have to leave Portland and move to Chicago or New York or another major city to earn the PhD that would allow me to accomplish anything significant. I'm pretty certain my family in this reality doesn't have the resources to let me do that. Then, it occurs to me I just might be smart enough to earn myself a fellowship.

"Ah! There you are," says Dad when the door swings open. "Eric, will you help me hitch Sal to the buggy? I want to ride over to the Jowalskis' place. There are a few matters I need to go over with Sam before he heads out to Salem and I'd like you to come along with me."

The Jowalskis? Is he talking about Erin and her family? In that same instant, I know that he is. Erin has a crush on Eric and he is similarly attracted to her. Up until now, however, he has been too shy to express himself. As that awareness strikes, I decide I need to change that aspect of myself by becoming a little bolder.

"Sure," I say, trying not to sound over eager.

"Good. If you'll lead Sal out to the hitching post, I'll go inside and see if the meal Ma's been preparing is ready."

To say that I'm pleased that I'm already acquiring the memories necessary to accomplish his request would be an understatement. One day earlier, I would have been at a complete loss at where the stable is, let alone how to even begin the task Dad has handed me. I love it when terms like "overcheck rein" and "crupper fork" leap to mind as I set about undertaking the complex task this world's Eric has been performing ever since childhood.

After insuring Sal's harness is properly secured, I roll the buggy out of the barn and wheel it close behind her. Feeling more confident now than I did yesterday, I back her between the buggy's shafts and run the traces around the breastplate, then between the girth and bellyband back through the breeching strap, and secure Sal to the buggy. After running the lines—what I used to call reins—through the terrets, or loops, in the gig saddle, I lead them back and over the dash rail, before wrapping them around the buggy whips handle the way I now know Dad prefers.

Dad steps out of the house with a rather large basket in hand and two jackets draped over his forearm. He flips up the lid of buggy's boot, then tosses the jackets inside. After eyeing my work, he gives an approving nod, then places our meal in front of the seat before grabbing hold of a handle and pulling himself aboard. On the side opposite from where he is standing, I use the two steps attached to the buggy's body to climb up and sit beside him. This is so far removed from driving an automobile I almost grin. Instead, I force myself to keep my face solemn, since this is part of our day-to-day, and nothing out of the ordinary.

"Would you mind driving?" he asks.

For a moment I worry about whether I can do it. I certainly wasn't up to it yesterday. Then the knowledge of how to handle a horse and buggy, as well as the route to the Jowalskis' settles over me, flooding me with confidence. I reply, "No, sir."

He hands me the lines and explains, "I have some reading to do," then flashes me a smile.

Dad always drives, so I expect this change in affairs is a result of my work on the bucket brigade and reflects a new level of respect that effort has given me.

Sal, who has been standing idle, flicking her tail at an occasional fly, perks up and steps forward when I flick the

201

lines across her rump. Responding to a gentle tug of my wrist, she wheels the buggy around and proceeds down the driveway. When I turn her onto the street, I make a clucking sound and flick the lines again, causing Sal to increase her pace to a trot. Dad withdraws a newspaper from the picnic basket, then settles back and begins reading. Despite my earlier trepidation, I believe this might indeed be a life I can learn to enjoy. I actually might fit in.

I realize that the journey toward a place that people in my original world will eventually call Wilsonville, will take about four hours. Since driving a horse does not require the attention to the roadway that driving an automobile does, I allow my attention to drift to my present situation and theories centered around multiple parallel universes.

Certain physicists believe that the number of possible universes is equal to the number of possibilities that arise out of every decision that every man, woman and child faces daily, with a new universe reflecting the differing consequences each choice produces. While that number staggers the imagination, it's in no way disproportionate to the number of factors that make up our physical universe.

Everything in the universe is made up of atoms. Most things feel solid in varying degrees. Hammer a nail into a piece of wood and there is a noticeable impact. A sidewalk's concrete also seems hard if one witnesses the effort and abuse a construction worker endures when using a jackhammer. In the face of all that, I find it astounding that the space between the atoms that form everything in the universe is comparable in scale to the distance between the stars. The world one perceives is, in fact, more emptiness than substance, more nothing than physical matter. This has been calculated to a mathematical certainty by scientists and verified by computers. The trillions or quadrillions of stars in each of the universe's two trillion galaxies, in their totality roughly equal the number of grains of sand comprising all the earth's beaches and all the oceans' bottoms. If that isn't astonishing enough, the number of atoms that make up one grain of sand outnumber all those nearly countless stars.

My mind turns to how many atoms there must be in our universe, in all those stars and all of the matter and anti-matter that fills up the space in between. Keeping this utterly incomprehensible, but completely possible number in mind, I consider the number of possible realities. While those numbers defy the imagination, they only do so because of the mind's limitations.

With this as foundation, I consider how to best understand multiple dimensions, since dimensional boundaries are what keep us from perceiving anything beyond our own three-plus dimensions: length, width and breadth, coupled with a fourth, that we refer to as time. Time is a dimension we are only dimly aware of. We detect it through both motion and change, although we can only perceive that thin slice of time we call the present. We are aware of our past and we can project our future, but we cannot step into either or travel between them except as the present allows. Something or someone who could travel through time the way we navigate our globe would appear to materialize out of nowhere if he were to suddenly move into the portion that our senses perceive. The often used example proposed in the 1884 novel, *Flatland*, written by "A Square," the pen name of author Edwin Abbott, illustrates why this is so.

While we are aware of the three dimensions we live in, Flatlanders occupy just two: length and width. If you were to suspend an object above them, they would be unable to see it, since the concepts of up and down are only theoretical in their reality. That said, if you were to set that object onto the plain they inhabit, it would—from their point of view—appear as an abrupt manifestation. Even then, they could only perceive the portion that touches their plain. Even the height of a single molecule or atom would be beyond their perception. The way Flatlanders perceive the third dimension

of height is similar to the way we perceive the fourth
dimension of time. That you and I are completely unable to
perceive a fifth, sixth or seventh dimension is the reason we
cannot perceive alternate realities, for they lie within them.
They exist here beside us, just beyond our ability to perceive
them. Should someone assert they are even as much as a
hair's breadth away would be to distance them too greatly.

Something draws me out of my daydream and back
into the present. The beat of Sal's hooves and the motion of
the buggy change, returning my attention to the present. A
fork in the road ahead confuses her, so I steer Sal along the
route leading off to our left.

Chapter
Twenty Two

We've been rolling through countryside west of the Clackamas River for quite some time when the landscape starts looking familiar. Dad, who nodded off an hour ago, gasps, makes a grunting noise, then abruptly stop snoring. Placing a hand on the buggy's seat handle, he pulls himself upright. He stretches, then grimaces and glances around.

"Looks like we're almost there," he observes.

I nod. "We should be there in another twenty minutes or so."

"Will you kindly pull over? I need to relieve myself." I comply, and, as the mare changes course, he asks, "Do you feel like eating?"

I nod and point to a low-lying grassy knoll just beyond a grove of cottonwood trees.

"That looks like it might work," I suggest.

He nods approvingly, then removes his cap and combs back his hair with his fingers. "That'll be fine," he says and I rein Sal toward it.

We have been riding since early morning, so we take time to stretch. While Dad vanishes into the bushes, I turn Sal free to graze before I walk to a shady spot and examine what Ma has packed for us. After unfolding the blue and white checkered table cloth I find inside the basket, I spread it out and retrieve two china plates and two sets of metal utensils. Apparently, we are to break our fast on local cheddar, sliced apples, day old bread and cold stew from last night's dinner. There is also a corked water bottle and two tumblers.

"You do realize that this will be our last day of freedom before the semester begins?" Dad asks as he emerges from the bushes and finishes buttoning his fly.

Since he rarely takes me along just for company in this reality, I suspect he's trying to ease into the reason he asked me to join him.

"Yes, sir," I reply, finding this new formality becoming easier to adapt to.

"You were acting a little strange last night," he says as he sits down beside me.

"I… I think it was because I was exhausted."

"Are you sure it wasn't because Erin Jowalski has taken a liking to you?"

"No sir. I mean, I'm pretty sure that wasn't it."

"I say that because I can remember when I was your age and your Ma took a liking to me."

I can see where this is going and it's starting to feel a little creepy. I hope he's not heading toward a discussion of the birds and the bees or something similar. Little House on the Prairie was fine on TV, but not right here in front of me. I understand Dad loves me and is trying to act fatherly, but I'm pretty sure I could teach him a thing or three if I wanted.

"No, Dad. I'm very comfortable with Erin."

"And you're not preoccupied?"

"No, Dad. I like her a lot and I'd like to see more of her, but I'm not having any difficulties on her account."

He raises an eyebrow and studies me with interest, as if trying to burrow into my brain to be certain what the truth is.

"Honest," I assure him and place a hand on his knee.

He begins nodding slowly and, after another moment,

gives two firm nods and adds, "Well, all right then. If that is the case, you should know she's going to be there this morning. I guess it will be all right if you two decide to spend some time by yourselves—out in the open, you understand."

I almost laugh, but instead I reply, "Yes, Dad. I understand."

We finish our meal, then clean up afterwards and stow away the plates, silverware and garbage. As we climb into the buggy, we are conversing cheerily about matters of no great concern. This time, however, Dad takes his usual place in the driver's seat. Taking up the lines, he gives a firm snap across Sal's backside—not enough to hurt, but strong enough to communicate that we are on serious business. It's growing harder by the minute to keep a straight face over this old fashioned world I've been thrown into. It's a little like the way Marty McFly felt in Back to the Future when he found himself confronted with earlier morals and ways of doing things. Somehow, though, I manage to contain myself as we drive toward the Jowalski house and I move another step closer to learning about Erin in this world.

We enter the Jowalski farm through a gate in a split rail fence. The summer has provided very little rain, so the fields of grass between here and the house have turned dry and golden. A border collie runs toward us, barking to greet the new visitors, and Dad works to keep Sal from bolting. Fortunately, our mare has a gentle disposition and, although initially startled, she isn't easily spooked, so Dad urges her on without much effort.

Fifty yards from the gate, at the top of a rise, sits a whitewashed, two story house somewhat larger than our own. In the wake of the dog's commotion, the front door swings open and a tall husky bearded man steps onto the porch and waves.

"Looks like he's expecting us," I comment, wondering, as he approaches, if he is as crazy as Erin's father was the last time I saw him.

The way that he greets us and the smile on his face says he isn't. His hair is combed and his shirt and overalls are pressed and neat. Furthermore, Dad seems relaxed and trusting. Still, the way one reality sometimes mirrors another leaves me somewhat uneasy. I take a minute to access this Eric's memories and find there is nothing to be worried about, so, realizing I've been holding my breath, I exhale and start to breathe easier.

"I talked to Sam early last week," says Dad, "about coming out today to discuss business." I glance at him with an inquiring look, to which he responds, "Depending on how our talk goes, I may tell you about it later."

When we have pulled close enough to hear, Sam calls, "Howdy, Walt." Glancing over at me, he adds, "Eric."

I tip my cap and say, "Hello, Mr. Jowalski."

He gives me a nod and turns back to Dad. "I was wondering if you'd forgotten."

"We got off to a late start," Dad replies and again I'm reminded how little time this trip would have taken on paved roads in an automobile.

"Eric," says Sam. "Erin's in the kitchen preparing dinner. I expect as she'd enjoy an excuse to step away from her chores for a while. Why don't you run inside while your Dad and I attend to business?"

"Thank you, sir."

Once Dad and I have tied up Sal beside a watering trough and Sam has brought her some grain and alfalfa, I do just that.

True to her father's word, Erin is in the kitchen, seated on a straight backed wooden chair. She is removing the strings and stems from a basket of green beans, tossing them into a bucket while placing the finished beans into a white ceramic bowel on the wooden table beside her. Noticing that I've entered, her eyes light up and she smiles broadly.

"Hello, Eric," she says and wipes her hands on her

apron. She stands, unties it, then folds it and places it next to the bowl. "Mother's spending time at the neighbors'." She gives me a mischievous look and adds. "Let's go for a walk. I want to show you the woods out back."

Grabbing my hand in a way that would have startled this reality's Eric, she leads me through the back door and into the garden, flashing me glances from the corner of her eye as we set off toward a grove of red oak and alder trees. Once we are far enough inside that the house is no longer visible, Erin stops and turns to face me.

"How did you convince your father to bring you here?" she asks as she takes both of my hands into hers and squeezes.

"What do you mean?"

"He's never left the two of us alone before. Even when Patricia invited me to your birthday party, he made sure there was always someone with us."

I access the memories of this dimension's Eric and realize Erin is right. My original father had never been restrictive. And although this reality's Dad had been, I tell her about the fire and the bucket brigade and how his behavior toward me has changed since then.

"Yes," she says, nodding thoughtfully. "He always has been impressed with demonstrations of manliness." She smiles and says, "Apparently, you've finally made the grade."

As she talks, I consider grabbing her and kissing her hard on the mouth, but decide against it for the moment. I think I can tell where things are going, but this reality's memories are making me uncertain. Still, she has taken me to this place in the woods, which gives me a clue to how she'll respond if I take things farther than the Eric she knows would have done, so I decide to go slowly, but nevertheless in a positive direction.

"Now," Erin continues, "if you just weren't so shy, I would also be impr… "

She stops short as I place my hands on her waist and pull her close without being rough. Touching her lips with mine, I begin placing soft, delicate kisses, one after the other, all over them. Without giving her time to think, let alone breathe, I press both of my lips against hers and dwell for a moment before opening my mouth and kissing her deeply. When her own mouth opens in response, I begin using my tongue to talk to her, to tell her how much I want her, how much I need her, and Erin responds by wrapping her arms around my neck. We go on like this for almost a minute, when Erin breaks away. Breathing hard, she takes half a step back, cocks her head and studies me with wide open eyes. I begin forming a word, but as I start speaking, Erin launches herself against me, embracing me the way I had considered doing to her only a few moments before. As her passion increases and her hands move across my back, neck, head and face, I press my body against hers and feel her reciprocate. After several more minutes, we separate and stare at each other, as if we are seeing each other for the very first time.

"My goodness you've changed!" gasps Erin. "Your father is right. Whatever happened on that fire line, you certainly *are* different."

I want to explain why this is so, to tell her the truth about myself, but I also understand that doing so would undermine her new regard for me because it would instantly destroy my credibility. Who in their right mind would believe I come from another universe? Certainly no one in this world, where the technology is preindustrial. Better to let her accept me for how I appear: someone abruptly transformed into the man she's been longing for.

And while I also understand she is not the Erin Jowalski I'd fallen in love with earlier, she looks and sounds like her and, for the moment, that's enough. I am terribly alone. My family, my friends and the world I once knew have vanished, probably forever. Better to have one person who cares for me, someone who loves me, than to remain isolated, separate and apart from everything that is doomed to remain a memory.

I glance over my shoulder and peer through the woods. "How much time do you think we have?"

"They have a great deal to discuss, so maybe an hour. Still," she says, looking back toward the house, "in case they finish sooner, we shouldn't stay here much longer."

We spend a few more minutes touching and caressing, then, suppressing our desires, we step out of the grove and return. We are holding hands now, the way I suppose our parents would approve. If our fathers were to see us, we would appear to be returning from a stroll through the countryside.

"Do you know what they're discussing?" I ask when we are halfway to the house.

"Father wants to start a new business and believes your father would make a good partner."

That takes me by surprise. "Dad's a teacher, not a businessman."

"No. But he has a good head and possesses integrity—two things my father believes are in short supply these days. That's why he wanted to speak with him. He wants to convince your father there is money to be made."

"Doing what?"

"There is a new invention that's growing popular back East called an automobile. It's some kind of self-propelled carriage. Father believes that when the invention catches on—and he's sure that it will—it will transform everything. Tomorrow, he is going to Salem to file articles of incorporation and he wants to add your father's name to them. He wants to be in on the ground floor before others begin applying to the automobile manufacturers for dealerships.

"What do you think about it?" she asks.

I have to pretend that I have only heard rumors about

what people are starting to call horseless carriages.

"I think it's a great idea." Remembering an article I had once read on the internet about their early capabilities and how people reacted, I add, "I've heard they can reach speeds of up to twenty-five miles an hour. Imagine how that will impact travel. Dad and I could have gotten here in just over an hour."

"Twenty-five miles an hour! That's as fast as a horse can gallop. But, of course, it couldn't maintain that pace for anything close to an hour." She turns and looks at me. "Can you imagine? That would make it possible to drive all the way to Seattle in—what?—seven hours, as compared to more than one day. I had no idea. Eric, do you know what that could mean?"

"It would completely transform our society."

"I mean for us. If what Father is projecting comes true, we could be rich. We wouldn't have to live on some crummy old farm trying to scratch out a living. If we were rich enough, your sister and I wouldn't have to spend the rest of our lives living like servants. We could have maids of our own."

I'm not sure how I like that idea and try to offer an alternative.

"Maybe you could continue on to college. You could have a career."

"Who wants to work? Imagine. I could have someone do all of the cooking and cleaning for me while I lie on a couch and have them bring me whatever I want."

These comments shine a new light on her. I'm hoping her statements are simply the result of someone who has grown up knowing her life will lead her down a path lacking any alternatives. If, on the other hand, the woman I'm walking with is someone who would exploit individuals less fortunate than she is, I don't want to spend the rest of my life with her. That said, I'll set that judgment aside until I get to know her better. For now, I'll enjoy holding her hand and, if the two of us can get together again, perhaps for some cautious lovemaking, since I'm certain this world hasn't invented any form of birth control.

Dad remains silent for much of the drive home and, as curious as I am about the outcome of his discussion with Mr. Jowalski, I'm reluctant to break the silence. For one thing, I don't believe I'm supposed to know what they had been talking about. For another, I understand how important his decision will be, since he's deciding between a certain future as a teacher that will provide security but limited income, and one that can open incredible opportunities, but carries extreme financial risks.

Halfway home, he turns to me. "What would you say if I were to tell you I'm considering leaving the world of education?"

"Depends."

"That's an ambiguous response."

"You've asked an open-ended question."

"Fair enough," he replies. "Sam has offered me a partnership in a brand new endeavor, one, I might add, that can greatly improve our lives."

Rather than offer a response, I remain silent in order to learn more about his thoughts on the matter. After a lengthy pause, he continues, "What have you heard about a new-fangled contraption they call an automobile?" When I respond by telling him the things I had told Erin, he says, "Those pretty much reflect my own thoughts on the matter. The reason I'm asking is that Sam wants to open an automobile dealership. He has already sent off letters of intent to three manufacturers: Ford, DeSoto and Chrysler."

"Does he have enough money to last if they're slow to catch on?" Before he can answer, I add, "I think it's a really good idea—the automobile, I mean—but without easy ways to fuel them, it might be years before enough people are ready to buy one."

He gives me a long appreciative look, then says,

"You have a good head on your shoulders. I hadn't considered that."

"That matter aside," I say, "I think it's something you should look into."

"I'm planning to see a business lawyer in town tomorrow morning. I intend to ask him his thoughts on the matter and find out if he's heard anything else that might be relevant." He slaps me on the knee and adds, "You're really starting to become quite the man."

He faces forward, then looks back at me. "I almost forgot. Before I drop you off at school tomorrow morning, I have to run by the bank. Do you mind coming along? It shouldn't take more than a couple of minutes."

"Not at all," I say, glad at the direction our relationship is taking.

Chapter
Twenty Three

During the night, the sky clouded over. A light rain has started falling as we ride into downtown Portland. So far, the precipitation is not enough to turn the roads muddy, but the wheels are beginning to throw up quite a spray. Before leaving home, Dad and I put on rubber boots, broad brimmed hats and oil cloth ponchos. They should keep us dry enough if the weather turns foul, and there is every indication it might. Wind coming out of the Columbia Gorge is already building and the trees along our route are beginning to shake.

"Is your trip to the bank really necessary?" I ask as we cross the Sellwood Bridge.

The Willamette river is already showing streaks of white across its waters. While they are not yet whitecaps, the water is already agitated.

Dad nods. "Yep. After the fire, since I had enough cash to pay for our groceries, I forgot to deposit my paycheck. I can't afford to lose it and I'll feel better once it's safely in our account. Like I said, it shouldn't take long." He looks at me sideways and asks, "You're not going to let a little rain keep you from attending classes, are you?"

"No, Sir."

Even though I'm not looking forward to returning home through an intensifying storm in an open, horse drawn buggy, I don't want to lessen his newly formed image of what his son has become.

"Fine," he says and clucks at Sal who has started to slow her pace heading into the wind.

As we leave Sellwood behind and draw closer to Portland, the traffic along the roadway gradually increases. Along with buggies similar to our own, there are enclosed carriages—probably owned by the well-to-do—riders on horseback and numerous wagons transporting goods. In the distance, I hear a train's whistle blow, reminding me that Dad refers to as a steam trumpet. It releases two long blasts, followed by a short and another long one. Closer into town, church bells ring and Dad pulls his pocket watch from under his poncho.

"Nine A.M.," he says, as we make our way uphill from the Willamette River's shore after crossing the Sellwood Bridge. "The bank should just be opening. We'll be there in another few minutes. What time do your classes start?"

"Nine o'clock, sir. I'm going to be late."

"Sorry, Son. Can't be helped. You'll probably get to class a little before nine-thirty. If you run into any trouble, have your teacher talk to me."

"Yes, Sir."

Dad was right. It takes us five minutes to get there. We tie the buggy to a hitching post and go inside. As we walk through the door, on my immediate left I notice a man in a uniform. He has a star on his chest, so he's most likely the bank's security guard. The bank's interior is not too unlike what I'm used to, given the technology. It's square-shaped room with a floor made of white and gray marble squares. It's walled in on two sides by a dark wooden panel six or seven feet high. Every few feet, a window has been cut into it. Each window, in turn, is fenced by a series of vertical brass bars, beneath which the bank's customers slide cash and paper documents. Lines have already formed in front of each of them.

On the third side of the room, a three foot high wood rail fence separates a small group of desks, where some bankers sit, from the rest of the room. I notice an office door standing open a few feet beyond them. Through it, I make out the front edge of a desk and a straight backed wooden chair positioned before it. Barely visible at the lobby's rear, behind where the tellers work, I can see the top of the vault's large steel door.

When we take our place in line, Dad shoves back his poncho and withdraws an envelope and a small book with cardboard covers. He notices me looking and says, "I had forgotten. You've never been inside a bank before, have you?"

I access Eric's memories and realize he's right. In this society, banking is left to the head of the house. With that realization, I also notice that most of the customers are men, as well as all of the tellers, since a woman's place is in the home, with certain exceptions. I suspect that the two women in line may be in charge of their households. This world's Eric is also aware that a small number of women either own their own businesses or, for various reasons, have found gainful employment as teachers or other minor occupations.

Opening the book he is holding, Dad explains, "This is called a passbook. The dates appearing on the left column of each page show when I have either made a deposit or have withdrawn funds. As you can see, the columns to the right are marked to indicate the type of transaction and the dollar amount. The last column shows the resulting balance and the teller places his initials in the square to its right."

Amazed at how primitive it is, I ask, "And that's all you have to show for how much money is in your account?"

"Pretty much. The bank does mail a statement at the end of each month. But in the event of a dispute, this is what I have to rely on. Regardless of what the statement or the bank may say, this passbook trumps everything."

217

"So, if you lose it… "

"I could wind up in a whole lot of trouble."

After another minute, a customer leaves a window and it's our turn.

"Good morning, Mr. Folder. How are you today?" asks the teller in a gray suit and bow tie.

"I'm fine, Lawrence."

"How can I help you on this gray and blustery morning?"

Dad starts to hand him the passbook, along with the envelope holding his paycheck, when there is a commotion behind us. I turn around to look and see three men and a woman standing in the doorway. They have on wide brimmed hats and are wearing bandanas over their faces. The man nearest the security guard takes him by the arm and presses the barrel of his revolver against his neck.

"Nobody move and this will go down easy," the man says. Glancing at the guard he adds, "You try to play hero and you're gonna wind up dead."

I know that voice, I tell myself. I can't place where I encountered it, but I've definitely heard it before.

"All we're looking for is some of your replaceable goods—cash, jewelry and whatnot. Take care not to lose your lives and you can earn back whatever we take in another month or so."

This comment elicits chuckles from the man's three companions, two of whose voices also sound familiar. Dad places an arm across my chest to hold me in place. He takes back the passbook and envelope and moves me away from the teller's window.

"Hold it right there," says the gunman.

"I'm just protecting my son," Dad replies.

"How admirable. Now, if you'll just hand over the things in your hand, you can keep on protecting him.

"Dan," the outlaw says to one of the men on his left. "Hold out your hat so he has something to put them in."

The second man steps forward, extending his hat as he was instructed. As he approaches, I get a good look at the eyes peering over the top of his mask and see they are an unusual shade of blue and the man at the door calls him… Dan? Under other circumstances, this pair of facts would hold no significance whatsoever. But since this world parallels my original one, as well as others I have visited, I have no choice but to believe the second man's surname must be Hastings. And now I recognize the voice at the door as well. It belongs to none other than Dan's partner in crime, Marco. Criminals in that world. Criminals in this. When Dad mentioned bank robbers over dinner, I should have seen this coming.

"Deposit those items into the hat, if you will," Dan says, giving a nod toward Dad's passbook and envelope. As Dad moves to comply, Dan tells him, "The pocket watch, as well."

When I start to object, Dad reminds me, "These are all replaceable."

"And both of your wallets," Dan prompts.

"I don't have one," I say as Dad adds his to the collection.

"Turn your pockets inside out."

As we comply, Marco says, "This is taking too much time. Dan, pass the hat around. Ladies and gentlemen, when it comes your way, be generous with your donations… watches, wallets and jewelry, people." He turns to the pair beside him, whom I now notice are carrying saddlebags. "Start from opposite ends of the teller windows and work toward the middle. Tellers, when my associates hand you their bags, I want you to empty the contents of your drawer into them. Don't be cute," he says as the man and woman associates move to comply. "If one of you so much as moves an inch away from your till, I'll shoot you dead on the spot."

One of the women standing in line breaks into tears when she's handed Dan's hat.

219

"But this was my mother's," she protests, grasping her necklace.

Dan knocks her hand aside and tears the article of jewelry away from her neck, probably breaking the clasp as he does so, then backhands her across the face.

I start toward them and Dad grabs a handful of my shirt, just below the collar, and forces me to stop. Our eyes meet and I grit my teeth and nod. The move, while purely reflexive and probably the result of pent up anger at all the injustice I have seen, would probably have been a fatal mistake. Fortunately, Marco fails to notice, since he is occupied with conducting the robbery.

"Which one of you is the bank manager?" he demands, glancing around, but finding only customers. "Alex," he says, and the woman robber turns to look at him. "There's someone in the office. Haul him out where I can see him. Len," he calls to her partner. "Step it up. I want to be out of here in no more than three minutes."

I don't recognize Len, but I'm not surprised that Alex is one of them. As she drapes the saddlebags over a shoulder, unholsters her revolver and makes her way toward the designated room, Len moves to the next window in line. A moment later, a man in a black suit emerges, hands high over his head. Alex follows with her gun pressed into the man's back.

"Are you the manager?" shouts Marco.

The man, who is sweating profusely, nods that he is.

"I want you to open the safe."

"I can't," he gasps.

"Can't? I thought you said you were the manager."

"It has a time lock," the manager explains.

"What's a time lock?"

I suspect Marco does not understand because this is recent technology.

"The lock is connected to a timer that allows us to open it only at specified times."

Marco frowns. "And just when is that?"

"We unlocked it an hour before opening. We can't do it again until just after closing."

"Len, make sure he's not lying. Grab one of the tellers."

Len orders the teller he is working with, "Keep filling 'er up. Then pass 'er over to the next one." He flicks his gun toward the man on his left to indicate which teller he means, then hurries along the wall of windows, only to find the teller cage locked.

"Open this thing," he demands of the manager.

The manager nods, reaches into a trouser pocket and produces a set of keys.

"Toss 'em over."

The manager complies and Len holsters his pistol. He starts sorting through them, trying the lock with each key in succession, but finding no success until his fifth or sixth attempt. Yanking open the door to the teller cage, he unholsters his gun, rushes inside and holds it to the first teller's skull.

"Tell me the truth, or I'll blow your head off," he says to the man who is standing wide-eyed and trembling. "Is what he says true, about the lock and all?"

The teller nods vigorously. "I- i- it's true." Glancing at Len out of the corner of his eye, he stammers, "H- he c- can't open the vault until th- three-fifteen."

Marco grimaces, then shouts to his associates, "Get what you can and let's get out of here."

Just then, a man comes in from the street. He brushes past Marco, then, seeing how everyone in the bank is standing stock still, their eyes riveted on Marco, he asks, "What's going on?"

Marco grabs him by the shoulder, shoves him into the lobby's center and shouts, "Get down on the floor!"

Taking advantage of the momentary distraction, the security guard yanks his arm free and, with his other hand,

221

grabs Marco's gun hand, forcing the six gun away in a broad sweeping arc. Two bright flashes accompany two loud explosions as Marco's gun discharges. All at once, I feel a sharp pain in my gut and realize I've been shot. I clutch with both hands at the bullet's point of entry and feel warm wetness spread across my palms. *Gawd, I hurt!* I did not realize how much pain a bullet could cause.

"Eric!" cries Dad. He grabs me by the shoulder and asks, "Are you all right?"

I can only shake my head and answer, "No," as my knees buckle and I collapse to the floor.

Am I going to die? I ask myself.

I understand in this instant that medical help in this world will be primitive at best. Since antibiotics had not been invented in my own world until the mid-twentieth century, I realize they probably do not exist in this one. I will likely die of blood poisoning, if I don't die from loss of blood. My only hope for survival is my aching head and the resulting shimmer that is building rapidly. As my head begins aching and my vision tunnels, with no other option before me, I reach out and tear at the barely visible strands of light. At first, I feel nothing, no sense of tendrils against my clawing fingers. Then, just as I begin losing consciousness, I feel the shimmer gain substance. With my strength ebbing rapidly, I use the last of what's left and pull downward.

Chapter
Twenty Four

I.

Am.

Alive.

I am standing.

Air moves in and out of my chest and the pain is gone.

As I recite these assurances, my hands move to my abdomen and discover no wound, no blood, no bullet hole. With that realization, I open my eyes and find myself standing on a broad grassy knoll above a forested countryside through which a river flows. Since each of my folds has landed me near the spot from where I departed the previous one, I suspect it must be the Willamette River near where the city of Portland should be. I say "should be" because there are no buildings, no roadways, nor any other sign of human habitation… anywhere. There is only forest, punctuated at intervals with grassy spaces similar to this one.

I suspect that the Eric I ousted from this world will have died on arrival, but I don't dwell on it. The will to survive is all that has kept me alive until now, and I intend to stay this way. Instead, I ponder on whether I am alone. Are there no other people anywhere? In the same instant this questions emerges, I know the answer. There are certainly others. No human comes into the world without parents, without generations before or other people around them. The Eric I have folded into could never exist in utter isolation. If I fail to immediately encounter the ones who live here, when I begin to access the memories that are hardwired into the brain I am using, the answers to where they are, as well as who they might be, will emerge and I will join them. This is all that keeps me from panicking. I deliberately calm myself and begin assessing my surroundings.

Gazing east, I spot Mount Hood, the ancient volcanic peak that stands watch over northern Oregon. Mount Saint Helens rises to the north. Turning toward the missing city, I notice Mount Tabor, a much smaller volcano that is situated on what would ordinarily be Portland's east side. It, too, is surrounded by forest. When the trees were cut down for the building of early Portland, their felling not only made room for the city's construction, but also provided the lumber for its earliest buildings. What remained after all those trees were cut down was what caused early settlers to nickname the city Stump Town.

Now that I have confirmed my location, I need to explore. There are no roads, save for one narrow dirt trail that is hardly visible as it cuts across this meadow. But since it runs in the general direction of where Portland State University will eventually be built, assuming it's ever constructed in this reality, I start walking in that direction.

Almost at once, a cry in the air above me—not that of a bird, but rather a sound that resembles a reptilian rasp— brings me to a halt. Looking up, I'm startled to see a winged creature, far larger than any eagle that ever flew. The knowledge I have acquired from Eric, the biology major, elicits the name archaeopteryx, a creature dating back to the Jurassic period, nearly one hundred fifty million years before people walked the earth. This can't be. There are people here and I am one of them. Still, if a creature from so long ago still exists in this world, what other prehistoric creatures might have survived the devastations that eliminated the dinosaurs in my own? I shall have to be very careful, indeed.

I smile when I realize that I'm retaining certain memories from each prior incarnation. Perhaps not all of them, but some of what was more important to each of my predecessors seems to carry forward along with my consciousness.

That thought slips aside as the beast overhead makes me wonder if this Eric Folder is armed to protect himself. I look down and see that I'm dressed in clothes fashioned from animal hides. I wear something like a coat that is secured at its front with leather thongs, a pair of pants of similar construction, and footwear like the moccasins native Americans once wore. A leather sack dangles from a strap running over my shoulder and down across my chest. I touch it and feel it holds a quantity of liquid that's most likely water. A foot-long knife made of obsidian, a black volcanic glass, is inserted into the belt around my waist. Unable to believe this is my sole means of defense, I search the ground around me. When I look back to where I was standing, I see a spear, perhaps six feet in length, that's also obsidian tipped, so I return to retrieve it.

Fine. Just great. And I thought the last world was primitive. I will be lucky if I live to see tomorrow in this one. Once again, I start to break down. I can't go on like this, shuttling from one dimension to the next, if I want to remain sane. I want to go home. I want to return to my original bedroom, sleep in my original bed and wake up from this nightmare. The problem is, this is no dream. The breeze across my face confirms it, as does the earth beneath my feet. Dreams are not made up of physical sensations, so this, like the others before it, constitutes my new reality. Since succumbing to despair will not improve things, I suck up the tears, then pick up the spear and head west into the forest.

From the length of my shadow, which points eastward, I can tell it's already several hours past noon. It will be unwise to remain in the woods much longer. I could become easily lost, so I work at maintaining a brisk pace.

Passing through the forest would be difficult going were it not for the deer trail. Whenever another one crosses it and I have to decide which path to follow, I take time to look back to observe where I came from before pressing on. I do this because it comes to me that if I'm to return this way, the woods will look completely different when approached from the opposite direction. I realize, on an instinctual level, that failing to do so is one reason so many people get lost when they are hiking. I smile at this understanding, suspecting that this Eric's knowledge is already beginning to seep through.

Another hour into my journey, the breeze becomes wind, the air starts to chill and the sky starts to darken. The trees and bushes rustle and falling leaves whirl past me. Fortunately, the clothes I am wearing will help keep me warm. Into the early part of the next hour, I emerge into a less forested area. The trees have thinned enough that I begin to acquire, from an occasional glimpse of the now distant river, a better sense of where I am. These views suggest that my destination is near.

Why I would choose to go to a place that might someday become a university campus is hard to understand. Perhaps it has to do with familiarity. In a strange land, with no knowledge of anything around me except in the most general of terms, being somewhere even remotely familiar provides a sense of security. Lacking bridges, or even a boat, I could not easily cross into Sellwood, so where else should I go? I begin looking for landmarks in a place that is so drastically different from the world with which I'm familiar.

By the time evening is falling, I am starting to grow hungry. My fingers absently reach for the belt at my waist and fall upon a pouch I hadn't noticed earlier. Glancing down, I spot the flap that's covering it is secured by a cord wrapped around a small piece of bone. Inside, I discover several pieces of dried meat, enough to get me through the night and tomorrow morning.

When I put a piece to my lips, I stop. My fingers encounter a thick growth of hair. Touching my face, I find I have a full beard and moustache. I'm not normally this hairy. Even in my last incarnation, I did not have enough facial hair to warrant using the straight razor that lay on my nightstand. This prompts me to run my hands through the hair on my head and I find it's tied into a pony tail extending down past my shoulders. Now that I think about it, a society as primitive as this would possess neither mirrors nor the tools for shaving or cutting hair. I chuckle and begin eating, pleased to find that these people have at least discovered salt.

I'm nearly finished when lightning flares and thunder booms. Almost immediately, rain starts falling in torrents. Ducking under an elm tree for cover, I secure the pouch, then search the area around me for better protection. Unfortunately, nothing offers more shelter than this, so I prepare to wait out the tempest. By the time the rain begins tapering off, I've had time to better assess my surroundings. During the time I've been waiting, it becomes apparent that I know this place, not from this current Eric's perspective, but from my own past experiences. Although I'm already acquiring small pieces of what this one knows, if this incarnation in any way parallels the previous one, it may take an entire day before my mind integrates sufficiently with this body's nervous system to fully access his knowledge.

As I study how the trails here intersect, as well as their spacing and the land's contours, it occurs to me that I'm at the heart of what, in my original universe, was the Portland State University campus. I'm certain of it.

All at once, there is movement around me. Shapes in the bushes are converging on the place where I'm standing. Their silhouettes suggest that they're animals. Without hesitation, I dive into a dense patch of vegetation, hoping to conceal myself.

When one of these beasts emerges, I see it's easily

twice the size of a bullmastiff. The scales on its body reflect the light of the now visible moon. Before the shifting cloud cover plunges us once more into darkness, several others like it appear and biologist Eric is unable to identify them. He is certain, however, that nothing similar has ever appeared in my world. When one of them raises its head and shrieks, two more appear and I'm suddenly terrified, knowing I can do nothing to defend myself should they find me. The inevitable regrets over the results of all of my folds begin to insert themselves, as well as a longing for the world I'll never see again. The wind increases and a sharp crack overhead makes me look up. It catches the creatures' attention as well. All of them turn in my direction and one of them starts walking toward me. I'm contemplating being torn apart and devoured when there is a second crack and a tree limb breaks, then lands a few yards to my right. The creatures study where it's landed, then return their attention to the original location. I am starting to relax when something lands on my shoulder and takes hold of me. I jump. Before I can cry out, a hand clamps my mouth shut.

"Shhh!" someone whispers. Then, a feminine voice says in a quiet but urgent tone, "Air, we have been looking for you for the better part of the day. What happened?"

Like the place around me, her voice is familiar. It belongs to Erin. What did she call me? Did she call me "Air?" Almost as soon as the question arises, I realize that, yes, this is my name in this dimension. It also comes to me that, in this world, her name is Wren. When I open my mouth to answer, she silences me again.

"We'll have time for that later. Come now, before they catch our scent and realize we're here."

Keeping ourselves low, we move through the bushes—slowly at first, in order to keep any noise we make to a minimum—then progressively faster as we leave the creatures ever farther behind. We are running hard now and I'm amazed at my body's incredible condition. My original version would have been winded after two or three minutes. Yet, all the while we are running, my legs pound the earth without effort, my lungs take in whatever air they need without forcing me to gasp.

After nearly twenty minutes like this, we are back where I started. Abruptly, Wren turns south. We begin following the ridgeline and I understand why we are doing so. Were we to traverse the hill's eastern face, rather than remain on its crest, travelling across ground made sodden by the night's heavy downpour, we would lose our footing and slide. It's a small understanding, but I believe it originates from Air's experience.

Suddenly, a dark shape moves in our way and confronts us, issuing a deep guttural growl. Without bothering to communicate, Wren and I separate, in order to avoid presenting a unified target. I don't know how good this creature's night vision is, but to my eyes, Wren and the creature are almost indistinguishable from the darkness. As she and I move to opposing positions, the creature pauses, as if deciding which of us to attack first.

Grasping my spear with both hands, I drop into a crouch, feet spread to enhance my stability. The beast roars and rushes at Wren. I run toward it, bracing myself against the inevitable impact, then drive my spear into its ribcage. The shaft halts briefly when it comes into contact, then changes direction ever so slightly when it encounters the smooth hard surface of the animal's scales. Even so, the weight of my body drives it forward and I feel the softer resistance of the underlying flesh. The creature whirls and I'm lifted off my feet and thrown to my right by the spear I refuse to release. The tips of what feel like several sharp blades—probably its claws—penetrate my leggings and score my left thigh, but I will not let go. The thing howls, then wheels to its right and I wonder if Wren has also impaled it. In the next second, several men cry out around us. The beast bucks and turns and I suspect it's finding itself under attack.

Suddenly, the obscuring clouds part and moonlight illuminates our surroundings. While I cannot see Wren, who is behind the animal, four men dressed in clothing similar to mine arrange themselves around the creature's flanks and hindquarters and are repeatedly driving their spears into it.

In the next instant, the animal breaks free and I can see it's the same as the ones in the university parkway. Moving faster than any of us can respond to, it backs away, then turns and retreats into the woods, emitting high pitched rasping cries as it flees, and taking my spear along with it.

For a moment, the six of us stare after it. Only when it has vanished does anyone move. One of the men approaches Wren.

"Where did you find him?" he demands.

"Where Water taught the initiates," Wren replies, and I understand she's referring to Dad.

The man scowls at me, then turns back to her and says in a loud and angry tone, "I told you he is a liability."

"Once he gets over his father's death, he will be fine."

Dad has died? How did this happen?

The man shouts at Wren. "I told you not to go after him. You could have been killed. We all could have been killed."

"Nonetheless, we were not," I reply.

Turning to me, he replies, "When a knife tooth cat killed my mother, I remained unchanged by her passing. I remained as I always had been."

"A parent's death affects each of us differently," argues Wren. "You know that. Look, Sky, before it happened, Air was among the best of us." As Sky glares at me, Wren adds, "After we cross the river and return home, I will speak with him. You can chastise him then, if it suits you. Now, however, every minute we remain on this side of the river increases our risk. Keep your anger inside until we are safe."

"It shall be as you say," Sky replies. Turning to

address the others, he says, "Home now. Let us not keep the canoes waiting any longer than necessary."

He turns toward the direction Wren and I had been heading and takes off at run. As the other three follow, Wren's eyes flash at me. I suspect she would like to add something pertaining to her and Sky's exchange, but she refrains from doing so and instead warns, "Don't slow us down."

She takes off in pursuit and I follow at the same pace as before.

The route to the river is steep and we all do our best to remain upright. Nonetheless, several times on the way down, the earth gives way beneath us and twice we all find ourselves tumbling through bushes before we can find a way to stop ourselves. If anyone plans to have words with me later, I'm sure these slides will not improve their disposition.

Two canoes are waiting at the shore. The men who are guarding them—one man per boat—begin shoving them back into the water even as we are approaching. By the time we arrive, we are calf-deep in water. Hurrying to board, the others toss their spears onto each canoe's bottom before climbing in. Taking up paddles, we place ourselves on each of the canoes' seats. Without hesitation, we begin driving them into the current, stroking as hard as we can. Even when we reach the river's midpoint, each of us continues to glance back toward the danger from which we've escaped.

Chapter
Twenty Five

We've arrived on the opposite shore and are carrying the canoes toward the cluster of bushes where we intend to conceal them. I look at Wren, who is walking in front of me. I am about to express how grateful I am that she came to find me, when she glances back and snaps, "How could you be so stupid?" then turns and leaves me with my mouth hanging open.

The hike to our village takes over an hour. By the time we've arrived, all of us are exhausted and no one bothers to criticize me. I suspect that what anyone has to say will wait until morning. Instead, we all separate and I have to find my way home on my own.

Although a light rain is falling, intermittent breaks in the cloud cover reveal a grouping of single story houses constructed from branches, tree bark and other readily obtainable materials. What I first perceive as a group of fragile structures, easily laid waste by any of the Pacific Northwest's winter windstorms, I can see, on closer inspection, they have been made to withstand whatever nature might throw at them. Sturdy leather strips lash panels of hides to corner posts that once were the trunks of young evergreens. The houses' thatch covered roofs remind me of photos of homes in some of England's rural communities:

straw tied into bundles with heavy leather thongs, each bundle in turn lashed to each of its neighbors. They have been laid in rows across what I can only assume are rafters similar to the corner posts. As further protection against the forces of nature, this community has been built in the midst of a grove of Douglas Firs.

I smile for an instant at this identification that biologist-slash-botanist Eric makes. In the next, I wonder if Air can inform me in which house he resides. When my eyes alight on one near the community's center, memories of family dinners emerge, and I believe this is the one.

"By the Goddess," Air's mother exclaims when I push aside the skin covering the entrance. "I thought I had lost you."

I almost fail to recognize her. Mom was always well-groomed, with short to medium length, professionally cut hair and carefully applied makeup. This world's counterpart wears neither. Her skin is tanned and lined from exposure to the elements and her uncut hair is staring to gray. This makes me wonder if Mom might have had her own colored without my knowledge.

It's Bee's voice that identifies her. Yes, I said Bee. While the pronunciation of her name is the same as Mom's nickname for Beatrice, here she's called Bee as a reflection of the honey gathering insect. My sister, Trish, is named Trees. And, though I find their names awkward, even uncomfortable, I realize that no one in a society such as this would be named the way I am used to. I also realize that Bee has not spoken to me in English—nor have any of the others, now that I think about it. Rather, it's some other language that my mind translates into these names that refer to either animals or aspects of nature. That makes me smile at they way these foreign sounding words end up resembling in any way those of my original family.

"I'm fine," I reply as I enter the house's combined living, eating and cooking space.

"I couldn't bear to lose anyone else."

"I understand. I miss him too," I reply as Air's grief over his father's recent death starts to wash over me.

We embrace and I feel her tears trace a path down the side of my neck. Air's dad, Water Fowl-Deer, used to instruct initiates—young men in the process of transitioning from adolescence into manhood—in our people's legends, poems and songs that have been passed down through generations, as a way of maintaining our people's cultural and historical identity. Despite the danger posed by the beasts that inhabit the river's western shore, Water felt the place he had chosen to teach them had a spiritual connection to the process of education. I now wonder if he somehow sensed its related use in other dimensions. When he failed to come home a few days earlier, a party was sent to search for him. They returned saying that the remains they found suggested he had been torn apart by one or more beasts. Was that what had compelled me—and quite likely Air—to return to the place of his death?

"Are you hungry?" Mom asks as we separate.

I tell her I am before adding, "I'm sorry. I didn't mean to make you worry. I just wanted to… "

She brushes the explanation aside with a wave of her hand. "Trees and I have already eaten. I've been keeping your dinner warm." Abruptly, she puts a hand over her mouth as she glances at a pot hanging under the chimney. "I hope it hasn't stuck."

"It will be fine," I insist. "Once I've finished eating, I'll fill it with water." When she begins to object, I assure her, "It's no trouble."

Air's knowledge is continuing to infuse through me. Since matters like cooking washing and carrying water are left to this society's women, I understand I am making what she considers an extraordinary offer when she replies, "You've always been such a good man, just like your father." Once again, she tries to conceal her grief with another embrace, burying her face in my shoulder until the tears pass.

When I finish eating the stew, I ask, "Where is Trees?"

"I've sent her to Cat's. Flower"—whom I recognize to be Cat's daughter—"has started a sewing circle. Trees has been working herself to the bone trying to deal with Water's passing and I thought it might be best to give her something else to do as a distraction. Besides, if she ever expects to attract a husband, sewing will add to her homemaking skills."

Just as in the previous reality, I'm struck by how restricted the women were in more primitive societies. This immediately calls into question Wren's fighting abilities and how she acquired them. What allowed her to break free from the limitations this society imposes is not yet clear.

I fill my bowl and the cook pot with water from two of the large urns my family keeps for just such a purpose. They will soak overnight and Mom will scrub them in the morning. Since it will be too dark to do anything after the cook fire is extinguished, whatever questions I have about my present circumstances must wait until morning. Consequently, I kiss her goodnight and retire to my "room."

Three sleeping spaces are built into the walls of the main room. Each is no more than an alcove separated from the living space by a leather flap that has been hung across each opening for privacy. Mine, like Trees', is only large enough to accommodate the stack of furs on which I sleep, as well as my half dozen changes of clothing and a few personal possessions, such as my knife, my spear—which I will have to replace—my bow, arrows and other tools of the hunt. The chamber belonging to Air's parents, of course, is larger and is situated between each of ours.

By now, even Air's superior body is exhausted, so I pull one of the skins over me and go to sleep.

Chapter
Twenty Six

Right after breakfast, I step outside, trying to decide how I should start my day. Do I begin by meeting these villagers, or should I try to locate Wren in the hope I can better understand what happened yesterday?

A sharp blow to the side of my face lifts me off my feet and dumps me hard onto the ground. Dazed, I'm attempting to rise onto an elbow to push myself upright when someone lands on top of me and starts pummeling me with his fists. When I encircle my head with my arms to protect myself, my attacker changes strategy and begins delivering blows to my midsection. With no other way to defend myself, I try to curl into a ball, but find only limited success as the body on top of me restricts my ability to move. A shimmer begins forming, but I elect to ignore it. Since the last two times I folded landed me in bizarre situations, I'm afraid of what the next fold will have in store for me.

"Stop it!" someone shouts, but the blows keep raining. "Sky, I said stop!"

A few more punches fall before Sky climbs off and I lie still as I listen to an angry exchange of words conducted by multiple voices. I'm in too much pain, however, to try and understand them, let alone to determine who's talking. My head, body, and the right side of my face are beginning to throb. Even breathing hurts and I gasp as the air passes in and out of my chest. Reluctant to open my eyes, I hear something land on the ground beside me. A hand grips my arm and I hear Wren asking, "Are you all right?"

"I don't know," I reply.

"Can you sit?"

"I don't know," I repeat and I'm genuinely confused.

On one hand, I'm furious, almost shaking with anger, at having been assaulted like this. On the other, since the memories of all that occurred early yesterday are still taking form, I think it's entirely possible that my previous day's misadventure might have been a grave enough mistake to have warranted this attack.

After a pause, Wren says, "Thunder, Bear, give me a hand."

Their hands take hold of my arms and shoulders and gently bring me upright while another hand supports the back of my head. When I finally open my eyes, Wren's face is less than a foot away and directly in front of me. She regards me intently, peering into one eye, then the other, before she begins examining my face. Shaking her head, she tells the ones who are supporting me, "He doesn't look good. Prop him against the wall."

As they attempt to move me, I cry out.

"Do you think this is wise?" asks the man on my left.

"It's all right," I gasp. "I just think some of my ribs are broken."

Wren nods and they continue. Once my back is supported and I am sitting upright, she asks, "Is your mother home?"

"No."

I am starting to explain that she has gone to pick apples and pears with a group of women when I hear Trees exclaim, "Dear goddess! What happened?"

I look up and see her remove the yoke from her shoulders that's been suspending a pair of water jugs. She sets them down, taking a moment to insure they are stable, before gathering up her skirt and rushing to my side. She kneels next to me and extends a hand to examine my cheek. When I wince, she glares at the ones surrounding us and demands, "Who did this?"

Wren answers with a question of her own. "Do you know how to make a poultice that can reduce the swelling?"

"Of course," Trees replies. "It's one of the things Air taught me."

"Good. Please do so at once. His right eye is starting to close, so we need to draw it down before it can no longer see."

Trees nods, then returns to her load. She squats and places the yoke across her shoulders. She straightens her back, then appears to concentrate as she pushes with her legs until she is standing upright again. Once she is stable, she begins walking forward, then turns sideways to complete the last few steps into our house.

Wren turns to Sky and rephrases Trees' question. "Why did you do this?"

"He nearly got us all killed."

"He did no such thing." Before Sky can object, Wren cuts him short. "Every one of us went of his own free will."

"But… "

"He would have done the same for you. In fact, if you will think back to last summer when you and Thunder were confronted by a bear, Air ran to your assistance. No one had to ask him. And now this is how you repay him?"

Sky falls silent, his next word dying on his lips before he can voice it.

As Wren turns back to me, I begin to apologize. She places a finger across my lips and says, "Hush."

Looking up at her, it occurs to me how striking she appears. Her hair, woven into dozens of pencil thin braids, all of which are beaded at the ends, hangs like a curtain as she peers down at me. She is wearing a triangular hat made of the

239

same tan, white and gray furs that make up her clothing. Her complete lack of makeup is more than compensated for by the elegant line of her lips, the contours of her nose and cheekbones, her sky blue eyes and a tan that speaks of countless days spent in the open. Further, she is regarding me with a tenderness that takes me back to the bed in our studio apartment.

"I'm sorry," I insist. "I wasn't myself."

If I weren't in so much pain, I would laugh out loud at the statement's underlying truth.

"I suspect it was your accident," she replies. "Head injuries can have a more profound effect than most people realize."

Yet another thread connecting each of the Erics I have been drawn into.

When I try to remember, which is to say when I try to access Air's memories about the event to which Wren is referring, thoughts begin to congeal into a coherent recollection. Mom and I had been discussing the roof's condition in the face of an impending rainstorm. Last winter, one section of thatch had started leaking. The leak had been small and infrequent enough that we could deal with it by placing a pot to catch the occasional trickle. Then, when summer arrived, the problem had slipped both our minds. However, once the days and nights had grown more equal in length and it had become cool enough for us to start wearing furs, the possibility of rain reminded me that I should try to identify the cause of the problem. It didn't take long. Something small, most likely a rat, had chewed through some of the thatching in an effort to establish a residence.

After taking down the affected sections, I spent an entire day gathering reeds. It took another day to bind them into bundles and replace the ones I had removed. I was just easing myself onto the ladder when two children playing a game bumped into it. My foot slid into the space between two of the rungs as the ladder fell backwards and I was unable to prevent myself from tumbling with it.

I'm still not sure how I managed to avoid breaking any bones, but I'm reminded, when I reach back to touch it, that the back of my head struck the ground. I paused to consider that, even though Air was puzzled by the shimmer that happened afterwards, he never mentioned it to Bee. If he had, she would have likely consulted with the village shaman.

"You're probably right," I reply. After a moment's thought, I add, "I'm wondering if it wouldn't be wiser, now that Dad is gone, to move the instruction of novices back to this side of the river."

"Who will teach them?"

"I can, for the most part. Dad and I went over most of the lore pretty regularly. My herbal knowledge is reasonably strong… " I add, surprising myself with something else I've unearthed. " …and I'm a competent hunter. Maybe I can talk some of the elders into filling in the parts of the education I'm not as strong on as Dad."

Wren nods, then glances back at Sky, Bear, and Thunder. "Until Air has recovered from your stupid assault, you're all going to have to help Bee."

The three of them nod, and I can see that Sky looks repentant. Sky, Bear, Thunder, Wren, and I pass the time discussing the logistics of transporting the scrolls and whatever else we might find. Several minutes have elapsed when Trees reappears with the poultice. In order to make it, she would have had to build a fire, then get a container of water to boil so that the essences of the herbs she would have added would have had time to diffuse into the liquid. I'm surprised to see she has wrapped it in some very special fabric—*precious* fabric I might add.

Three summers earlier, Cat's sister-in-law brought a new invention with her when she came to visit. Someone had forged a twin bladed cutting tool from bronze and she taught Cat how to use it to shear wool from a sheep. The sister-in-law then taught her how to spin those fibers into thread. For the rest of that season through the following fall and early winter, she helped Cat build a device for weaving threads into cloth. It's a tedious, time consuming process, so I'm more than a little surprised to see that Trees has used some of that material for wrapping the poultice.

The morning is cool, so columns of steam are rising through the fibers. When Trees is beside me, she hands Wren the ceramic dish on which the poultice is resting, then kneels down and studies my face.

"These herbs will help a little, but what we really need is ice." She laughs and asks, "Couldn't you have waited until winter?"

I start to laugh along with her, then wince at my injuries. Trees shakes her head and reaches for the bundle. She squeezes the excess liquid into the dish before placing it over my eye.

"Please hold this in place," she instructs.

I expect the preparation will be hot, but instead find it pleasantly warm and soothing. My nostrils fill with the predominant aroma of comfrey—one of the herbs I cultivate in our garden—but I also detect plantain and arnica.

Trees adds, "I preserved all of the remaining liquid in a small pot next to the cook fire. Please see that the fire doesn't go out. If you need to further treat yourself, you can warm it, then resaturate the poultice."

"Thank you," I say, more than a little grateful for the work my sister performed on my behalf.

It becomes clear how I'm going to be spending the rest of the day.

Chapter
Twenty Seven

Three weeks after the beating, I set off to the place where Dad conducted his instructions, accompanied by Wren, Trees, Sky, Thunder, and Bear, along with two young men named Elm and Oak, and a young woman named Dawn. I wanted to leave earlier, but my balance was off. I was wobbly on my feet and I suspect I sustained a concussion, which probably added to my previous head injury. Although we were uncertain how many people we might need to recover Water's possessions, Wren and I decided that Sky, along with the two who stood by and watched but did nothing when he attacked me, should do something to make amends. I had not expected any of them would play nurse during my recovery, and they did not. We concluded that this little journey seemed to be something they would associate with either their actions against me or their failure to prevent the attack. And while I didn't see the sense of having the girls join in, since they were not parties to the assault, Trees wanted to come because of the undertaking's emotional connection. As for Wren… well, she just wanted to be a part of anything having to do with me. Since I enjoy her company, who am I to refuse? We invited the remaining three in order to be certain a second trip wouldn't be

243

necessary.

During the weeks leading up to this expedition, I made inquiries about the night hunters—the name my people gave the monsters from which I'd been hiding at what would have been the university campus in the original Portland— and why they remain on the Willamette's west side and never cross to the eastern shore. The reason, it turned out, is extremely simple: they are unable to swim. As a result, the river provides an effective barrier. But since it doesn't protect us from any of the other denizens that prowl the Pacific Northwest, the village's men, young and old alike, take turns patrolling the perimeter by day and keeping watch by night, either alone or in pairs. Unlike many community efforts in the world where I started, such as Neighborhood Watch, the nationwide crime prevention organization whose chapter in Eldorado which, while effective, presents virtually no risk to its participants, these patrols sometimes incur casualties. As recently as ten days ago, our village's residents were awakened by the early morning sounds of a woman screaming. On her way to take some laundry to a nearby creek, she came across the disemboweled remains of her husband and eldest son. Paw prints suggested that the predator had been a giant cat, smaller than *Smilodon populator,* whose skeleton I encountered at the SRTC, but no less deadly. Its size suggested it was probably what scientists in my world would call the American lion. Although creatures like these are sometimes encountered by day, they are typically nocturnal as are, of course, the aptly named night hunters. Consequently, understanding it might take hours to inventory all of Water's scrolls, ceremonial totems and other items before we packed them, we decide to leave early enough to perform our task, then return home with adequate daylight remaining.

When we reach the place where our canoes are hidden, a curtain of fog sufficiently dense to obscure the western shore hangs over the river. As we remove our crafts from the concealing bushes and carry them to the water's edge, I wonder who would want to steal them. Air's memories inform me there are several likely candidates, from a village as far to the south as Lake Oswego, to half a dozen others bordering the Clackamas River, as well as a similar number up and down the Willamette.

In this world, everything is crafted by hand. Since all are the result of intense labor, it is to anyone's advantage if they can obtain something already made, then put it to immediate use. In this regard, my own village is no better than any of its neighbors. Everyone steals whatever they can whenever possible. Needless to say, this unnerves me.

As we wade out and float the three canoes we have chosen, I become aware how much swifter the current has become since the last time we crossed. The intermittent rains that are presaging an early winter have increased the mountain runoff. The current will grow swifter as Winter progresses, reaching its peak by late Spring.

When we have passed the river's midpoint and are beginning to discern our destination through the fog, we see a shape moving south across the landscape. We withdraw our paddles and conversation halts. I would like to ask Thunder, who is seated in front of me, about its possible identity. But since all of the others remain silent, hoping that our scent will not carry due to the stillness that allows the fog to persist, I keep silent in hopes that the creature will pass without noticing us. When I glance to my right, I see Wren scowling, eyebrows furrowed. I nod in acknowledgement. We all understand that some breeds of cat and certain other predators can and do swim. The questions that hang in the air are: Will it detect us? If it does, will it be hungry enough to come in after us? If that happens, will it be sufficiently out of its element that we will have the upper hand? Even so, what happens if it tips a canoe? We all hold our breath, hoping we won't have to find out.

Several minutes pass after it has vanished before we

resume paddling, and still no one speaks until we haul our crafts on shore.

"We will have to paddle hard against the current when we return," Sky observes, remaking how far downstream the current has carried us.

Before I can voice the question I'm sure is on each of our minds, Trees asks, "What was that thing?"

"An early morning hunter," Sky replies.

She frowns and gazes upstream. "Do you think it might have been a group of people?"

As we take up our backpacks, the men retrieve their spears and the women their bows and arrows. Sky shakes his head and points to tracks running along the embankment.

"Large cat," he replies, but elects not to elaborate.

It takes us nearly two hours to complete our hike. When we arrive at the place where Dad instructed the initiates, I notice that the site appears unremarkable. If one were unaware of this place's purpose, one might have walked right past with only a glance at the sweat lodge and each of the three adjacent huts. There is nothing to indicate it as a place of importance, yet that is exactly what it is.

In this reality's culture, every young man passes into adulthood over the course of his adolescence, beginning with its onset and culminating at his approximate eighteenth summer. I use the term "approximate," because the various birth dates of the youths involved range from early autumn through the summer that follows. For those who are born shortly after one initiation ceremony, it might be their nineteenth summer when they are finally welcomed into manhood. During the course of these years, each of us is placed under the care of a group of dedicated elders. They teach us all of the techniques we will need in order to protect and provide for our families, from the basics of how to chip volcanic glass into knives, arrow heads and spear tips, to hunting skills ranging from tracking prey, to killing, then skinning and cleaning their carcasses. I should note it is our women who stretch and tan the hides, then either prepare the meat for cooking, or else cure and dry it for storage.

We also learn the various uses of edible and medicinal plants. When we locate varieties we can eat, we alert the women, who will then forage and collect them for our meals.

Construction skills, which can range from building canoes to erecting a house, are also passed down. In addition, all of our young men and women are schooled in hand-to-hand combat. Our men are also entrusted with maintaining our culture and history. This is where Dad entered the picture. In order for us to preserve our identity as a people and remind us how we fit into the place we inhabit, he taught us the important events in our past that have been preserved in the songs we sing and the stories we tell each other on warm summer nights around our campfires. To insure that future generations remember, lest memory fails to preserve all of the details, he created scrolls with symbolic depictions of these events. We have no written language, but Dad created pictures to help tellers of the tales remember these stories with a degree of accuracy.

Finally, because it is important that we have a set of laws to govern our behavior and a common code of ethics on which to base them, Dad curated all things legal and religious. We are here to preserve what he has left before others can either steal or destroy them.

We've considered the possibility of returning for a second trip at some later date. My Dad, Water Fowl-deer, was able to keep the initiates safe, despite the danger of being on this side of the river, because a party of warriors and hunters kept watch over the encampment, guarding it from whatever marauders, animal or human, might present themselves. This, however, is the height of hunting season and any possible protectors will be occupied with other duties until winter arrives.

The huts are arranged in a semicircle around the

sweat lodge, a structure whose function is essential to the rites of passage. My father understood its use far better than I do, so I will only tell you that in it our initiates are purged of their bodies' impurities and put into a state of mind that facilitates spiritual communion and establishes the nature of their journey into manhood. Although I suspect it contains none of the things we have come for, I glance inside and confirm that the lodge is indeed empty. This leaves only the huts for our consideration.

"Let's begin with this one," I say, indicating the one on our immediate right.

Before I can issue any additional instructions, Trees dashes into it. I go in after her and find her kneeling in the hut's center, staring at the array of containers arranged along its walls. I am only slightly surprised to find she is crying.

"Wh- what are they for?" she asks when I drop down beside her.

I study the objects that have captured her attention and it takes only a few seconds to determine their nature. While the lids on the many boxes are closed and all the jars are stoppered, two flutes are displayed above two racks of antlers.

"They contain sacred musical instruments like rattles and gourds," I tell her. "I suspect the jars contain scrolls relating to ceremonial songs."

"I always wanted to be a part of it," she sobs. Turning to face me, she asks, "Why aren't women allowed to participate? It isn't right. We are people too."

I cannot arrive at any sound argument. Air might have been able, having grown up in this culture, having been inculcated with this society's beliefs, but I haven't occupied his body long enough to have gained enough understanding.

Instead I say, "I can't disagree with you. You should have the right to fully participate in everything we do."

"Really? Do you really mean it?" When I nod, she throws her arms around me and says through her sobs, "I feel as if I was robbed. This is the part of our father that meant the most to him, and I was never allowed to see any of it."

Behind me, I hear Wren ask, "Is everything all right?"

I glance over my shoulder and see she has just passed through the doorway and Bear is peering in after her.

"We're fine," I assure her. "Just give us another minute or two, then we can begin."

Wren returns a tight smile, then glances at Trees, who is already starting to calm down.

"We'll be waiting outside," she replies.

She nods to Bear, who is looking on with a furrowed brow, and motions him to back up so she can make her way out through the narrow opening. Although he still looks concerned, he complies and she follows him outside.

"I'm sorry," Trees apologizes when we are alone again. "I didn't plan to do this. I just… " She pauses, unable to complete the thought.

"I understand. Let me know when you feel ready."

"Give me another minute." She inhales deeply, then releases her breath with an accompanying noise that sounds halfway between a sob and an embarrassed laugh.

Once she gives me the word that she is ready to begin what we all came for, I summon Wren and Bear and ask Trees to assist them. There is clearly enough here to fill all of this trio's backpacks. These are not backpacks of the kind I grew up with. Instead, they are sacks with straps attached that serve the same function. I find myself wondering if we should have brought a few more, then I dismiss the thought, understanding we will take what we can. Hopefully that will be everything, I tell myself as I turn to join the others.

"Something is bothering me," I tell Sky, once I'm beside him. "I have the feeling we shouldn't take too much time."

Our original plan was to sort through and organize everything. Then, after having decided what was indispensable and what could be left behind if we determined

249

we could not take all of it, we would pack what we could and go. There is something about this morning, however, that nags at me. It isn't just the cat we saw earlier. Something in my gut tells me we should clear out of this place as soon as we are able. I am relieved when he accepts my decision.

"I agree," he replies. "Something doesn't feel right."

Over the years, I have learned to listen to my gut, even when there was no logical explanation to back up my instincts. Whenever I have felt that I needed to do something other than what I had initially planned, whether or not I listened, my inner voice has always been right. This is one of those times and it feels good that someone else senses it too.

I direct Sky, Thunder, and Oak to deal with the second hut, which I quickly confirm holds the totems sacred to our religion. Once they begin, I ask Elm and Dawn to accompany me to the third, which I now know holds all of the historical documents.

Packing the scrolls is taking longer than I like. But since many are old and therefore fragile, we need to insure we do not destroy them by being hasty. Even so, some of the parchment tears when we attempt to wedge the last of the scrolls into our packs. I can only hope that I or someone else can duplicate their contents, should it prove necessary. When we have completed task, I am pleased that the three of us are leaving nothing behind and hope the other six also share our success.

When I step outside, I discover my earlier suspicions were right. A dozen or more men Air has never seen before are passing not far from here. They are heading up from the river and moving westward, past where we are standing, so clearly this is a chance encounter. However, when one of them notices us emerging, he points us out to the others in his party. They change direction and begin walking toward us.

The ones who are in the other two huts have smaller and more numerous articles to collect than Elm, Dawn and I did and they are still working. I go to each of them, poke my head inside and alert them to the looming confrontation. They emerge a few seconds later, securing their backpacks as they step out to join us. If they haven't already gathered up everything, the items they have collected will have to suffice. I suspect our visitors will want to see what we have been up to once we've departed, since their expressions indicate this is not going to be just a neighborly encounter.

After spending a moment or two appraising us, one of the newcomers separates himself from his comrades and draws to within a few feet of where we are standing. While most of these strangers are in their early to mid-twenties, this man is closer to forty and the apparent leader. I say this because the rest of the group are watching him closely. After spending a few seconds appraising Wren, Dawn and Trees, the man turns his attention toward Sky and me.

"It appears you have found something of interest," he says. "Would you care to share your discovery?"

"These are my father's belongings," I reply. "They don't concern you."

He raises his eyebrows. "That's a little harsh. What if I were to tell you they interest me a great deal?"

"Then I would have to disappoint you."

Up until now, his companions have either been either holding their spears at their sides or else have them pointing upward with their ends planted on the ground. However, as the tone of the conversation changes, some of them shift their weapons into both hands, as if preparing to use them. Even so, the party appears to be divided. Some of their faces grow more intent, while others in the group glance at their comrades as if to inquire what they're being drawn into.

While keeping my own eyes fixed on our visitors, I hear some of the members of my group shifting stance. I imagine that they are unshouldering backpacks and setting them aside in order to unencumber themselves should matters escalate and they need to use their weapons. As all this transpires, I am somewhat relieved that the ever present

251

shimmer intensifies only slightly. I'm growing tired of being thrown out of the reality I'm getting used to, only to be thrust into a different one.

"This doesn't have to happen," I tell the man.

"And I should point out," he counters, "that we outnumber you."

He smiles, then, faster than I can react, he attacks me. I see his spear come up and, in that same instant, I hear a simultaneous *shiss thunk*. The man halts, cries out and looks down at himself. I follow his gaze and see an arrow imbedded in his right thigh. A glance to my left shows Wren nocking another arrow to her bow while Trees and Dawn raise their own. Wren's eyes flick toward me, then quickly return and remain on her target.

"She could have killed you," I tell him. "Be grateful she's more civil than you are."

When he looks up at me, I immediately comprehend what people mean when they say, "If looks could kill."

I study his followers and see that all of our would-be assailants have halted. Any ideas they might have had to join his attack have ended, if only for the moment. Spears that were pointing toward us only an instant before, are slowly descending, pointing earthward. On either side of me, Sky and the others in our group have already raised their own weapons and are keeping them either poised and ready to use, or else are keeping them aimed at the enemy.

"Take my advice," I tell the man, "and turn a bad idea into something better. Go back where you came from and we'll forget this ever happened."

Without removing our eyes from them, we recover our packs and begin backing away. Once we've gone far enough that they can no longer see us, we turn and start running.

At one point, Wren catches up with me and offers apologetically, "I had to stop him."

"You did what was necessary."

I add a smile to this assurance before glancing back to be certain we're not being followed. Once we are safely in our village, I tell myself, I will have to find a way to be alone with her. I want to find out whether, in this world, we have enough in common to strike up a relationship. Air never did and I have no clear idea what, if anything, was at the root of it.

We are nearing the hillside's crest when the river comes into view and Sky calls, "We need to get the canoes into the water as quickly as possible."

Although we have had no sign up to this point that the strangers are following us, I nod in agreement. But just as I begin turning my head away, Sky's knees buckle and he pitches forward with a spear sticking out of his back. Those bastards have caught up with us and are now coming out through the trees.

"Run!" I cry.

Not only do they outnumber us, but only five in our party are armed for hand-to-hand combat. With our attackers almost on top of us, the girls' bows are useless, since they will not have time to nock arrows, aim, and shoot. And since our attackers' position above us gives them further advantage, I realize that our only chance at survival depends on our arriving on level ground where, at least, our footing will be stable.

We are running hard toward the bottom when the goddamned filaments begin expanding across my field of vision. It is hard enough dodging trees and bushes as I plummet downhill, without having to see through the increasingly brilliant lines of light. Suddenly, my foot catches on something and I fly through the air and crash into a thicket of bushes. With dust in my nose and a mouthful of leaves, I am struggling to disentangle myself when someone clutches my jacket and pulls me free.

"Hurry. They're almost here," urges Wren.

Virtually blind, I attempt to turn downhill.

"Not that way! What's wrong with you?"

Before I can answer, I hear our pursuers' footsteps and voices. There is the sound of a struggle, then I hear Wren cry out in pain. Unable to see clearly, I nonetheless turn in her direction, letting the sound of her voice guide me. Shapes beyond the shimmer are moving, but I'm unable to tell which one is Wren and which ones belong to the others. I grab at a shape that appears to be moving toward Wren, when I'm struck in the face and find myself toppling out of control. Another shape moves toward me. With no way to determine if this is friend or an enemy, with no way to help Wren and unable to defend myself, I claw this reality down and fold into the next one.

Chapter
Twenty Eight

Another strange place.

"GODDAMMIT!"

I'm furious at what I've done. Another fold and I've left someone else I care about behind and in a terrible situation. Is this always what's going to happen when things turn bad? I want to hit something. I want to hurt myself. I look around for something I can use… and then I realize how stupid that would be because there was nothing I could have done to defend myself. There was nothing I could have done to defend Wren. Although I'm angry over of how helpless I was when she needed me. I can't imagine what other course of action I could have taken, except maybe allow those others to kill me. And what would that have accomplished? I know it doesn't seem fair, but how else should I deal with it? Should I die like a sitting duck because I'm blinded and unable to protect myself? I can tell you right now that offering myself up as a sacrificial lamb in order to sooth a guilty conscience is unacceptable. I know that one day all of the resulting guilt will pile up and I'll have to deal with it. For the present, though, all the pain seems to balance out whatever actions I've taken to keep myself alive.

Aside from all that, this shuttling between dimensions is starting to wear on my nerves. How many more realities must I visit in order to find a situation that isn't life threatening? I feel like sitting down and just giving up, except that won't work either, because if past situations are any indication of what my future holds, something bad is going to catch up with me regardless of my action or inaction.

I sigh and look at where I am.

I'm standing at the end of a cul-de-sac on the ridgeline overlooking yet another version of Portland's South Waterfront. I'm sure it's not one of the previous South Waterfronts I've visited because the number of residential towers are greatly increased and there are two mirror-faced needle-like spires rising to the heavens in their center. I suspect the neighborhood where I'm standing is similarly transformed, because I remember looking up here and seeing trees and lots of one and two story houses. Now, however, the streets are lined with chic-looking clothing stores, nightclubs, bars and restaurants.

As I gaze out over the Willamette to locate Mount Hood, a strange sort of aircraft coming out of the south and flying toward Mount Saint Helens appears a few hundred feet above me. Its body is wingless, flat and semicircular, with a straight edge at the rear where I suspect its propulsion system must be. Is this somewhere in the future, or, like the Little House on the Prairie iteration, a world that developed at a different rate from my own?

"Thank God! I've finally caught up with you," says a woman's voice behind me.

Startled, I turn to look and find myself facing someone whose name I cannot recall, but who, nonetheless, has a vaguely familiar look about her. She stands about five feet six and appears to be in her early to mid-twenties. Her hair glows bright copper in the sunlight, and her eyes are a deep emerald green. To my eyes, she is an unearthly beauty, a walking daydream.

That's it! She is the one I saw in the dream I had in

the hospital room… except that would be impossible. Dreams never turn into realities. Still, the resemblance is uncanny and I've never met anyone else with eyes like hers. I wonder if she is also the one I saw during one of the folds.

"What do you mean 'caught up with me'?"

"Our paths crossed in each of the interstices," she replies.

"The… "

"The interstices: the spaces between the dimensions."

"The spaces between… " I repeat, suddenly confused.

"They are almost immeasurable. Then again, how much space do you think your soul requires?"

"My soul?" I ask, before I realize I'm starting to sound like a parrot.

I'm grateful when she ignores my momentary idiocy. Then, instead of calling me out, she explains, "I'm not referring to the soul in any religious sense. I'm talking about that weightless, dimensionless intelligence that inhabits the body."

Before I can ask for more detail, she changes the subject.

"You completely surprised me that first time I ran into you. Until then, I was aware of only one other person who could cross between dimensions like I can. After you avoided me, I was afraid I might never catch up with you again, until Mark assured me he could track you. Once he established your where-when, as he likes to call it, he helped me locate you. The second time, I also tried to speak with you, but you slipped away again before we could communicate and I vowed to learn more about you.

"I was afraid you would avoid me this time as well, so I decided to follow you in when you moved into this reality. It's important that you and I talk, in view of our mutual gift. For the longest time, I thought Mark and I were the only ones born with this ability."

"I wasn't born with it."

She throws me a curious look, so I give an account of how the automobile accident altered me, some of what happened afterward and my term for what I do.

"That's remarkable," she says. "Still, I'm wondering if your ability to fold, as you like to call it, necessarily required a trauma to initiate it. I'm wondering if it might have eventually emerged on its own."

"Does it really matter?"

"I suppose not. Whatever the cause, you've been handed a remarkable gift."

I shake my head. "I'd call it a curse. Why would anyone want to step blindly into an unknown situation? Every time I do, something terrible happens."

"It's not like that for me." She pauses to consider, then offers, "I think you're locked in a loop."

"What do you mean?"

"Every situation is as likely to occur as it is unlikely to occur. Just as you decided to visit the library that first time, you might have elected to simply go home and nothing more would have happened… nothing remarkable that is. You might never have discovered your ability, or something else might have triggered it at some later date."

She puts a finger to her lips and appears to be thinking. After a moment, she says, "My instinct suggests that when you stepped—that is to say, folded—out of one bad situation, then later folded into another one, you somehow set up a chain that would move you through a series of similar circumstances."

"Is that really possible?" I ask.

The woman nods.

"You know as well as I do that horrible events rarely happen to the same person on a regular basis. And while we like to think that the universe is truly random, we both know that our frame of mind can make certain kinds of occurrences more likely to occur than they would have otherwise.

"For example, optimists are more likely to create

favorable outcomes than pessimists. A person with low self-esteem is, in all likelihood, going to continue to find himself going from one bad situation into another that's equally bad, if not worse. It's the same sort of guiding principle that self-help books are based on. They all assert that each of us creates our own reality. It's a deeper truth than you might think and it makes me wonder if we—Mark and I, and possibly you—might be able to find a way to change what you're going through."

I find the possibility intriguing. Still, I wonder, "But what happens if I find myself in a bad situation with no way out?"

"That has already happened."

"What?"

"Every possible situation has already occurred, or else will occur at some time in the future. But that doesn't mean you—the person I'm talking to—have to be part of it. While most people travel along either one path or another that their decisions create, what makes you, Mark and I special is that we can jump across realities that only roughly parallel our original ones. From what you have told me already, it's obvious that each fold moved you into a stream of events that, while increasingly removed from your initial reality, retained certain similarities."

"If what you say is true and there are so many parallel universes… "—a conclusion I arrived at earlier—" …how can this guy, Mark, help me find my way to something better?"

"I don't know how he does it," she says. "He just can." When I smile, she says, "Of course, you won't be able to completely avoid all of life's pitfalls. Nobody can. Still, I'm just wondering if we can shift your path toward more favorable circumstances, the way Mark helped me steer my own situation so that you and I could meet right here, right now."

When I present a blank look, she explains, "He just

had to find a set of realities in which I planned to visit Portland, then find the one that would intersect with your trajectory here."

My head is beginning to spin and I'm sure that I show it. She smiles and says, "While you and I possess remarkable gifts, Mark is in a class by himself. Just as there are people who can remember everything that ever happened to them every day of their life, or chess masters who can win against fifty or more opponents without seeing any of the boards, Mark has a way of locating realities with specific circumstances, then guiding me to them. There's no one in the universe like him. Although I have to say, since you surprised both of us, Mark and I now know that he isn't perfect." She chuckles and adds, "That's made him a little easier to live with. Before you came along, he thought of himself as the closest thing to God. Now he sees himself as a little more human."

I start to reply, then stop and say, "I just realized I don't know your name."

"Liana," she replies. "Liana Foxworthy."

"Eric Folder."

"Ah! Now I understand where the term 'folding' comes from. Nice to meet you, Eric."

"Back atcha, Liana." When another aircraft, similar to the first one, flies by, I ask, "Can he help me get back to where I started?"

Liana's eyebrows come together. "Why would you want to? I mean, now that you've seen what's possible, do you really want to go back to college?" Before I can answer, she adds, "Who there would understand you? You'd be an outsider. You could never share anything about yourself—the part that sets you aside from everyone else, I mean—with anyone. They would think you were crazy."

"But I had a girlfriend."

Her expression darkens a bit, then changes to something brighter. "We could still arrange for you to see her. I don't see where that would pose a problem."

"But you have something else in mind."

Liana nods. "I'm not suggesting that I replace her. Far from it," she says, although I wonder if that is not entirely accurate. She's obviously intelligent. She understands what I do and takes on a look that says she has a special attraction whenever she looks at me. She goes on to say, "There is just so much more that we could do together."

"Such as… ?"

"We could make thought-out changes." I cock my head and she elaborates. "We have the ability to alter unpleasant outcomes."

"Like… ?"

She sighs in exasperation. "We can put ourselves in exactly the right place at exactly the right time and put the right word in the right person's ear… Think of the possibilities, Eric. This could be the start of the greatest adventure anyone has ever embarked on."

In less than a second, I realize that if alternate realities don't occur until someone is faced with a decision, then she is right. We could make changes.

"But how will we learn about them?"

"Again, this is where Mark comes in."

"Look. If he's so great, why doesn't he simply take care of them himself?"

"I once asked him about it. The way he explained it, it's so he can retain his perspective. He needs to keep himself separate and apart from everything else. If he were to participate on an intimate level, he would lose the broader vision. Until he met me, he had to remain a spectator. I became the tool he could use to make changes. Your addition to the mix opens many more possibilities.

"So what do you say?" Her expression becomes mischievous. "Will you join me as… how should I say?… a partner in crime?"

When I become alarmed, thinking back to Drug

Dealer Dan, she takes a figurative step backward.

"I'm sorry. It's just an expression. I didn't intend it to come out sounding like that. What I meant to say is, will you combine your intelligence with ours and help us do some real good?"

I pause for a second to consider. If I could eventually return to the Erin of my dreams while creating a better universe for us to live in, why wouldn't I? Faced with no better answer, I tell her…

"Yes!"

ABOUT THE AUTHOR

Raymond Bolton lives near Portland, Oregon with his wife, Toni, and their cats, Max and Arthur. His epic fantasies are published by WordFire Press, publisher of the Dune and Star Wars novels, and have received endorsements by the late Mike Resnick and award-winning author Paul Kane.

You can find his other titles on his Amazon author page:
https://www.amazon.com/Raymond-Bolton/e/B00HMY0B6U/